Fr

"Is that it?"

Comes

V i r g i n i t y

"Is that it?"

by

KAREN LOUISE TAYLOR

I don't claim to write literature I just want to tell my story.

Acknowledgements

FROM YOU KNOW WHO I AM
TO YOU KNOW WHO YOU ARE.

My love and thanks go to all who know me.
For their patience, understanding, LISTENING
and contribution towards not just this book but also all
the fun and happy memories you have etched into my life.

THANKS FOR BEING GREAT FRIENDS.

Front and back cover illustration.
With love and thanks to a dear friend
Sue Grafflin

Coming next

L o v e

"Is it that?"

&

T h e b i g

4 0

That is it...

Sponsored & Published by
Condom Clive International Marketing Ltd.

First published in Great Britain in 2002 by
Condom Clive International Marketing Ltd

All characters in this publication are fictitious and any resemblance to real persons, living or dead, is purely coincidental.

ISBN 0-9542600-0-7

Typeset in Times Roman 12/14pt
Printing and binding in Great Britain by
Perfect Print, 81 High Street South, Dunstable, Beds.

For all sales inquiries contact
Condom Clive International Marketing Ltd

At

www.condomclive.com

A note from the author

In the days I attended school, family and older people constantly reminded me that, 'Your days at school are supposed to be the happiest days of your life.' I still today question if they were.

This story will introduce five girls, their families and friends to you. It could be any school in Great Britain and at any time, but one thing it has in common with you, the reader, is that you yourself have experienced school life and met the Karens, Amandas, Sallys, Wendys and Samanthas of this world.

As you read, see if you can find your friends in them, and maybe you might find yourself?

Karen L Taylor

A note to readers not accustomed to reading
in the present tense
(He/She says)

Is read as He/She sez.

Virginity "Is that it?"

Chapters

Virginity "Is that it?"

Samantha

"It...is for the love between two people, not a subject to be discussed in a classroom of boys and girls."

"Mam, do you mind! I'm trying to get dressed." Samantha's 14-year-old sister Ann, kneels in front of the coal fire trying to keep warm, as she gets ready for school, embarrassed by the conversation between her older sister and mother.

"They're only going to show a film, then talk about it," Sam explains as if apologising on behalf of the government for teaching sex education to fifth year pupils.

"I still think it's best left to parents to decide, not some perverted male teacher to stand up and preach it."

Sam's mother always substitutes the word sex with the word 'It.' As a teenager once herself in the late fifties, you could understand her reluctance for saying that word.

"Anyway mam, it's just going to be us girls, Mrs Summers will be giving the lesson."

"Mam have you seen my plimsolls?" Bobby, Sam's twelve-year-old brother dashes into the lounge.

"Come on Bobby or I'll miss Wendy and Paul!"

Sam fastens her coat.

Ann jumps up, "I'm ready," and heads for the door.

"Here they are, oh you haven't white washed them!" A mundane weekly task Bobby deliberately forgets to do, expecting his mother to have them gleaming white ready for sports day.

"That's your own fault, don't expect me to clean your sports shoes," mam vanishes back into the kitchen, seemingly uncaring, only to face the start of her mundane daily routine that is her life. Washing up the breakfast dishes.

Outside Sam holds open the front door, while Bobby scurries out dropping a plimsoll as he tries to stuff them into his rucksack.

"Come on Bobby!" Sam picks it up and hands it to him as she shuts the door.

"I'll get the slipper from Mr Butcher now," Bobby shudders at the thought.

"Well, you should have cleaned them last night, shouldn't you," Ann lectures Bobby.

"Shut up!" Bobby snaps.

"Stop it you two!" Samantha tells them as she hurries down the garden path from the family's nine-teen sixties council house.

Samantha is an intelligent girl, tall, plain looking with long blonde hair and is quite mature for a sixteen-year-old. She has to be, to undertake the pain-in-the-arse duty of chaperoning her brother and sister to school every morning, which always causes her to be late meeting up with her closest friend, Wendy.

Wendy

"Yes mam, bye mam see you tonight."

Wendy leaves her home, a nineteen thirties three-bedroom semi- detached private dwelling.

Wearing a long black duffle coat that just manages not to trail along the pavement, she walks quickly to the end of the cul-de-sac to meet Paul, her long time school sweetheart.

Wendy, a small perfect girl, bright and bossy, always meets Paul in the morning to walk to school. Paul and Wendy met on their first day at Redcar High Senior, finding they shared the same birthday it seemed they were meant to be together. Four and a half years later, now both coming up to sixteen, they still walk each other along the same route to school.

"Hi Paul," Wendy shouts.

"I'll see you later," Paul's mate rides on ahead.

"OK mate I'll see you in first lesson, Hi Wend," Paul climbs off his bike.

Wendy stands looking at him. "Haven't you forgotten something?"

"Oh Yeah," Paul kisses her on the cheek.

"That's better. Isn't it slippery."

"Yeah, I nearly came off my bike riding here."

"Why do you always bring your bike, you only live round the corner?"

"I don't want to wear my shoes out."

"Paul!" Wendy laughs and gives him a gentle nudge as he pushes his bike along the path. With his right arm draped over Wendy's shoulders, they make their way to school like they always have done, every morning come rain, shine, sleet or snow.

Amanda

"Amanda, have you got everything?"

"Yes mum," Amanda runs down the concrete stairs from their two-storey council maisonette to her mam waiting in their old blue mini.

"Come on love, we don't want you to be late on your first day."

"Wait a minute," Amanda stops to check her satchel, "I can't find..."

"Don't forget your school report!" her mother reminds Amanda as she starts the engine.

"No, I've found it, it's here," Amanda jumps in the car.

"I hope I can remember the way, it's been a long time," her mam remarks.

"When did you and grandma move from Redcar?"

"Oh I was your age love, sixteen, it seems so long ago."

"It's a lot different than back home mum." Amanda looks through the passenger window as they drive out of the rundown Lakes Estate, which had just recently become their new home.

"I know love, but this is just a stepping stone before we buy our own house."

"I know mum...it'll be OK," wishing she could be back home with her step dad in their five bedroom London house.

Average in height, slightly overweight with shoulder length wavy brown hair; Amanda is a caring young girl with a pretty face to go with her personality, pretty enough to wow the boys.

"Now remember if I'm late home, go to Betty's next door and have your tea there."

"Yes mum."

Karen

"I'll decide what I wear," Karen storms out of the house and down the drive muttering under her breath.

"Madam you change your attitude before you come home tonight...I don't give a damn if you catch your death," her mother slams the front door leaving Karen to freeze as she walks to school.

"Fuck off," Karen curses. With her arms folded to keep warm, dressed only in a school blazer, white shirt and black skirt, Karen defies her mother's orders to put a jumper on and heads for school.

Karen lives in a newly built five bedroom detached house with en suite bathroom, situated in Redcar's wealthiest housing estate, Wheatland's Park.

Although she has two wardrobes full of clothes, like most 16-year-old girls who go to school, she wears as little as she needs to.

Sally

The Robinson twins step out on to the pavement from their nineteen twenties street house... SLAM!

"Sorry mam," Sally shouts through the letterbox.

"Bloody door... you have to slam it, it's warped," Sue moans.

"Corr, its cold this morning," Sally links arms with Sue.

"Yeah... you'd think it would get a bit warmer in the mornings," Sue remarks, fed up with the cold.

Virginity "Is that it?"

Sally and Sue, both sixteen, hurry to school. Even though they are twins, there is a noticeable difference between them. Sally has long soft blonde hair, blue eyes and a beautiful complexion, whereas Susan has curly wiry blonde hair, blue-green eyes and suffers from facial acne.

"I've nearly got enough money for that tank top," Sue says chirping up a bit. "You know, the one I've been after for ages."

"Not the one with the red sequins on?" Sally looks at Sue. "I wanted that!"

"Well…it's mine…it doesn't matter, you always end up wearing my clothes anyway."

"You wear mine!" Sally defends the accusation. "At least we don't have to wear the same clothes any more."

"Yeah, remember Christmas three years ago? I could have died when mam bought us those duffle coats," Sue says giggling.

"She hasn't noticed yet, I took mine to the charity shop," Sally confesses to Sue.

"You didn't tell me, I wondered where your's got to."

"Don't tell her Sue!"

"Only if you don't tell her I put mine in next door's bin."

"You didn't!" Sally and Sue burst out laughing as they walk faster, not wanting to be late for school.

At The School Gates

"Oh no! It's running season again." Paul moans. "You come back to school after Easter and find all the goal posts gone and running tracks chalked out everywhere."

"All you ever think about Paul is football," Wendy says voicing her disapproval. "It's about time us girls get to have some fun... Are you running in the 800 metres Sam?" Wendy asks.

"If I qualify."

"You always qualify... Mrs Summers is asking me to compete in the County finals at Clairville Stadium," Wendy announces proudly.

"You'd better start running to the stadium now, you don't want to miss the start of the first race," Paul jokes.

"Are you implying I'm slow?" Wendy looks at him, squinting her eyes in anger.

"I'm off," Paul pedals away to escape the wrath of Wendy.

"You wait till I see you at break Paul!" Wendy laughs.

"Come on Wend it's nearly nine," Sam eggs her to get a move on; the girls walk on through the school gates passing Alison as the bell rings.

"All right Kaz... you're early for a change the

first bell's just gone." Alison one of Karen's friends, the school gossip, stands resting her weight on one leg, chewing gum whilst combing her hair with a fluorescent pink comb.

"So what," Karen walks past.

"Who got out of bed the wrong side this morning then!" Alison snides at Karen.

"What's first lesson?" Karen asks slumping against the wall, openly taking a drag from her cigarette.

"Maths I think," Alison replies. " Have you done your home work?"

"What do you think?" Karen snaps.

Alison sees Sharon approaching. "Here comes Sharon… Shaz did you see Julie over the holiday she has a black eye!"

"No, tell me more!" Sharon wants to hear Alison's latest gossip.

"Well…She told me she fell over, but I reckon Bri's been hitting her again."

"She's always getting thumped by him, what d'yer reckon Kaz?" Sharon asks.

"All lads are bastards." Karen stamps her fag out.

"Decker dumped you again?" Alison asks.

"What's it to do with you?" Karen looks at her with a threatening gaze.

"Nothing only asking."

"Well keep your big nose out."

"Here comes Decker now Kaz," Sharon spots them.

"Hi Deck," Karen says hopefully. Decker and his mate Bradley walk past ignoring the girls. "Fine, don't speak then!" Decker and Brad walk on laughing to themselves. "Come on, I'm not standing here to be laughed at."

Karen, Alison and Sharon start to walk towards the school.

Amanda and her mam pull up in their car at the gates alongside the girls. "Excuse me girls, is this Redcar Senior High School?"

The girls stop and look at each other. "No that's back that way missis," Karen says pointing to the direction they had just driven from.

Amanda leans over her mother from the passenger seat. "Could you step aside please?" The girls part from each other revealing behind them the sign, Redcar High Senior School est. 1956. "Thank you..." Amanda sighs looking at her mother as she drives on into the schoolyard leaving the girls laughing amongst themselves.

They pull into a parking bay. "Well it took a few wrong turns but we got here in the end. Now let's get you inside, I mustn't be late for my job interview." Amanda steps out from the car and follows her mam to the school's main entrance.

The second bell rings and a rush of late pupils shove past Amanda and her mother almost knocking them over. Amanda holds the door open not noticing the next person walking through is Karen. They stare at each other. Karen smiles at her sarcastically, then pushes past followed by Sharon and Alison.

"Amanda come along," her mam stands by the secretary's office window tapping on the glass panel. It slides open.

"Hello," an important looking secretary looks over her spectacles. "Can I help you?" she politely asks.

"Hello, My name is Mrs Wright, my daughter Amanda is due to start school today."

"I'll let Ms Blakemoore know you've arrived, please wait around the corner, there are chairs you can sit on," the glass panel closes sharply.

"Yes thank you...come along love."

Registration

Karen and Alison walk into the classroom. "See yer at break," Alison calls to Sharon as she heads to her own classroom.

"Don't forget you owe me a hot chocolate," Sharon reminds her.

"No I don't," Alison shouts back quickly

following Karen to the back of her class.

"You're in my chair," Karen stands over Sally.

"No she's not," Sue tells Karen.

"Get out now!" Karen pulls Sally's chair forcing her to stand up.

"OK." Sally submits.

"Stay there," Sue tells Sally pulling her back into the chair.

"Yes… listen to your sister, do as she says, you don't want to upset her."

Sally gets out of her chair. "Come on Sue, it's not worth it," she moves two desks down.

Sue follows. "Yeh, I wouldn't sit in a chair she uses either," Sue says to her sister.

Karen stands behind her desk. "Easter hols might be over but I've just started with you Bonnie and Hide."

"You and whose army?" Sue snaps back.

"Do you want to say that again?"

Just then the teacher enters the classroom. "OK now everyone…" two girls push in past the teacher. "Come on girls be quick about it," the class sits.

Karen pushes Alison into another chair. "Karen Sinclair, have you got a note from your doctor?" the teacher asks.

"No! Why, should I?" Karen stands looking puzzled.

"Well that will mean you don't have a problem

with your posterior so please sit on it," the classroom fills with laughter.

"Very funny," Karen snides as she sits down.

"And where's your school tie."

"It's in my pocket."

"Put it on then," the teacher orders. "And when I have called registration, you can then make a nuisance of yourself to other teachers in the school."

"Piss off," Karen mutters under her breath.

"OK! Andrews?"

"Here!"

"Addison?"

"Here!"

"Bradley?"

Ms Blakemoore's Office

Outside the headmistress's office Amanda sits nervously twiddling with her last school report.

"You're not nervous are you love?"

"No." Amanda sits up and straightens the report.

The door to the headmistress's office opens, out steps a tall stocky woman with dark hair. "Good morning, my name is Ms Blakemoore and you must be Amanda," Amanda and her mam stand. "And you must be Mrs Wright." she holds out her hand to greet them both.

"Yes, hello," they all shake hands.

"Come on in, I'll send for some tea."

"If it's OK, I'll skip the tea… I have a job interview to get to."

"Oh very well… is the job local?"

"Yes it's at the Stead Hospital, I'm applying for the receptionist vacancy."

"I wish you well, it will be handy to know someone there, we often send over our pupils."

Amanda looks at her mam puzzled. "Oh don't think the school is out to maim its pupils, but we do have the occasional sports injury." The headmistress smiles at Amanda, she smiles back shyly. "Now Amanda, you will be with us for the last three months of school, mainly for your exams, you will already know that all exams nationally are set to the same standards, so don't worry about changing schools it should not cause any adverse effects on your results, do you have your last report?"

"Oh yes," Amanda hands the creased report over to the headmistress to look at.

"Oh sorry! I was erm..."

"Let me see," Ms Blakemoore scans through the report.

"You'll find Amanda's results are very favourable, she's always reading and finds it very easy taking in information."

"Mum!" Amanda gets embarrassed.

"Sorry love… I am very grateful you have allowed my Amanda to join your school," Amanda's mam pauses and starts to get upset. "It hasn't been easy these last few months, with the divorce and all."

Ms Blakemoore hands over a box of tissues. "I understand, sadly for a number of reasons divorce seems to be on the increase these days, but don't think for one minute that we would let Amanda down, we will make sure she gets all the help she needs… Did you live in London long, Amanda?"

"All my life."

"Yes…so you will find our northern accents a bit strange?"

"Yes a bit."

Amanda's mother interrupts again, "I've always kept mine… I was born in Saltburn myself, I moved south some sixteen years ago."

"Well, now you are returning home to a new life and I hope Mrs Wright that you do not hesitate to call me if you would like to have a chat about the old days, as I myself was born in Saltburn and went to the Priory Girls Grammar."

"Oh, the same school as me."

"Well let's keep that thought… Now I expect you, Amanda, will be eager to meet your new classmates, I have asked a girl, her name is Wendy, she's a lovely girl and I hope a friend to be, she will help you find your way around school, now… Mrs Wright, let's move on to the important paperwork then you can get away to your interview."

Maths Lesson

"Quarter of an hour back and no one can tell me the square root of sixty four," Mr Evans calls out to the class, frustrated at the lack of intelligence in the room.

"Is it the second turning before route sixty-six, sir?"

"Is it what, Bailey?"

"You know sir, America's route sixty-six." The classroom bursts into laughter.

"Bailey this is not a geography lesson, but I'm sure if you drove down route sixty-six you would get lost inside of five minutes."

The class laughs more at the teacher's joke. "Now I'll ask you all to open your maths books to page twenty-seven, and we will go right through this chapter again!" The class opens its books with moans and groans.

There's a knock at the classroom door. The headmistress pops her head around the door. "Mr Evans, can I trouble you for a moment please?" The class all stand except for Karen who slowly decides to.

"Yes, Ms Blakemoore, come in please."

"This is Amanda Wright the young lady I was telling you about." A wolf whistle comes from the back of the class.

"Bailey was that you?"

"Sorry sir."

"Don't apologise to me, apologise to the young lady this instant."

"Sorry."

"See me in my office at break."

"Yes Ms Blakemoore."

"Is Wendy here?"

"Yes Ms Blakemoore," she holds up her hand.

"Amanda will sit next to you," Mr Evans tells her. "And Samantha you can sit next to Julie."

"Yes sir," Sam gets up and moves to the next desk not happy at the move.

"What happened to your eye Julie?" Ms Blakemoore inquires.

"Oh I fell over."

"It looks very painful!" Ms Blakemoore comments. "Thank you Mr Evans I will leave you to get on with your lesson." The class all sit.

"Now Amanda I am not just your maths teacher but also your year tutor, if there's anything you need to know just ask. Tell me Amanda do you know the square route of six hundred and twenty-five?"

"Twenty-five sir." Amanda replies without hesitation.

"As if", Karen whispers to Alison.

"Very good Amanda, I can see you are going to show that our southern friends are just as clever as we northerners...now page twenty-seven top left hand corner, Amanda you share with Wendy."

Alison looks at Karen.

"What are you looking at?" Karen snides.

Break Time

Wendy, Amanda and Sam walk out on to the playing field. "Well...it's actually Pinner, which is just outside Harrow," Amanda explains.

"I have an aunt who lives in Harrow," Sam mentions. "It's where the rich live isn't it?"

"Parts of it," Amanda replies.

"So how long have you been here?" Wendy asks.

"A week."

"Do you like it here?"

"It's all right, I haven't had much of a chance to see the place yet."

"We'll show you round," Sam offers.

"Hi Wend," Paul and Geoff join the girls.

"Hi Paul," they kiss.

"Who's this then?" Paul asks looking at her admiringly.

"Amanda, she started school today," Wendy

replies not happy at Paul's interest. "Meet Paul, my boyfriend," Wendy makes it clear so Amanda knows he's taken.

"All right Paul."

"Hi Amanda," Paul smiles.

Paul's mate Geoff approaches. "Ello, 'ello, 'ello the policeman said to his wife in bed with three men."

"What?" Amanda looks at Geoff puzzled.

"That's what the wife said, what, what about me!"

"Oh, this is Geoff…Paul's mate, we just put up with him, don't we Sam?"

"Leave me out of it," Sam steps aside.

"Like what is there to say, other than I'm free and single."

"I thought you fancied Sam," jokes Wendy.

"I've got to keep my options open," Geoff licks his thumb and wets his eyebrows.

"As long as that's all you keep open." Amanda quips.

"This girl's funny," Paul laughs.

"Come on let's go up the field, maybe the fresh air might clear your head Paul," Wendy says as she drags Sam and Amanda up the playing fields.

Geoff and Paul follow play fighting with each other.

"I might work on her, nudge nudge, wink wink, you know what I mean," Geoff nudges at Paul.

"You haven't got a chance Geoff," Paul jumps on him and throws his arms around Geoff's neck. "Not with your acne."

"Thanks mate, I love you too," Geoff replies as they both tumble to the ground.

The Coffee Machine

"Give me my money back," a first year pupil kicks the coffee machine and bangs the money return button trying to retrieve his money; he has no luck and walks off to the secretary's office.

Sally and Sue approach the machine. "Watch this," Sue walks to the side of the machine and kicks it, a five-penny piece drops. "What drink do you want?" Sue asks.

"I'll have a hot chocolate," Sally requests. Sue successfully puts the five pence coin in the machine and pushes the button for hot chocolate. "That Karen's going to get you one day Sue."

"She's all talk, if you face up to her she backs off."

"She frightens me."

"Well don't be, anyway with that new girl starting she'll have a new victim to play with."

"I guess you're right, I feel sorry for her, she's in for a rough time." Sally and Sue walk down the corridor sharing their free hot chocolate.

"I think she'll survive, we all do, come on let's go to art I want to see Mr Quibley about my exam piece." Sue heads off with Sally to the art rooms brushing off her sister's concerns.

The first year pupil returns with the secretary, she opens the machine door. "There's no money in the slot," the secretary points out to him.

"I put five pence in, honest," the poor lad, pleads his case.

"Well, it's not there now, is it?"

He walks away unhappy muttering to himself. "That was my last five pence." The secretary closes the coffee machine door sharply.

Behind The Bike Sheds

"Well you owe me one," Karen stands with her hand out waiting for a fag.

"OK...but remember, it's your turn to buy the next ten, I'm not nicking them from my dad all the time," Sharon hands her a cigarette.

Karen lights up. "Do you want a drag," passing it to Alison.

"No ta," Alison rejects her offer as she combs her hair looking around, chewing gum.

"I forgot, you don't smoke do you?," Karen says sarcastically.

"I'm not polluting my lungs! Any how what's got into you, you've been like shit all morning?"

"What do you mean by that?"

"She means you're like a bad smell you can't get rid of," Sharon tries to light up her fag. "Bloody matches."

"Reckon its 'cos she won't let Decker shag her…that's why he's finished with her," Alison bitches.

"Hello…am I invisible?" Karen shouts. "Shut your gobs you two it's nothing to do with you."

"Well I think you're right not to give into him he's only using you," Sharon backs Karen up.

"I said it's got nothing to do with you."

"I'm only sticking up for you," Sharon leans against the bike shed still trying to light her fag. "I was dumped after I did it."

Karen and Alison turn and stare at her. "What?"

"What do you mean after you did it?" Karen asks, stunned by her revelation.

"Oh that was two years ago when I was thirteen, this lad I was seeing took me into the farmer's field in Green Lane and we did it there."

"You didn't tell me," Alison complains.

"I didn't want the school to know." Sharon replies.

Alison looks away. "I wouldn't have."

"I would have thought you'd tell me, what was it

like then?" Karen asks puffing intensely at her cigarette.

"It hurt, I told him I didn't want to do it again so he dumped me the next day. Don't tell Brad, he thinks I'm still a virgin, anyway I'll just deny it."

"We won't tell him," Karen looks at Alison."Will we Alison?"

"What makes you think I'll say anything!"

They both stand speechless looking at Sharon.

"I wish you'd leave your hair alone Alison. You're getting on my nerves combing it all the time," Karen snatches the comb from her.

"Give's it back!" Alison grabs her comb. "At least my hair looks nice!"

"There's nought wrong with my hair, it's called punk if you hadn't noticed," Karen educates Alison.

"Yeah, and it's going out of fashion if you hadn't noticed," Alison returns fire.

"Give's a light from yer fag Kaz, these matches are crap."

Karen helps her finally light up. Sharon takes a big drag on her cigarette and smiles back at Karen who stares at her as if she was a different Sharon from the one she thought she knew.

"I wanted my hair cut like yours but my mam wouldn't let me." Sharon tells her.

"My mam will let me," Alison brags about her independence.

"I bet," Karen snides, snapping back into reality.

"Here's Decker and Brad," Sharon sees them coming over.

"All right Kaz?" Decker calls to her.

"You're talking to me then!" she replies.

"Shaz come here," Brad walks round the bike shed.

"Why?" Sharon asks.

"Just come here!"

"No! I don't trust you."

"Get here," Brad pulls her round the corner.

"Mind me fag," Sharon stumbles around the bike shed.

Decker stands in front of Karen. "Ha way Kaz, I was only mucking about," he goes to kiss her.

"Not with Alison here," She pushes Deck away.

"Bugger off Alison," Decker orders.

"No I won't."

"I said bugger off Alison," Decker stares at her.

"It's alright, I'll see you back in next lesson."

"You're mad Kaz," Alison walks off not happy.

Decker tries to kiss Karen again. She turns her head away. He steps back. "Third time lucky," he says making another attempt. This time he succeeds and they kiss, washing machine style. "There that's better."

"Why haven't you bothered seeing me over the hols?" Karen asks.

"Had things to do."

"More important than seeing me!"

"What you doing tonight?" Decker asks changing the subject.

"Nothing…why?"

"I'll meet you at Borough Park then. Seven o'clock!" They snog for a while. Decker moves his hand over Karen's shirt and feels her tit, she pulls his hand away.

"I told you," Karen warns him.

Deck looks into her eyes. "Brad come on we're going."

"Where are you going?" Karen asks him.

"To see a boy about some dinner money." He walks back towards the school.

"See yer at seven then." Karen shouts.

Decker raises his hand in the air as if to say OK. Brad runs after him.

Sharon reappears from behind the bike shed fastening up her shirt top. "Made up then?"

"Come on let's go," Karen walks off. "I'm sick of this place."

Amanda Has Tea With Betty

"Here you are Betty," Amanda enters the lounge from the kitchen with a pot of tea.

"Oh you are a dear…thank you…it is nice to have company, people are far too busy to call round these days."

"Thank you for letting me stay," Amanda pours the tea.

"If your mother is ever late home always give me a knock, you can stay here until she gets back…now can you just pop those net curtains down for me, there's a girl, I like to wash them regularly it keeps the room bright."

"Can I use this chair to stand on?"

"Oh no dear there's a proper set of steps in the kitchen, we don't want you falling over do we?" Amanda returns from the kitchen struggling to open them. "Can you manage dear, they can be a bit difficult?"

"Yes I've got it now," Amanda climbs the steps and easily pops the nets off their hooks. "There…where do you want me to put them?" Amanda asks.

"Oh just leave them on the chair dear. I'll see to them later… I think you and I are going to become good friends, don't you dear?"

"Yes Betty, I think so too," Amanda agrees smiling.

"Hello… anybody home?" Amanda's mam enters Betty's.

"Oh! Hello Norma, come on in and have a cup of

tea with us."

"Has my Amanda been taking care of you?"

"Yes, she's been a great help, she's even got my net curtains down for me."

"That was sweet of you love," Amanda's mam gives her a hello hug.

"Pour your mam a cuppa."

"Sorry Betty but I have work to prepare for tomorrow."

"You got the job!" Amanda jumps with excitement.

"Yes love and guess what...the car's passed its M.O.T."

"Oh mum," Amanda hugs her, relieved the old blue mini has passed. This seems to make Amanda feel things are going to be OK.

"See everything turns out well in the end," says Betty pleased for them both.

"Thanks for having her Betty."

"Oh any time dear, I've told her she is welcome here when ever she wants and that goes for you too."

"Come along love, thanks again Betty, goodbye."

"Bye dear, take care," Betty closes the front door behind them.

"Now... I'll just put these nets into soak."

"How was school love?" her mam asks as she puts her arm around her.

"Oh all right… I made two new friends, Wendy and Samantha."

"That's lovely, you didn't meet up with those silly girls we met this morning?"

"Her name's Karen she's the bully of the school." They walk into their house entering the hallway, Amanda reels at the décor.

Early seventies wallpaper consisting of orange and brown squares; the lounge was no better, avocado green lines crossing over paler avocado green lines.

"When are we going to decorate mum?"

"Soon love, just let me get settled into my new job and when we have enough money to buy wall-paper, we'll make it feel like home… now have you had something to eat?"

"Yes, Betty made mince, peas, carrots and pota-toes."

"I'll have to give her some money for food."

"I don't think she'll take it," says Amanda as she slumps down on to the settee. "She enjoys the company."

In the kitchen her mam tidies up. "I must admit, I don't look forward to growing old here," she falls silent.

Amanda gets up and walks through. "Oh mum Wendy's going to show me around town at the weekend can I…mum are you all right?"

She stands looking through the window. "Yes love...silly me," she wipes a tear away with the tea towel.

"Everything will be OK," Amanda puts her arms around her. "I like my new school, you've got that job and Ethel's passed her M.O.T."

She turns and hugs Amanda. "You're so precious to me I couldn't have made it without you." There's a knock at the door. "Oh can you see who that is love?" Amanda goes to the front door and opens it.

"Hello there," a tall dark haired man about forty stands almost filling the doorway. "Do you own the blue mini?" the man asks.

"Yes," Amanda replies.

"You've left your parking lights on." Amanda's mam enters the hall wiping her face and straightening her clothes. "Have I," she laughs. "With all the excitement I must have left them on, be a love," she picks up her handbag from the hall table. "Run down and switch them off," handing Amanda the keys.

"OK," Amanda squeezes past the stranger and runs down to switch them off.

"OK then," the man turns and starts to walk away.

"Oh thank you." She steps out on to the balcony. "Do you live here, sorry of course you must do," she laughs.

"Yes number thirty-seven... You've been here a

week now."

"Yes and still trying to get sorted out."

"Norman is my name." The man introduces himself.

"Oh yes… Norma… pleased to meet you," she holds out her hand, Norman shakes it.

"Oh! Isn't that a coincidence my name is Norma and your name is Norman," she laughs again.

"Actually Councillor Norman Pritchard, pleased to meet you."

"Oh a councillor… how exciting!"

"If there is anything you need you can always give me a knock," he says helpfully.

"Thank you I must say everyone is very friendly around here."

"Yes, it's not a bad place, a few pensioners, single mums, single dads."

"And which category do you fall into?

"Widower, my wife died in a car accident."

"Oh I am sorry," she replies embarrassed.

"I have a son, he's at university studying to be a doctor."

"That's good… you must be proud."

"Yes! I suppose I am really."

"I must crack on," Amanda's mam makes an excuse.

"Yes OK… are you doing anything later?" Norman asks.

"Sorry!" she says surprised at the offer of a date.

"I mean would you like to go out for a meal?"

"That's very kind but..."

"Don't worry, the offer stands open, maybe another time?" says Norman embarrassed at the rejection.

Amanda returns bouncing up the concrete stairs, not wanting to leave mam alone with a strange man for too long.

"Yes, maybe some other time... I'd like that."

"What's going on?" Amanda asks.

"Pardon!" her mam responds annoyed at the tone in Amanda's voice.

"By you were quick switching those lights off," Norman says jokingly.

"Not quick enough!" Amanda takes a dislike to Norman and walks past him and her mam into the hall.

"OK... I'll maybe see you later," Norman asks feeling awkward.

"Yes, thank you again... Goodbye," Amanda's mam enters the hall and shuts the door; Amanda steps out of the kitchen eating an apple.

"What are you doing?" Amanda asks taking a bite out of the apple.

"Sorry!" Her mam responds amazed at the question she has just been asked. "I was about to ask you the same thing, that was very rude the way you answered Norman when he was clearly being friendly."

"Norman… is that his name? You've only just met him and you're on first name terms," Amanda walks upstairs to her bedroom.

"Now listen madam, if I wish to talk to people, even if they are men, I will not have you being rude to them," Amanda slams her bedroom door.

"Stay in your bedroom and don't come out until you apologise to me, do you hear?" Her mam slams the kitchen door behind her.

Borough Park

"Go on," Decker tries to persuade Karen as they hide in the park bushes. It's 8pm and getting darker by the minute.

"No!" Karen replies.

"Touch it, it won't bite."

"Arrr," Karen screeches.

Decker laughs loudly. "What's wrong?"

"It moved."

"It does that… go on hold it!"

"I can't see it's too dark."

"Here give me your hand."

"Err."

"Now what's wrong?"

"It feels…"

"Wait until it's inside you."

"No way! I'm not putting that…"

Karen's interrupted by Alison approaching the bushes.

"Kaz are you in there?"

"Bugger off Alison," Decker shouts.

"You bugger off," she replies.

"Are you coming then?"

"No such luck," Decker moans.

"Yeah, I'll be with you in a minute, wait at the Park gates," Karen shouts.

"Don't be long then," Alison leaves.

"Come here Kaz."

"Watch where you're poking that," Karen tells him. "I'm going home now, I'm starving."

"Here have a nibble on this," Decker hints.

"Err, no thanks, put it away!"

"Give us a snog then before you go."

"Argh!" Karen screeches again.

"What now?"

"It's still sticking out."

Decker laughs. "Here I'll put it away… there."

"Why does it have to be so big?" Karen asks.

"That's why they call me donkey dick."

"Well no way is that entering any part of my anatomy, not until you cut it down a peg or two."

"What!" Decker reels, horrified by the thought.

"I'll see you at school tomorrow."

"Don't go Kaz," he pleads with her. "I haven't finished yet... what are you doing?" Decker asks.

"Looking for my school tie, shit where is it?"

"While your bending down!"

"Argh, fuck off Deck. I'll come back tomorrow and find it," she leaves the bushes and walks off.

"Kaz don't go yet... I'm not cutting a millimetre off it! For no one not even you," Decker shouts. "So don't you worry my golden rod."

Brad approaches the bushes. "Decker I'm going to the club, it closes at ten."

I thought you were with Sharon?" Decker asks.

She's gone off with Alison."

"Wait there a minute... Orr."

"What are you doing?" Brad asks.

" Yeh...I'm having a... oh yeah!"

"Fuck off Deck, I'll see you tomorrow."

"Don't go Brad... oh yeah! Yeah!" There's a silence.

" Orr...I needed that."

Breakfast At Sally's

"I won't tell you again, get up... now!" Sally's mam stands at the bottom of the stairs yelling. "Do you hear me?" she walks through the dining room into the kitchen. "Stop that Adrian or you'll get a smack."

Adrian, Sally's three-year-old brother sits at the dining table playing with his breakfast. "Me don't like," he calls out.

"Shut up and eat up," mam shouts from the kitchen.

"I hate yucky stuff," he calls again.

"What's for breakfast Mam?" Sally asks as she enters the room.

"It's on the table and cold I expect," mam hurries backwards and forwards between the kitchen and dining room preparing breakfast in her usual harassed state of mind.

"Porridge again," Sally sits down looking at it.

"Some people have nothing, so eat it." Her mam tells her.

Sue walks in yawning and sits in the armchair.

"You, out of your father's chair, now! Your porridge is on the table," mother walks back into the kitchen.

"I don't want any breakfast."

"Sit down and eat," mam shouts. "I don't cook food for a hobby you know."

"Well I'm not eating it." Sue replies adamantly.

Mam carries a pot of tea in and puts it on the table. "Adrian!" she slaps his hand, "if I've told you once, I've told you a hundred times don't play with your food."

"Don't hit him," Sue gets up to comfort Adi as he starts to cry.

"When you have kids of your own, I won't tell you how to bring them up, so don't tell me, now take him upstairs, his nappy needs changing and no if, buts, where's or why's about it." Mam heads back into the kitchen.

"He might as well be mine," she picks Adi up. "I'm always having to change him… come on Adi let's get you clean."

"Just get on with it," mam shouts.

Dad stands in the doorway stopping Sue and Adi passing through.

"Well I'm not moving," dad looks at Sue. She steps aside so dad can enter. "Is my breakfast ready?"

"In a minute dad," mother calls to him.

"I want it now, I'm going out in a minute."

Mam enters with a plate of bacon, sausage, eggs, tomatoes and toast. "Stop your whingeing, your breakfast is always ready, you should know that," she hands it to him as he sits in his armchair.

Dad eats it like it's his last meal.

"We have no nappies!" Sue calls down.

"Just clean him up and put a pair of undies on him," mam shouts up the stairs.

Sally smells burning. "Mam the toast!"

"Oh shit!" Mam dashes back into the kitchen.

"Where's my shoes?" dad demands with a piece of bacon half in his mouth.

"Where you left them, under the television set," mam shouts as she throws the burnt toast into the bin.

"You could have cleaned them woman," dad shouts as he puts them on.

"Sports day is coming up in a few weeks dad, will you be coming to watch?" Sally quietly asks.

"I haven't got time!" he says with his mouth full.

"I wish you would dad, I'd love you to see me, I'm running in the one hundred metre hurdles."

Dad looks at her, his eyes saying, 'I've answered your question, don't ask me again,' and carries on eating.

Sue carries Adrian back in the dining room; she sits at the breakfast table with Adi, sitting him on her lap.

"I want eater bix," Adrian can only say parts of his words.

"Eat what you're given boy!" dad shouts.

"I don't want," Adrian cries.

"Don't answer me back boy!" dad shouts even louder. "And stop yer crying."

"Don't cry Adi, here let's put some more sugar on your porridge."

Mam brings dad a fresh mug of tea. "Where are you off to love?" she asks.

"None of your business."

She hands him his tea. "Listen I've just cooked you your breakfast, the least you can do is let me know what you're planning to do today." Dad looks at her saying nothing. "Oh eat your food," she heads back into the kitchen.

There is a silence in the room only Adrian whines to himself as Sue feeds him.

"I said stop your crying!" dad shouts spitting his food.

"Don't yell at him dad… I don't think he's feeling well, Mam! I don't think Adi's well," she calls.

Mam marches back into the room. "What's wrong with him?" she snaps.

Sue feels his forehead. "He's got a temperature."

"Well if you feel sick you can go upstairs back to bed, without any breakfast," mam takes his porridge back into the kitchen. Adrian sobs quietly into Sue's arms.

"Bloody cry baby!" Dad talks into his mug as he gulps his tea.

"There's a part time job at the hairdressers' in Park Street," Sally tells Sue. "Do you fancy coming with me to see about it."?

"You do that, then you can help pay towards your keep," dad says as he finishes his breakfast.

"At least she'll work for her money," Sue mumbles under her breath.

"What did you say!" Dad throws his plate on the floor.

Mam rushes in. "What's going on?"

"Come hear you slut," dad jumps up and raises his hand. Sue stands with Adrian in her arms.

"Stop it dad, stop it sit down," mam steps between them.

"I'm not staying here to be disrespected," dad grabs his jacket off the back of his chair and storms out the back way into the alley.

"Now look what you've done, you clean that up miss before you go to school."

"Clean it up yourself," she puts Adrian on the chair and grabs her bag, running out the front door.

"Sue!" Sally runs after her.

Adrian pulls on the tablecloth as he tries to climb off his chair, he laughs as the plates and cutlery fall to the floor.

"Bugger the lot of yer," mam storms into the kitchen, leaving Adrian now sitting on the floor crying.

Outside Sally catches up to Sue in the street, "Sue wait on."

"It's about time that bastard was…" Sue starts to cry.

"Sue what's wrong… you know what dad's like, just ignore him."

Throwing her bag down Sue slumps on to a doorstep, "I hate him."

"Why do you…"

"I hate… the yelling every morning, always having to keep him happy."

"Sue don't cry," Sally is worried, this isn't like Sue.

"Why is it yell, yell, yell…"

"That's just the way they are," Sally tries to calm her down.

"It's dad's fault, he's always causing the arguments, Mam has to keep him happy all the time," Sue picks up her bag and stands. "Come on," she wipes her tears away. "We'll be late," she and Sally walk on together.

Wendy And Paul Talk Biology

"It's our biology lesson today, they're showing us a facts of life film," Wendy informs Paul as they stroll to school. "Mrs Summers is going to explain all about…contraception."

"That should be interesting," Paul smiles.

"When are you going to see the film?" Wendy asks.

"Tomorrow I think."

"I heard they were going to show all the whole

year at the same time," Wendy says, horrified at the thought.

"That should steam up the hall windows," Paul jokes.

Wendy laughs. "Has your dad told you the facts of life yet Paul?"

"No I don't think he knows what they are."

"He must have known something, they produced you didn't they!"

"Exactly!"

"Hi Wend, Paul!"

"Hi Sam," Wendy waves to Sam.

"Say Sam, have your parents told you the facts of life yet?" Paul asks.

"Paul!" Wendy stops him. "Don't be rude."

"No!" Sam replies embarrassed.

"My mam started to tell me about the birds and the bees," Wendy explains. "But the milk man came, so she had to see to him."

"Did she come back and finish?" Paul asks.

"No she just told me to continue with my jigsaw."

Paul quickly jumps in. "Now let me get this straight, you were doing your jigsaw while your mam was seeing to the..."

Wendy stops him. "Don't go there Paul."

Karen's Office

Amanda enters the girls' toilets, seeing Karen, Alison and Sharon she stops and turns to leave.

"Well look what's just popped into my office, stop her Shaz," Sharon blocks the doorway with her arm.

Amanda turns and faces Karen. "What do you want?" she asks.

"I'll tell you what I don't want," Karen walks up to her.

"And what's that then?" Amanda stares at her.

"I don't want southern slags swanking into my school showing they're cleverer than we are."

"And I've done that have I?"

"Ooohhh she's witty as well," Sharon remarks.

Karen walks round Amanda. "What shall we do with her?"

"Put her head down the toilet!" Alison shouts.

Karen pushes Amanda into the toilet cubical. She falls on to the seat. Karen stands in front of her. "You'd better realise I run this school, so you can start by doing what I tell you."

"Take a running jump," Amanda stands up.

"Get her girls," Karen gives the order to flush her.

"Get off me, get off me!" Amanda shouts trying to fight them off.

At this moment a teacher enters the toilets. "I

hope no one is smoking in here," the teacher calls. Seeing the commotion she asks. "What's going on?"

The girls leave the cubicle. "Nothing miss just playing," Alison replies.

"Well playtime is over go to your lessons." The girls start to leave, the teacher grabs Karen by the arm. "Where's your tie?"

Karen puts her hand to her neck remembering where she lost it the night before. "I've left it... at home," she lies.

"Well make sure you wear it tomorrow, now get to your lesson, break's over," Amanda emerges from the cubical straightening her clothes and hair. "Aren't you the new girl who's here to do her exams?"

"Yes miss."

"Well if I can give you some advice."

"What's that miss?"

"Keep clear of girls like Karen Sinclair, those types end up as nothings," Amanda smiles and walks past the teacher. On the way to her lesson she meets Karen waiting in the corridor.

"I haven't finished with you yet," Amanda pushes past ignoring her.

Sex Film Or Education

The girls file into the science lab. "Right settle down!" Mrs Summers prepares to address the girls. "Mrs Kidman could you turn off the lights please?" There is much excitement and talk amongst the girls as to what they are about to see. "Now girls, quiet please, first we will see a short film on the make up of the male and female reproductive system, then we will discuss contraception and I will answer any questions you may have, so settle down." The film starts.

After a short while Karen gets restless. "Oh this is boring," she whispers to Sharon. "Miss...Miss."

"Yes Karen."

"I'd like to know how sperm...you know the stuff boys have," the class giggles. "How does that reproduce, do they shag each other and have baby sperms?" The class laugh.

"OK Karen that's enough."

"If the baby sperm come out first instead of the older ones is that what pre-ejaculation means?" The class are now laughing aloud.

"I said that's enough."

"What happens to the old sperms, do they just keep growing in the lad's bollocks until they can't fit any more and that's why they have wet dreams?" The class is now hysterical.

"Karen if you don't shut up, I'll ask you to leave," the teacher warns her.

"It's the blind leading the blind," Karen whispers to Sharon.

"I don't want to see this anymore," Sam tells Wendy,

"Your not embarrassed are you?"

"No! But I'll faint if any of that stuff comes out."

"I said quiet," Mrs Summers shouts.

"Here Sam," Wendy, whispers. "When boy's play with themselves the stuff that comes out wriggles about on their tummies."

"Oh don't, I'll be sick as well... how do you know anyway?"

"Trust me..." Wendy nods her head looking around. "I've seen the stuff."

"Wendy...you haven't!"

"Samantha if you say another word you can be the first to leave," the teacher shouts.

"Sorry Miss."

"Yeah shut up, he's coming...I mean the good part's coming," Karen shouts out as the class laugh again.

"Right settle down," the teacher is now annoyed. "Karen! Any more talking and I will switch off the film."

The class go into protests of, "Oh no miss, don't do that it's interesting" and "We'll shut up miss promise."

"Right all of you shut up and watch then," she orders.

"I feel faint," Sam tries to stand.

"They haven't shown any stuff yet," Wendy informs her.

"Ooohhh."

"Sam, sit down, breath deeper," Wendy holds Sam's arm whilst still watching the film. "You'll be fine, just look away if it comes out… look away, look away now it's coming out."

Sam faints, falling to the floor.

"Miss, Sam's fainted," Wendy calls out.

"Lights please Mrs Kidman," Mrs Summers picks up Sam and takes her outside.

"Typical, someone's got to faint and guess who, plain Jane herself," Karen laughs.

"Karen, you're on detention tonight."

"Shit, can't anyone have fun anymore?"

"Now the rest of you quiet! While we help Samantha, this always happens, we expect another two to faint before the film finishes," the class goes quiet looking at each other. 'Who's next?'

Outside Sam is sat with her head between her knees. "Shall I go and get some of that smelling stuff from the first aid room Miss," Wendy asks.

"Stuff, stuff no I don't want to smell it," Sam faints again.

Virginity "Is that it?"

"Oh dear," the teacher says. "She's delirious."

Dinnertime

"Do sperm shag each other?" Paul laughs hysterically, Wendy looks at him as to say 'keep it down I don't want the whole dining hall hearing,' he stops laughing.

"So Sam's gone home then?" Paul asks looking serious.

"I know we shouldn't laugh but it was funny," Wendy giggles. "Especially when she woke the second time screaming get it out, get it out of my nose," they both laugh aloud.

Geoff butts in. "What's this stuff you're talking about?"

"Get a life Geoff," Paul says still laughing.

"Well… what is it?"

"So Saturday's OK for you Amanda?" Wendy asks changing the subject.

"I don't know, mum and I had a bust up last night, I haven't said sorry yet."

"When will you be saying sorry?" Wendy asks.

"Tonight I suppose."

"So Saturday's still on then?"

"Yes, I think so."

At the back of the dining hall Sharon is holding

up a sausage, she bites into the end leaving an inch long piece of meat. "That big," Sharon laughs.

"What about you Kaz, did Decker get his out?" Alison asks.

"It was dark I couldn't see," Karen dismisses the question.

"You told me you touched it!" Sharon questions.

"No!" Karen replies staring at her.

"Liar," Sharon accuses her. "Come on how big is it?"

"I've heard they call him donkey dick," Alison remarks.

"Well, it's for me to know and you never to find out!" Karen picks up three sausages together and bites off the ends, they all laugh.

At Sally and Sue's table, talk is more sombre.

"Games next!" Sally looks at her timetable.

"It'll be running I bet," Julie moans as she sits with the twins. "Which race are you entering Sal?"

"The one hundred metre hurdles, I hope."

"What about you Sue?" Julie asks.

Sue in a world of her own looks out of the dining hall window. "What?" She replies.

"Are you all right?" Julie asks.

"Yeah, why shouldn't I be?"

"Sue, are you coming with me to apply for this hairdressing job?" Sally asks her.

"I suppose so!" Sue says, not really interested in having a conversation.

"They're looking for two people, it'll be fun if we both get the jobs," Sally tells Julie.

"Leave it out!" Sue snaps. "Come on, I'm going down the shops before break ends."

Games Lesson Or A Running Hell?

Looking over the school field, the fifth years train for sports day. One third of pupils sit at the side of the running track, talking and waiting, hoping not to be chosen next. Another third warm up; they are usually the star pupils, the teachers always pick them for the best teams. The remainder, throwing javelins, discus or hop skip and jumping, are all trying to look professional.

"Come on Andrews run don't walk," Mr Butcher the games teacher yells.

"Sir!"

"Yes Peterson."

"Have you put me down for the one hundred metres?"

"Everyone gets to try for the one hundred metres Peterson," Mr Butcher looks at him. "But you'll be fine," he winks at the boy.

"Thanks."

"Sir, Peterson, sir."
"Thanks sir."

Geoff sits next to Paul discussing the unfairness of games lessons. "Well! Are you down for it?" Geoff asks Paul.

"No," Paul replies.

"I bet he puts me in for it."

"No chance you couldn't run down your garden path," Paul jokes.

"You're telling me," Geoff looks to the sky and yells. "I want to do the javelin, why won't they let me do javelin, I'm lousy at that as well."

"You're not very confident in sports are you," Paul asks.

"No! But I make up for it elsewhere…like girls, that's my sport."

"You're lousy at that as well," Paul laughs.

"Can we have all the girls please," Mrs Summers calls out. "Now take your places for the four hundred metres girls and remember run your hearts out, we want to win, win, win."

The girls gather together Karen, Alison and Sharon push past Wendy. "Where's your friend? Chickened out of sports… because she's fainted," Karen snides. Wendy says nothing. "Move over freaks," Karen pushes Sally aside.

"Who are you calling freaks?" Sue snaps at Karen.

"Leave it Sue," Sally again tries to stop any conflict.

"That's the freaky part…you talk to one and the other answers," Karen, Alison and Sharon laugh as they get into their lanes.

Mrs Summers holds the whistle to her mouth. "Ready, set," she blows the whistle; they all set off Karen in front, Sharon soon takes over.

"Come on Kaz," Decker shouts.

"Away Shaz! Move it!" Brad hollers as he and Dec run alongside the track.

"Come on Kaz, I've got a spare baton you can use for the next relay race," Decker whips out his Willy.

"Piss off Decker," she yells.

Brad laughs as he watches Decker's antics."Remember girls Brad and Decker have got the best tools in town," Brad boasts as he starts to get his out.

"Put it away," Sharon runs on.

"Come on Shaz," Brad shouts. "Who's your daddy, who's your daddy?"

"I'll kill that bastard," Sharon curses.

"Deckland, Bradley do you want to run around this field picking up litter?" Mr Butcher shouts at them.

"No sir," Decker and Brad discreetly put away their tools.

"Fuck off queer bastard," Decker curses under his breath.

"Why do you call him that?" Brad asks.

"He's always looking at yer dick when he talks to you in the showers."

"I've noticed that."

"Jacqueline Bailey's coming along nicely Mrs Summers."

"Yes, I hope she does as well as last year, I want her in the county finals Mr Butcher."

"The new girl runs well, she's overtaking Karen, Mrs Summers."

"Come on girls this is your chance to prove yourselves... dinner Saturday Mr Butcher?"

"That depends, Mrs Summers."

"Depends on what Mr Butcher?"

"Where, Mrs Summers."

"I thought we'd try the new restaurant in Station Road Mr Butcher."

"Eight o'clock it is, Mrs Summers."

"OK Butch!" She smiles walking away.

As the race nears its end, tired Karen drops back as Amanda overtakes her.

"So you can run too then?"

Amanda ignores her, Sue runs alongside Karen.

"Freaky watch your step," Karen puts her heel

out, tripping Sue up, she falls bringing down two other girls. "Hat trick," Karen laughs running on.

"Ahhhhh my ankle," Sue screams.

"Sue are you all right?," Sally stops running and rushes to her aid.

"Oh no! What's happened now?" Mrs Summers shouts as she runs towards them. "Stop running girls," Mrs Summers tends to Sue.

"Karen deliberately tripped Sue," Amanda says approaching the teacher. Mr Butcher runs up to assist.

"My ankle, my ankle!" Sue screams.

"What's wrong, can you move your toes?" Mr Butcher holds her ankle. "Let me take a look," he starts to take off her plimsoll supporting her leg with his hand under her knee.

"Is it broken Mr Butcher?" Sally asks.

"Just sprained I think," he replies.

"Get off!" Sue suddenly yells and pulls her leg back. "Aaaagh!" she screams in pain.

"Sorry did I hurt you,?" Mr Butcher apologises reaching out putting his hand under her thigh to help her.

"Get off me! Don't touch me again," Sue scowls.

"I'd better take you inside" Mrs Summers steps in to defuse the situation.

"I was only looking at your ankle!" Mr Butcher defends his actions.

"Dirty pervert," Sue accuses him.

"Sue!" Sally questions her reaction.

"Now we'll have less of that madam," Mrs Summers helps her up.

Mr Butcher walks back over to the lads looking back, concerned about what had just happened.

"The rest of you girls join the boys while I tend to Susan." Mrs Summers and Sally help Sue back to the changing rooms.

"Now where does it hurt?" the teacher asks sitting her down on the bench.

"My foot, now I won't be able to run," Sue protests.

"Don't worry about that, we'll get you to the Stead Hospital and have it checked first, I'm sure in a few days we'll have you back running again."

"It was that Karen's fault she caused it!" Sally complains. "It was deliberate."

"These things happen so quickly Sally, let's not jump to conclusions, now take care of your sister, rest it for five minutes in a bucket of cold water, then get showered and dressed, after that I'll run you to the hospital. OK! I'll be back in ten minutes."

"Yes Miss," Sally looks at Sue's foot.

"Arghhh, get off it hurts," Sue screams out.

"I've got to get your sock off," Sally tells her

sister. "There's a bucket over there, I'll fill it with cold water."

"I'm gonna get that fucking Karen, she's pushed me too far now," Sue threatens.

"What was that all about with Mr Butcher?" Sally asks filling the bucket with water.

"All men are perverts," Sue states.

"You can't say that, he was only trying to help, here give me your foot," Sally gently puts Sue's foot in the water.

"Take my word for it, they're only after one thing and that facts of life film didn't explain that fact."

"No! But it did leave a lot to the imagination." Sally jokes trying to cheer her sister up.

"Yeah it did, didn't it," Sue laughs. "Ouch my ankle."

On the field Karen is not happy. "That cow spragged on me and got me disqualified," Karen looks around. "She's in the changing rooms, are you coming Alison?"

"It's not time to go in yet."

"Shut up, are you coming or not?" Karen walks towards the school.

"Kaz," Alison calls her then follows.

The door bursts open to the changing room, Karen storms in followed by Alison looking behind herself checking no one is around. "Where are you Gobshite?"

Sally jumps up.

"Sit down Sally, she's all mouth."

"I'll show you who's all mouth," Karen kicks the bucket of water, spilling it everywhere.

"Arghhh my foot," Sue cries.

"Come here you," Karen grabs Sally's hair and drags her off the bench; they both slip on the water and tumble to the floor, Sally bangs her head on the floor. Still holding her hair Karen slides round and kicks her in the side. "That's for getting me disqualified."

Sue, in agony with the pain in her foot jumps at Karen. "Leave my sister alone." Alison stands by the door watching as Karen rolls over and punches Sally in the mouth, not before Sue grabs Karen's hair and pulls a chunk of it out.

"Argh! You bitch," Karen yells. They both clamber to their feet. "Hold her Alison!" shouts Karen. Alison grabs Sue's arms from behind. "Split on me would you, I'll split you," Karen kicks Sue in the crutch.

Sally still lying on the floor with blood running down from her head cries out. "Sue!"

Alison lets go of Sue's arms as she collapses screaming in pain. "Go on Kaz, kick her again," Alison instructs.

Karen kicks her in the face, blood splatters up the changing room wall. Sally lies on the floor crying. "Stop crying, cry baby, when I've finished with your sister you're next."

"Go on Kaz, kick her as well," Alison shouts.

Sally screams out as Karen's foot lays into her back.

Sue screams from across the room. "Argh! I'm bleeding, I'm bleeding," as she looks down at the blood running between her legs, spilling and mixing into the water.

Karen turns to Sue. "Oh dear, cut yourself? Come on Alison... they won't be running for a while yet."

Trembling, Alison looks at Karen standing between the girls, her clothes all wet from fighting in the water, breathing deeply, her face screwed up in anger.

"What have you done? We'd better call an ambulance, she's bleeding like mad." Alison starts to panic.

The changing room door tries to open but Alison is stopping it. "Open this door," Mrs Summers yells. Alison moves away from the door, the games teacher enters, stops and stares in horror seeing Sally crawling to Sue as she screams out her name doubled up in pain. "What the hell has been going on in here it looks like a blood bath? Alison, go get the school nurse and get a secretary to call an ambulance,

NOW!" Alison runs out crying, Mrs Summers walks over to Karen. "What do you think you're playing at?"

Karen stands and starts to giggle looking at the carnage she has caused. Mrs Summers grabs her by the hair. "Fuck off," Karen yells.

"You cow." The teacher thumps Karen in the face throwing her across the room. "You spoilt little bitch," she calls Karen. Mrs Summers turns to Sally, "You didn't see that! And you Sinclair get yourself down to the headmistress's office NOW!"

"I'm telling her what you..."

The teacher approaches her raising her arm again to strike her, Karen dashes out.

Mrs Summers slams the door behind her and falls against it, she looks back to Sally and Sue, and shock sets in. She begins to shake putting her hands to her head she cries out. "Oh God no..."

Heads Again Tails Karen Loses

Karen stands in the headmistress's office with her arms folded looking to one side not interested in what is happening, Alison standing next to her snivels twiddling her hair with her fingers feeling sorry for herself.

"Stop snivelling," Karen tells her.

"Thank you for your help," Ms Blakemoore replaces the receiver. "Stand up straight you two," she carries on with her lecture. "Do you realise what damage you could have done to those poor girls?" Ms Blakemoore sits back at her desk, the games teacher stands behind the girls. "That was the hospital on the phone lucky for you Susan will be alright, she'll suffer no permanent damage." Karen giggles. "What on earth do you find so funny…?" Karen looks to the ceiling tutting. "I will not tolerate violence in my school."

"It's not your school." Karen mumbles to herself.

"One more word from you Karen and I will have you suspended indefinitely and to hell with your exams are you listening to me?" Karen says nothing. "As for you Alison, I am amazed you would participate in such a sick attack, now because exams are nearly upon us, I will write to your parents suspending you both for one week…now get out of my sight."

Alison turns and walks to the door, Karen follows then stops, turning back she looks at Mrs Summers. "I want to make a complaint."

"A what?" The headmistress looks up in amazement.

"That cow there," she points. "Attacked me in the changing room, I've got the bruises to show for it," Karen points to her chin and pulls down her shirt revealing a bruise to her shoulder.

"I think, Ms Blakemoore, you'll find she got those through fighting with the girls."

"Quiet!" Ms Blakemoore stands for a second and thinks. "Get out of here," She looks through some paper work. "You're pathetic."

"You're all the fucking same," Karen turns and leaves following Alison. "Stop snivelling… cry baby."

Sitting quietly the class read their textbooks while the teacher scribbles on the blackboard, suddenly Karen bursts in and marches over to her desk.

The teacher turns and looks at her. "Excuse me Karen, do you mind going back out and coming in, in the proper manner?" Karen ignores her.

"Stop right there!" The teacher orders.

"Oh why don't you shut the fuck up!" Karen yells collecting her things out of her desk.

"Watch your mouth madam!"

"Always picking on me that's all you've ever done, picked on me since I came to this fucking shit hole of a school."

The class gasp in amazement at the language as Karen heads for the door. "You've never given me a chance, always fucking knocking and ridiculing me in front of everyone."

"I think you'll find you have managed to do that all by yourself Karen."

"Oh fuck off you ugly bitch!" Karen slams the door behind her; one of the glass panels smashes on to the floor.

The teacher walks over to the broken window, "I knew nothing would come of that girl, let her be an example to us all as to what happens to people when they think they are better than everyone else."

The class sit in stunned silence. "Now Bailey go and get the caretaker to clear up this glass, the rest of you get back to your work please." The teacher turns back to the board and carries on with her work as if nothing had happened.

Simultaneously the class all cheer, the teacher turns and looks at them, they stop. "Don't stop on my account!" The class laugh, cheer and bang their desk lids.

Karen storms out of the school into the playground, hearing the banging and cheering she runs home crying.

Home Bittersweet Home

Arriving home, Karen walks in through the front door, no one's in but for Blackie her pet Labrador. "Hi Blackie, surprised to see me eh?" She cuddles the only true friend she has, who came to her as a present from her father on her tenth birthday.

Karen wanders into the kitchen and opens the fridge; she takes a mouthful of milk from the bottle, grabs a chicken leg from last night's leftovers and wanders through into the lounge. Turning on the TV she notices two £1 notes on the set next to the milk bill, she picks them up and scrunches the bill into her pocket, she sits down and watches a game show. It's three o'clock in the afternoon, she glances at the photo of her and her dad on the mantelpiece, remembering the holiday to Disneyland when it was taken last February, it was the last time she saw him, her sixteenth birthday. She starts to cry looking out of the window from her chair.

An Evening Stroll

Karen walks around the many amusement arcades on her own playing the machines with the milk money she's stolen from her mam. After losing her last ten pence she decides to head for home.

It's 8 o'clock, there's a chill in the air, walking along the seafront she buttons up her school blazer and crosses her arms to keep the cold North Sea air out. A dozen motorbikes roar past with the biker in front doing a wheelie. "Wow!" Karen stops, impressed with the lead rider, she crosses the

Esplanade road and sits in a shelter to watch them as they park their bikes opposite the lifeboat station, one of the biker girls walks past her.

"Hello!" the girl nods to Karen.

"Nice bike you're riding." Karen tries to make conversation but the girl carries on by.

Most of the bikers head off to the amusements. Karen walks to one of the bikes. A Yamaha RD250 the nameplate reads on the red petrol tank; she glances over the mass of chrome that makes the bike look powerful and reaches out feeling the need to touch this impressive machine.

"Get off kid!" the biker snaps at her.

"Sorry… I'm only looking… and I'm not a kid!," she replies.

"Just leave it."

Karen walks on looking back at the biker. Is he the lead biker she thinks to herself noticing his clean long wavy dark hair. Dressed in full leathers together with his boots he looks tall and handsome.

Later sitting in the amusements cafeteria, Karen watches the bikers leave and enter the arcade, including him. They play fight, bang the machines and most of all chat up the girls. Karen gets up and wanders around; she plucks up the courage to approach the biker. "How old is your motorbike?" she nervously asks the tall dark rider.

"What?"

"I said, how old is your motorbike?" she asks again.

Another biker approaches from behind. "Chatting up little girls are we Dave?"

"I was only wanting to talk with him, I like bikes," Karen explains.

"Run along, come back when you're old enough," David tells her. Karen stands not moving. "Did you hear me?"

"I'm allowed to stand here," she says. "Anyway I'm not going anywhere until you answer my question."

"Look at the registration number and work it out for yourself, if you can read the letters that is."

Some bikers laugh at his jibe. "Come on we're getting together at Saltburn!" a biker shouts from the street door, they all start to leave.

One shoves past Karen. "Watch it!" she snaps.

Karen follows them to the door and from inside she watches as they roar off doing wheelies down the Esplanade.

The Postman Delivers Bad News

"Any mail Mum?" Amanda runs downstairs finishing getting dressed.

"Only a letter from your Aunt Lil. Are you

coming shopping with me to Middlesbrough?" her mam asks.

"I'm meeting Wendy and Paul down town, I told you."

"Oh sorry love, I forgot."

"How's Aunt Lil?" Amanda asks as her mam reads the letter.

"Oh dear, your Uncle's not very well."

"What's wrong with him?"

"Cancer I'm afraid love," her mother breaks the bad news.

"Uncle Peter's got cancer! What are we going to do?" Amanda asks approaching her mam upset.

"There's not a lot we can do love, even with the treatment these days it's not guaranteed."

"Uncle Peter's my favourite," Amanda takes the letter.

"I'll tell you what! We'll go and visit them next weekend shall we? York is only a forty-five minute drive down the road."

"Oh yes mum, I'd like that."

There's a knock at the kitchen window, Norman waves. "Come in the door's not locked," Norma calls to him.

"Hi Norma, say it's a lovely day how about us all going out together, I can show you around, nothing much has changed."

"No thanks I'm already busy," Amanda goes upstairs.

"She doesn't like me much does she?" Norman whispers.

"You have to understand, it's too soon since her father and I split."

"I understand… so what shall we do?"

"I fancied shopping in Middlesbrough," she suggests.

"Middlesbrough it is, there's a new shopping centre they've built! The Hill Street centre, why don't we go there?"

"That'll be nice," Norma agrees.

The Saturday Meeting Place

Situated on the middle of Redcar Stray is a lonely but important café, simply called 'the Stray Café'. It has provided the young of Redcar over many years a regular meeting place, especially for Wendy and co.

"Hey that's mine put it back!" Wendy grabs the spoon and hits Paul on the back of his hand demanding he puts the marshmallow back into her hot chocolate.

"Hi you two," Samantha joins them.

"Tell him to give me back my marshmallow Sam."

"Paul give it back!" Samantha commands.

"Yes miss, I won't do it again miss, open wide." Paul spoons the marshmallow into Wendy's mouth.

"Have you…finished your…" Wendy coughs, "Dance lesson?"

"Yeah, and do my feet hurt," Samantha kicks off her shoes.

"What's cooking?" Paul asks.

"Cheeky," Sam kicks Paul.

"Ouch! Wend she kicked me."

"I was trying to do this new dance routine, you know from the film Fame."

"Hi everyone," Amanda joins them. "Guess who I bumped into on the way down?"

"Ello, ello, ello as the policeman said."

"We've heard it," Paul, Wendy and Sam shout together.

"Oh yeah you've heard that one," Geoff sits leaving Amanda standing.

Amanda coughs. "Any room for me?" she looks at Geoff.

"Shove up Sam," Geoff pushes Samantha up into the corner. "Let this gorgeous girl sit down."

"Hey! I'm not a sardine you know," Samantha complains.

"So what's the plan today?" Amanda asks squeezing in the seat.

"Paul and me fancy going to the pictures this

afternoon it starts about two o'clock."

"That sounds good," Amanda looks round to Geoff and Samantha. "You up for it?" Amanda asks them.

"Yeh!" Sam agrees.

"Sounds good to me," Geoff nods in agreement.

"I'm off to get an inner tube for my bike," Paul says getting up from the table. "You girls go off and do the things you girls do, Geoff and I will meet up with you at two o' clock."

"Yes! We'll do what you say," Wendy quips. "Anything you say Paul."

"All right with me," Amanda looks at the girls.

"Well that's settled, see you later then," Paul kisses Wendy. "Away Geoff."

"See you later dudes," Geoff clambers slowly over Amanda to get out from the seat.

"When you're finished Geoff?" Amanda looks at him.

"I haven't started yet."

"Come on Geoff, she'll eat you for breakfast," Paul grabs his jacket and drags him out of the café.

"Promises, promises!" Geoff shouts.

"That's got rid of them," Wendy laughs. "My mam said I can have my ears pierced so I'm going to get them done today, I haven't told Paul yet," Wendy whispers across the table to Sam and Amanda.

"You're lucky, my mam won't let me," Samantha

complains. "I can't see why not."

"I've had mine pierced but let them heal over."

"Let's see?" Amanda shows them her left ear. Wendy looks up close. "What does it feel like? You know when you had them done."

"It hurt really bad that's why I let them heal up."

"It didn't!" Wendy's worried.

"Only kidding, no you don't feel much just a little jab, I left the stud out that's why they healed over."

"Did you see those lads on TV last night they had a chain from their nose to their ear," Samantha reels with the thought. "They called it body piercing."

"Body piercing! That'll never catch on," Wendy comments.

"Shall we go then, I like to see blood?" Amanda gets up.

"Ey!" Wendy looks at Amanda worried again.

"Only kidding, come on let's go."

Saturday At The Flicks

"No I'm not doing it!" Wendy protests outside Redcar Regent cinema.

"Come on Wend it'll be a laugh," Paul eggs her on.

"What will happen if we get caught?" asks Amanda.

"They'll only throw us out," Paul tries to persuade the girls.

"Come on Wend," Sam encourages her.

"Sam! I didn't think you were like that," Wendy says surprised.

"Well is it on then?" Geoff asks.

"Yes," Paul whispers to Geoff. "Here's the money to get in when the coast is clear open the fire door we'll be waiting outside."

"Don't forget the popcorn," Samantha reminds him.

"I'll pay to get in! Why does Geoff get to do it?" Wendy asks protesting at the fact that Geoff will be the only one going in legally.

"Because you can't go into the gents loos to open the fire doors."

"Why can't we go in through the ladies fire door?"

"Because it will look funny two lads entering the cinema from the ladie's loo!"

Wendy says nothing.

"OK! I'll see you inside you bring the cokes," Geoff hands Paul the cans of drink.

Geoff heads into buy himself a ticket, stopping at the sweet counter; he then buys five bags of popcorn then walks into the cinema passing a very large lady attendant. "Hungry are we?"

"What?" Geoff stops and looks up at her. "Oh yeah… can't get enough of the stuff."

"Follow me please," the attendant leads him down the aisle to his seat. Geoff makes his way to the middle of the row. "Sorry, sorry, ta," he sits and watches the attendant leave then climbs back out dropping his bags of popcorn as he struggles past the other punters. "Sorry, I err sorry." He moves out of the seats and makes his way to the gents toilets, looking back checking all is clear.

Outside Paul and the others wait impatiently.

"What's taking him so long?" Wendy complains, just then the door opens.

"Stop yer moaning, hurry up then before the attendant sees the security light's on," Geoff orders.

They all pile in. "I can't believe we're doing this," Amanda laughs.

"Phew! It stinks," Samantha complains.

"This is not going to work," Wendy thumps Paul.

"Ouch what was that for?" Paul looks at her.

"For forcing me into a man's toilet and for not noticing I've had my ears pierced."

"Oh! They do look nice Wend, when did you have them done?" Paul tries to be nice.

"Oh shut up," she snaps.

Geoff looks through the curtains into the arena. "Quick hide, the attendant's coming."

"What! Hide where? Oh we're going to get caught," Wendy panics.

"Quick inside the cubicles," Paul shoves the girls.

"What!" Wendy cries out.

"You're joking I'm not…" Samantha resists.

"Shut up and get in," Paul pushes Wendy and Samantha into the cubicle with him. Geoff and Amanda go into another cubicle.

The attendant walks in and checks the fire doors. "Who's in here?" She calls out.

"We're the ghosts of the crappers, who dooooo you think?" Geoff calls out in a spooky voice. "Can't we take a craaaaap in peeeace?"

The attendant looks under the doors and sees in each cubical a pair of legs with trousers around its ankles.

Paul sits in the middle with Wendy and Sam balancing on the pan behind him holding on to each other trying not to slip off.

In the other cubical Geoff is sitting the wrong way, with his trousers around his ankles facing Amanda as she balances on the pan, hitting Geoff on his head with her hand as his face stares smiling into the crutch of her trousers.

"Hurry up in there the film will be starting in a minute," the attendant shouts before leaving.

"Thank yooohhh," Geoff smiles; Amanda hits him on the head again. "Ow!" Geoff looks up at her.

"But it's worth it," she pushes him aside and clambers over him to get out of the cubicle. "Mind my ticket," he protects his privates from her foot with his hand.

"Your what?" Amanda asks.

"My ticket to ride."

Amanda ignores his remark. "Just pull your trousers up please."

"Has she gone?" Wendy asks.

The girls leave the cubicles as the lads do up their pants.

"We can't stay here all day!" Wendy moans.

"I hope my clothes don't end up smelling of this toilet," Sam says as she sniffs her shirtsleeves.

"Geoff, check the curtain! You girls get ready," Paul instructs.

"She's looking this way, I'll go and distract her," Geoff leaves still clutching the popcorn.

"He calls it his ticket?" Amanda questions.

"Oh his mam called it that when he was a kid," Paul looks through the curtains scanning for an empty row of seats. "Once when he was six, travelling on a bus, the bus conductor asked his mam if he could punch the boy's ticket, it caused such a laugh he's kept calling it that ever since. "I think it's a deep psychological thing, don't tell him I told you." The girls giggle. "Hold on! Geoff's talking to the attendant… quick follow me." They dash out from the gents, Paul pushes the girls to the front row and they each dive into a seat.

Geoff joins them. "She thinks I've moved to the back," Geoff briefs Paul.

"See I told you it would work," Paul puts his arm around Wendy.

The film starts as they tuck into their popcorn and coke, suddenly the attendant appears in front of them. "Can I see your tickets please?" The girls spit out their popcorn and coke laughing.

Geoff looks at them. "What's so funny?"

The Amusements Are Free

"Well it would have been a rubbishy film anyway… the attack of the giant tarantulas."

"Yeah but I paid for a ticket," Geoff complains, the girls giggle to each other. "What have you been saying," Geoff whispers to Paul.

"Nothing! Let's get the bus home," Paul suggests looking at the girls, they all burst out laughing.

"Very funny, I'm going to the musies," Geoff walks on sulking.

"That's a good idea let's all go," Wendy links arms with the girls and they follow Geoff.

Standing next to Paul, Geoff watches him play the

fruit machines, where the highest prize is three bells in a horizontal line paying one pound fifty in tokens, inside twenty minutes Paul has accumulated winnings of one pound eighty pence. Geoff on the other hand is down one pound twenty and skint.

"I don't know why I bother," Geoff says fed up with losing. "You always win, I lose every time I come in here, how do you do it?"

Paul gets another three nudges; he holds the buttons and lines up two bells in the window. "You have to memorise the reels!" Paul says putting another ten pence in the slot. "Then when the nudges come you know what's behind them… hold!" Paul gets a hold straight after the nudge. "Watch this… if you get a nudge and hold straight away, you hold the reels and the trick is to cancel the hold," Paul pushes the buttons then cancels.

"No!" Geoff shouts. "You should of held the two bells in case the third one comes in." The reels spin and all three bells line up, again a one pound fifty win in tokens. Paul looks at Geoff and smiles.

"How do you find these fiddles?"

"I have a cousin who tells me the tricks of the reels," Paul collects his winnings.

"Lend us ten pence so I can have a go?" Geoff asks.

"Here! Now bugger off," Paul gives him some tokens and Geoff buggers off.

Wendy, Samantha and Amanda are sitting in the cafeteria drinking coke. "Are you liking it up here?" Sam asks Amanda.

"It's all right, Geoff and Paul are a good laugh."

"Yeah sometimes I crack up seeing the stupid things they get up to," Sam remarks.

"I miss my friends though," Amanda looks into her glass of coke.

"Did you have a boyfriend when you lived down south?" Wendy asks.

"Well you could have called him a boyfriend of sorts but he hasn't written to me yet… he did promise."

"What's his name?" Wendy asks.

"Robin, Robin James Tomlinson."

"RJT sounds like a motor oil," Wendy jokes.

There's silence from Amanda as she sits in a daydream state.

"Sorry," Wendy apologises. "I didn't mean to make fun of him."

"No, it's OK, I was thinking about my mum, she's met this bloke."

"What's he like?" Sam asks.

"He's called Nooorman."

"Norman, that's a silly name," Wendy laughs.

"I don't like him much, he's always hanging around the house."

"What happened with your step dad?" Sam asks.

"He ran off with one of his models, he's a fashion photographer."

"I bet your mam was upset," Wendy enquires.

"Devastated, she couldn't stop crying for weeks."

"How did you feel about it?" Wendy asks.

"I was upset, but a lot of my friends' parents have split too, anyway it was better than all the arguments that went on."

"Why move up here?" Sam asks.

"Oh mum felt it would be good to make a new start, she says it's much more quiet up here, less hassle up north not like down south traffic jams, houses as far as the eye can see, you've got it made up here, open countryside, forests and the sea… I like the sea."

"She's not wrong about it being quiet, there's never anything to do," Wendy points out.

"What with beaches and countryside!"

"I suppose," Wendy replies. "But when you live here you don't notice it as much."

Geoff approaches the girls. "There you are, I've been looking all over for yer, lend us ten pence, I've got two plums and a possible hold on 'em."

"No! Go away," Sam snaps.

"I'm skint," Amanda checks her pockets.

"What about you Wendy?" She just looks at him.

"Oh thanks!" He walks off.

"Don't drop your plums it might hurt," Amanda jokes.

"Don't you girls ever give up!" Geoff shouts back.

"Talking of plums there's one over there looking at us," Wendy whispers to Amanda and Sam.

"Where?" Amanda turns to look.

"Don't turn around he'll see you looking… over there by the space invaders, he's got a motor bike helmet in his hand."

Amanda turns slowly to look at him then quickly back to Wendy. "He saw me looking!"

"Oh no! He's coming over, away let's get going," Wendy gets up to leave, Sam and Amanda follow. As they walk down the steps from the cafe the biker stands in front of them.

"You're not going now are you?" he asks.

"We're…erm… we're going to see our boyfriends," Wendy pushes past. "They're not your boyfriends I've been watching you for the past hour…anyhow I haven't seen you in here before."

"No it's my first time," Amanda replies, Sam shoots her a look.

"I thought so your accent's not from around here, where yer from?" The biker steps closer to Amanda.

"Pinner… in Middlesex."

"What's yer name?" he asks.

"Well nice talking to you but we have to go," Sam

grabs Amanda's arm and drags her away from him. "Come on Amanda."

"Amanda...nice name, might see you in here again?" the biker calls out as she's dragged off.

"What's wrong Sam?" Amanda asks.

"He's a biker, you don't talk to them."

"I know bikers down south, they're OK."

"Not up here they're not, they're only after one thing," Sam states.

"What's that then?" Amanda says innocently.

"It!" Sam replies as they join Paul and Wendy. "Are you ready for home Wend?"

"In a minute Sam, Paul's won three pounds sixty," Wendy announces proudly.

"I suppose I'd better get back, I promised mum I would help her strip the wallpaper in the hall, what are you doing tonight Wend?" Amanda asks.

"Me and Paul are babysitting my sister."

"Where's Geoff?" Sam asks looking for him.

"Oh he's trying to nudge some pennies from the waterfall," Paul tells them.

Just then Geoff comes running up. "Away lets get out of here, I've just kicked the penny machine and set the alarm off."

"Typical," Sam says as they all scurry out of the amusements.

I'm Home Mum

Walking slowly up the concrete stairs tired from a fun day, Amanda smiles to herself, remembering the antics of Paul and Geoff. She finds her keys in her pocket and opens the door. The hall has half its wall-paper stripped off and laying all over the floor. Laughter and giggles come from inside the lounge, Amanda quietly opens the door, it squeaks. Norman's head pops up from behind the settee then her mam's, Norman looks at Norma embarrassed.

"Oh hello love, I didn't expect you back so soon," her mam pushes Norman off her. "Was the film good?" They both stand fastening their overalls.

"We were doing some stripping," Norman says innocently.

"I can see that," Amanda stares at them both.

"Wallpaper love," they both stand looking guilty.

Amanda turns and runs upstairs. "Save it," she shouts.

Her mam approaches the bottom of the stairs. "We… err… it's not…"

Norman walks up to her. "I think we'd better call it a day Norma."

"OK, thanks again," Norman starts to leave. "Norman," she calls to him, he turns and looks at her. "I'm sorry, I'll see you later?" she questions.

"Wild horses wouldn't stop me," he winks at her.

"See you tomorrow."

"Bye," the front door closes. Amanda's mam stomps upstairs angry, then stops and pauses, she walks back down thinking to herself then goes back upstairs slowly to Amanda's room. Opening her bedroom door she sees her lying on the bed and walks over to sit next to her. "You and I need to talk love."

"How could you?" Amanda sobs.

"How could I what?" her mam tries to stay calm.

"Leave dad… bring me to this place."

"Now listen Amanda, for one thing your father left us and gave me no choice as what was left to do, and for another," her mam runs her hand through Amanda's hair fighting back the tears. "I thought you liked it here… you've made new friends… I've left my friends and a beautiful home too, we both have to make a new start… listen love, believe me I didn't want to go but I had to and that's that, we have to make good with what we have now… after two years your father and I will get our divorce then we will have enough money from the sale of the house to buy a new home, with a garden, not that it matters you will most probably be in university by then making new friends… you'll be able to visit your father in his new home, your friends will still be there and you'll have the benefit of having two places to live, in two different parts of the country."

"What about him?" Amanda questions. "Where does he come into your plans?"

"Amanda! Norman is a friend to me, yes we are becoming close and I could call him my best friend, like you have your best friends… I won't tell you who to see and who not to see it's up to you to choose, so please don't make choices for me. Norman is in my life, he's good to have around as a companion."

"You mean boyfriend," Amanda turns her head away from her mam.

"Yes love if that's what you want to call him," her mam strokes her hair. "I'll make us some tea, come down when your ready." She leaves the room closing the door and stands on the landing, tears welling up in her eyes, she walks into her own bedroom and sits on the bed crying quietly so Amanda won't hear.

Amanda lies on her bed; she closes her eyes and cries herself to sleep.

Mondays Bloody Mondays

"If you're going out tonight make sure you get something to eat!" Karen's mam slams the front door on her way out to work.

Karen wanders through to the kitchen fastening her school shirt; she opens the fridge and looks in.

"Yeh! What with?" she takes out some orange juice and pours herself a glass, she hears the letterbox rattle, putting down the orange she races to pick up the mail. "I'll take them!" She runs up the hall and tries to snatch the letters from her brother who gets to them first.

"What you doing?" Her brother pulls them back.

"Its nothing to do with you, give us em here."

"Its not another letter from your head is it?" He smirks.

"So what if it is?" She takes the letters and searches through them to see if it's arrived, she finds it and puts it in her pocket.

"You'll never get a job with your school record," her brother says.

"And you care?" She walks back into the kitchen opening the letter.

"You're right I don't care!" He follows her.

"Why aren't you at work anyway?" Karen asks.

"Day off…so what have you been up to, to get another letter?" He creeps up behind her as she reads it and snatches it out of her hand. "Let's see it then?"

"Fuck off, that's not yours to read," her brother quickly scans the letter.

"Its addressed to mam so it's not yours either." He reads the letter as he runs round the kitchen being chased by Karen. " You beat up a girl and she had to go hospital."

"Give me back that letter," she hits him on his back.

"And suspended for a week... mam'll love you."

She tries to grab the letter from him. "Give it back or I'll tell..."

He turns putting the letter behind his back, "tell who?"

She stops and glares at him. "Piss off, do what you want." She grabs her blazer and runs out of the front door, her brother looks at the letter and smiles to himself then crunches it up and throws it in the bin.

School Gates The Meeting Place

"Hi Sue," Jackie jumps up and down waving. "How you feeling?"

Sue and Sally walk together up to the school gates. "All right I suppose." Sue informs her.

"It was just she..." Sally starts to explain.

"Do you mind!" Sue stops her.

"Sorry... hey we got the job," Sally announces.

"The hairdressing job?" Jackie asks.

"Yeah."

"Lucky bastards, you can do my hair from now on," Jackie requests.

"Give us a chance we haven't learnt how to yet,"

Sue snaps. "Come on Sall let's go." They walk on into the school.

Amanda and her mam pull up at the gates. "Bye." Amanda steps out of the car.

"Listen love," her mam leans over the passenger seat to talk to her. "I know you miss your father a lot, but Norman is a friend, someone for me to talk to, give him a chance… eh!"

Amanda looks around not taking much notice of what her mam is telling her. "Yeh bye." She turns and walks into the school.

"I'll cook you Ravioli tonight your favourite… OK?"

Amanda stops and looks back at her mam. "If you want," she carries on walking. Her mam watches her as she walks into the school then drives off.

Karen approaches the gates.

"All right Kaz thought you were suspended?" Sharon walks up to her. "Want some gum?"

"Yeah ta… I've come to show the teachers that I'm having fun being suspended, as if suspension is going to hurt me."

"You'll miss lessons," Sharon points out.

"One week yeh! That's gonna to kill me, anyway exams will be here soon so I'll do them and then the school can go fuck itself."

"What you going to do all week then?" Sharon asks.

"Walk around have fun down the musies."

"Lucky you, I must admit I'd rather be with you than stuck here," Sharon says fed up.

"I might call for Alison."

"She's coming to school, her mam's pissed off with the head for suspending her, she says she shouldn't be suspended because you beat up a girl."

Karen stands looking around and doesn't comment. "Where's Decker and Brad?" she asks.

"Don't know late as usual."

"I'm off then," Karen walks away. "See yer sometime."

"I'll give you a call tomorrow night if you want?" Sharon calls to her.

"If you want," Karen waves back to her.

Karen spends most of the day walking through Redcar High Street, feeling hungry she pops into Woollies and nicks a Marathon and a Mars bar. By now, four o'clock she's fed up, nothing to do and no money, she walks around the corner to the sea front amusement arcades and spots the bikers congregating outside the Ritz café, a regular meeting place for tea and bacon sarnies.

When the tide's out some of them would show off and race their bikes on no man's land, the sand between high tide and low tide where the police can't touch them. Many kids, teenagers and passers-by would stand around the sea walls to watch them put on a show with their fast powerful machines.

Karen sees Dave polishing his bike. She wanders over to the shelter on the sea front and sits watching him.

"I was like you," the biker girl Karen had spoken to the other night steps from around the shelter eating chips out of newspaper covered in curry sauce.

"What!" Karen jumps in her seat startled.

"I said, I was like you once, looking at the bikes wishing I could have a ride with one of the lads…ever been on a bike before?"

"Yes." Karen lies.

"What kind?"

"What?"

"What make of bike?"

"I don't know, but it's my brother's."

The biker girl sits next to Karen. "What's your name?"

"Karen… Kaz to my friends."

"All right Kaz! I'm Jenny."

"All right."

"Wanna chip?"

Karen takes three and dips them in curry sauce. "Ta, I'm starving."

"You like the bikes then or the bikers," Jenny asks Karen as she grabs a few more chips and stuffs them in her mouth.

"They're alright, I don't like him much," she points with a chip dripping curry sauce.

"Who?" Jenny looks at the bikers.

"The one with the red bike."

"Who Dave... oh don't worry about him he doesn't like talking much but he's alright."

"Do you have your own bike?" Karen asks pinching another chip.

"No, can't afford one, I'd like to have one, one day, I ride with Nick on his."

"Is Nick your boyfriend?"

"Sort of... how old are you?" she asks Karen.

"Sixteen, why?"

"Still at school?"

"No!" Karen looks down at the uniform she is wearing. "Well, we finish in two months."

"If you want my advice," Jenny leans back on the bench. "Don't have anything to do with them."

"Why?" Karen asks taking another chip.

"They use girls like you, I've seen them come and go."

"You're with them!" Karen states.

"Nick's different, he treats me better than the other lads."

"It must be fun!"

"Yeah we party a lot, ride all over the country, meet up, go camping."

"That's what I'd like to do, get out of this crummy town."

"We all say that, but only some of us do."

"How can I become a biker girl?" Karen asks.

"You really like bikes then?"

"Yeah," Karen says enthusiastically.

"Well, don't say I didn't warn you..."

"So how can I get to ride with one?"

"Well...basically... shag one of them."

"Do what!" Karen says taken aback by her answer.

"See I told you, these lads don't sit around having tea and biscuits with girls, they just wanna screw them."

"Does Dave have a girlfriend?" Karen enquires finishing off Jenny's chips.

Jenny scrunches up the newspaper. Throwing it on the ground, she gets up to leave. "Dave never has girlfriends," she walks on.

"Is that what you did?" Karen asks.

Jenny turns around. "Did what?"

"Let one of them shag you."

Jenny smiles at her. "Sort of," then heads back to the bikes.

Karen walks towards the amusements smiling to herself that she's made a biker friend.

The week passed slowly for Karen she would walk up and down the sea front every day hoping to see Jenny and the bikers again, but for some reason they never came, leaving Karen to do the odd shoplifting and fag scrounging from people down the amusements.

Back To School For Karen

The class assemble for registration, chairs scrape along the floor as pupils settle down for the next lesson, girls giggle amongst each other, and boys throw school notebooks at each other. Karen bursts in her head held high, the classroom hushes as they all turn to look at her, she walks to her seat glaring at Sue and Sally, then turns her attention to the rest of the class. "What are you lot fucking looking at?" The class goes into a whispering chatter. Alison is already sitting at her desk, watching Karen but not wanting to get involved, Sally looks at Karen and whispers to Sue. "What did you say?" Karen shouts at her. The girls turn their heads and say nothing. "What did you say Miss spragger of the year?" Karen kicks a chair it slides over to Sue hitting her leg. The classroom falls silent.

"No she's not," Amanda says turning in her chair to face Karen. "I spragged on you so that makes me the spragger of the year, in your case the millennium." The class laugh.

"Ooh Miss Toughie eh!" Karen walks over, Amanda stands and faces up to her.

"Hit her," Alison shouts, out of habit. "No! Forget I said that," she remembers she's to keep out of trouble.

"I'll see you after school tonight," Karen threatens Amanda then turns away to walk back to her desk.

"No you won't," Amanda replies.

Karen stops and looks at her and walks over to her again.

"No you won't what?" Karen faces up to her.

Amanda smacks Karen in the face. She goes sprawling over the back tables, there's a loud cheer from the class.

"What is all this racket?" The teacher stands at the door, the class settle back into their seats. "Sit down now!" he shouts. "I will not have shouting in my classroom."

"Sir," Alison puts up her hand.

"Shut up Alison I don't wish to hear it!" He opens the registration book as the class giggle.

"Sir," Alison again puts up her hand.

"Alison after I have finished registration you can see me then."

"Yes sir, but sir..."

"But nothing, anyway where's Karen isn't she supposed to be back at school today?"

"That's what I was trying to tell you, she's on the floor next to me."

The class bursts out laughing.

"What's she doing on the floor?" He stands to look.

"Being unconscious sir," Alison lowers her hand.

Outside the headmistress's office Amanda sits one side of the corridor and Karen with a green blood-soaked paper towel covering her nose on the other, the teacher stands between them.

The office door opens. "Send Amanda in first please," the headmistress orders. Amanda walks in closing the door behind her; Ms Blakemoore stands behind her desk and slowly lowers herself into her chair. "I am very disappointed Amanda, you have come to my school with a clean record only within a number of weeks you have already accrued a black mark."

"Girls like Karen have to have a taste of their own medicine," Amanda states.

"In this case I will agree with you, but as I have already told Karen I will not tolerate fighting in school time, ask Karen to come in please."

Amanda opens the door. "Can you come in now." Karen, still holding the towel to her swollen nose enters and stands next to Amanda followed by the teacher who stands behind them with his arms folded.

"Now Karen! The fact your mother has made the choice not to come into school, let alone bothered to contact me and tell me so, it makes me wonder if she cares about your education."

"She doesn't!" Karen mumbles through the paper towel.

"I'm sorry Karen I did not hear that?"

Karen moves the towel away from her mouth. "I said she doesn't care!"

"That's a pity… now Karen, suspended last week, what action in light of this incident do you think I should take?"

"She hit me, I didn't do anything!" Karen defends herself.

"That's right miss I thumped Karen, she didn't make the first move," Karen turns her head and looks at Amanda surprised at her confession.

"Well! In light of your honesty and this time Karen, for once, you are not totally to blame, I will give you both one last chance and put you on one hour's detention every day this week… if you miss one, I repeat one, detention you can both kiss goodbye to any hope of attending your exams… you may both leave."

Outside the headmistress's office Karen faces up

to Amanda. "Don't think because you took the blame lets you off the hook."

Ms Blakemoore checks the detention register, "Who's on detention duty…? Ah Mr Butcher."

There's a sound of crashing chairs from outside her office. "What was that?"

Amanda pops her head around the door "Miss… Karen's unconscious again."

Amanda sits at the front of the classroom, Karen at the back with a bruised nose and now a black eye. The games teacher Mr Butcher sits with his head buried in a book.

"I've finished sir," Karen closes her book.

"I've finished too sir," Amanda puts her book into her satchel.

"Right! You can both go your hour is nearly up."

"Sir can I leave first? She might hit me again!" Karen asks.

"I won't be hitting you," Amanda replies.

"I don't believe her sir."

"Both of you get out of my sight," Karen ups and makes for the door.

Amanda watches her as she slowly follows her out. "Goodbye sir," Amanda says politely.

Karen walks quickly down the corridor, Amanda calls out. "Karen stop!"

She stops and turns. "What do you want?"

"I want to say sorry… sorry for hitting you."

There is a pause between them as Amanda catches up with her.

"Yeh! Why should I believe you?" Karen questions.

"Because I'm honest."

"I didn't do anything to hurt you."

"No but you threatened me, when I was already having a bad morning." They look at each other, Karen laughs.

"So I'm forgiven?" Amanda asks.

"Yeh… as long as you don't hit me again."

"Only if you don't threaten me… shake on it." Amanda holds out her hand.

Karen looks at her. "Deal." They walk together down the corridor. "Where did you learn to hit like that?" Karen asks.

"When you live down south you learn a lot in city schools, come on let's get out of this place eh!"

Amanda laughs. "I'll even buy you a Pepsi at the corner shop."

"I prefer Coke."

"OK! Coke it is…does this mean we're friends?" Amanda asks.

"Yeah why not…we still have four detentions to do…because of you."

Amanda stops and looks at Karen. "I'll have a

word with Mr Butcher tomorrow after detention."

"What will you say?"

"You'll see, come on."

The girls run out of the school laughing, now friends.

Finishing their second detention, Karen and Amanda get up to leave. Amanda waves Karen on and then approaches Mr Butcher. She talks to him, which makes him jump up out of his seat and yell at her. Amanda steps back with a worried look on her face but carries on talking. Mr Butcher listens then points to her to leave, she quickly walks to the door, he calls to her. Amanda stops, turns and looks at him, he thinks for a moment then nods his head; she smiles and hurries out into the corridor where Karen is waiting.

"What did you say?" Karen asks.

"Oh I just asked him how a certain games teacher was doing these days, and if he would like the school to know."

"Know what?"

"It doesn't matter, but not much escapes me."

"Does that mean we've been let off detention?"

"I think so." The girls run off laughing as Mr Butcher steps out of the classroom with a worried look on his face.

Come Round For A Drink

Amanda arrives home with Karen. "Mum are you home," Amanda calls. "Looks like she's out, that's a good thing I suppose."

"What do you mean?" Karen asks.

"Oh if she recognises you, she won't be happy."

"Oh yeh, I remember," Karen grins.

"Do you want a cup of tea?"

"You got anything else?"

"Have a look in the fridge I'll just pop upstairs to the toilet," Amanda dashes upstairs while Karen walks into the kitchen and looks in the fridge.

"Hey I've found some wine!" Karen shouts.

"What! I can't hear you... help yourself," Amanda calls down.

Karen picks up a glass from the sink drainer and pours the last of the wine into it; she takes a mouthful and strolls into the hallway.

"The wallpaper looks good." Karen looks at the one strip that has been pasted on.

"What?" Amanda calls down again.

"The décor," Karen shouts.

"I can't hear you... help yourself," Karen laughs and takes another drink.

Amanda scurries down the stairs. "What did you say?" she asks.

"The wallpaper," Karen points with her glass.

"Oh Norman's doing it for my mum."

"Is that the Norman you told me about?"

"Yeh." They walk into the lounge Karen sits putting her feet up on the coffee table. "Where did you say you were going tonight?" Amanda asks.

"To meet my new boyfriend and his mates."

"I thought you were going out with Decker?" Amanda puts on some music.

"Well in school I kick around with him but I sort of have a boyfriend out of school."

"What a 4-10?" Amanda asks.

"A what?"

"We call them, 9-4's & 4-10's down south, you know a 9-4 is a boyfriend for school and a 4-10 is an older boy with money for after school… what's that you're drinking?"

"Some wine... you said help yourself."

"I didn't mean that… give it here! Mum will kill me." Amanda walks back into the hall with glass in hand as her mam arrives home.

"Hello love, sorry I'm late tonight we've had a lot of school sports injuries to attend to." Her mam stops and stares at Amanda holding the glass of wine. "What's that in your hand?" Amanda looks at the wine then her mam. "That's my wine if I'm not mistaken," her mam takes it from her. "What do you think you're doing drinking alcohol?" Karen walks up behind Amanda. "And who are you… do I know you?"

"No!"

"Yes I do! You're that silly girl who doesn't know where her own school is."

"I'm not staying here to be insulted," Karen pushes past Amanda to leave.

"You're right, get out! Amanda, upstairs to your room," Amanda's mam walks into the kitchen and pours the wine down the sink.

"Mum," Amanda tries to explain.

"See yer later eh," Karen walks out on to the balcony stopping by the kitchen window to listen, she hears yelling and shouting, Karen smiles as she walks away.

You Can't Pick And Choose Your Bikers

The sun sets over Hartlepool across the Tees bay reddening the evening sky, Karen walks the length of the promenade for the fourth time looking and hoping she'll see the bikers return, suddenly there's a roar of bikes, fifteen, eighteen, twenty thunder from around the boating lake passing the cinema, cruising along the esplanade stopping outside the Ritz café.

Karen runs as fast as she can hoping to see if Jenny will be there with them, out of breath her heart pounding excited, she sees Jenny pull up. She must be with her boyfriend Nick, Karen thinks as she ponders over what to do next, she slows down fastens up her blazer to look smart. "I wish I'd changed before I came here," she curses. "No! I'll leave it undone, yes and undo a couple of buttons on my shirt, boys like that."

Walking at a fast pace she approaches Jenny. "Hi Jenny."

"Hi yer.... What happened to your eye?"

"Oh nothing... you wanna see the other girl," Karen laughs.

"Nick, this is Kaz! The girl I told you about."

"Hi Kaz," Nick nods his head.

She remembered my name, Karen smiles thinking to herself.

"Where you off to?" Karen asks Jenny.

"Nowhere, we've just got back from a week's rally at Brighton."

"Rally!" Karen says excitingly. "What was it like?"

"Just like you, lovely," a biker approaches.

Karen looks round at him. "Oh you," she says recognising him.

"Oh is that what I get for being polite?" he replies.

"Last time you took the piss out of me," Karen accuses him.

"Oh that was just a bit of fun, listen I'm Ian let's start again," she ignores him. "Come have a look at my bike."

"What makes you think I want to look at your bike?" Karen plays hard to get.

"Please yourself," Ian walks away.

"OK then if you insist," Karen follows him. "I'll see you later," Karen waves to Jenny.

"Hey," Jenny calls.

"What?" Karen looks at her.

"Watch yourself."

"I'll be all right," Karen strolls up to Ian crouching beside his bike checking the chain.

"You like it then?" Ian asks.

"It's OK," she says trying not to be impressed.

"OK! Suzuki 250, moves like shit off a shovel."

"Can I have a go?" Karen asks.

"Do you have a licence?" Ian looks at her.

"Do you need one to have a croggi?" Karen questions.

"No, I'm only joking."

"Yeh! So was I." She laughs embarrassed.

"OK climb on, here I always keep a spare." Ian passes her a helmet; she puts it on struggling with the strap. "Here I'll help you," Ian tries to help her.

"I can do it," Karen fiddles with the strap. "See, do I get on first?"

"No I'll get on."

"OK."

Ian straddles the bike and holds it steady as Karen climbs on nervously, she puts her hands on his waist while he kick starts the bike, as he settles in the seat he lunges forward and brakes hard.

"Oh!" Karen screams at the sudden movement of the bike.

"What?" Ian shouts back to her after hearing her voice.

"Nothing, where are we going?" she shouts over the noise of the engine.

"You'll see, now hang on to me and when I lean you lean with me, right!"

"Right!" Karen shouts thrilled to bits she's going to have a ride on a bike.

Ian turns the bike round and roars down the slipway on to the beach, the tide is fully out, his motorbike headlight beams brightly as the night sets in reflecting over the wet packed sands, he revs up to speed, Karen screams with excitement as they race along the beach zigzagging, Ian leans with the bike but Karen tries not to.

"Lean with me, lean!" Ian shouts.

"I daren't, I'll fall off!" Karen screams.

"No you won't, here we go full circle."

"Yeah!" she screams.

"Like it!" Ian calls out.

"Do I, I'm pissing me pants," Karen laughs.

"Not on my seat!" Ian shouts.

Shooting up the slipway Ian skids to a halt outside the café,

Karen removes her helmet. "That was great, can we do it again?"

"Another time, shouldn't you be getting home? It's late."

"No!"

Ian removes his helmet. "Where do you live anyway?"

"Wheatlands Park… will you give me a ride home?"

"Put your helmet on then."

"Ta." Karen puts the helmet back on and grabs Ian tightly, he looks at her and smiles, she smiles back to him.

"See you later you lot," the other bikers, acknowledge him as he rides off down towards the coast road.

"Stop here, stop here," Karen shouts tapping him on the shoulder.

Ian pulls up and removes his helmet. "Which house is it?"

"I live down there," she points. "I don't want my mam to see me on a bike." She climbs off and hands her crash helmet back to him.

"Thanks… see you later." Karen heads home.

"Don't I get a kiss then?" Ian asks.

"No... but I'll see you again," Karen still plays hard to get.

"Thanks for nothing," Ian mumbles fixing his helmet.

Karen watches him ride away, "Yesssss!"

Fag break

Amanda, Wendy and Sam walk by the bike sheds; as usual Karen, Sharon and Alison are hanging around them.

"Hi Karen, sorry about last night, did you go down town in the end?" Wendy and Sam look at Amanda confused.

"Yeah! You should of come," Karen stamps out her cigarette.

"Amanda!" Wendy calls her.

"Oh she's all right once you get to know her."

"We'll see you later then," Wendy and Sam walk on not wanting to associate with Karen and her kind.

"See you in class," Amanda shouts to them as she walks up to Karen. "What are you doing this Friday Karen, do you fancy coming down the amusements?"

"Not with them," Karen watches Wendy and Sam walking away looking back at her, whispering to themselves.

"No you and I, Sharon and Alison can come too."

"Thanks," Alison says sarcastically.

"OK! Friday, what time?"

"Seven o'clock…see you there! Wendy, Sam hold on," Amanda runs after them.

"You're not hanging around with her are you?" Sharon asks Karen.

"She's cool when you get to know her," Karen replies.

"As long as she doesn't smash you in the gob," Alison laughs combing her hair.

"Shut up Alison."

"Here comes trouble," Alison says walking around the shed.

"Where are you going?" Karen asks.

"Well I'm never wanted when they turn up," she replies.

"Well you're wanted now so don't go." Alison vanishes around the corner and heads back to the main building.

"Hi Shaz," Brad calls. Sharon walks up to him and they snog each other tonsil tennis style.

"All right Kaz?" Decker goes to snog her she pulls away.

"What's this? I haven't seen much of you lately being suspended and all."

"So!" Karen snaps at him.

"Well I get the impression you're avoiding me."

"I'm not."

"So come here then," Decker pulls Karen towards him.

"I have to get back to class." Karen puts her hand between herself and Decker to keep him away.

"Since when have you been interested in class?"

"Well I've got stuff to do haven't I, exams are up soon I have to study."

"Study! The only studying I'm hearing is your interest in bikers."

"Who says?"

"A certain school gossip."

"She should shut her gob shouldn't she?"

"Well is it true." Karen says nothing. "You seeing someone else? Because if you are I'll sort him out first, then I'll sort you."

"Go away Decker you're all mouth," she pushes him back.

Decker slaps her around the face. "Argh!" She falls to the ground.

"What did you do that for?" she shouts.

"What's going on?" Sharon runs to help Karen.

"Keep your nose out of it," Decker warns Sharon.

"Just like Jackie's boyfriend are we, slapping girls around," Sharon kneels beside Karen.

Decker stands over Karen waving his fist at her. "I don't like being used or taken for a sucker," he yells.

"Fuck off you fat bastard," Karen glares at

him.

"Are you looking for a good slapping?" He slaps her hard around the head.

"Stop him Brad," Sharon shouts.

"Away Dec she's not worth it," Brad pulls him away.

"I'll have you Kaz, if you're seeing someone else behind my back."

"Come on Dec." Brad walks off with him. "I'll see you after school Shaz."

"Slag, fucking slag," Decker shouts back at her. "I'll have both of them when I see them."

"Are you all right Kaz?" Sharon helps her up.

"Yeah, it didn't hurt, where's Alison?"

"She's gone in."

"Fucking big mouth, get off me, I'm not a kid," she shoves Sharon aside.

"OK... I was only trying to help."

"Well don't, piss off, leave me alone," Karen walks towards the school.

"Kaz!" Sharon shouts.

Down In The Amusements

"You look down," Amanda joins Karen sitting at the table in the amusements café, blowing bubbles with a straw into her Coke. "Where are Alison and

Sharon?"

"They couldn't come out… I'm fed up with them anyway, they just hang around me all the time, they can't do anything on their own...I always have to tell them what to do."

A biker approaches them. "Hi again," he leans over the rails to talk to the girls.

"Hello," Amanda recognises him.

"You know him?" Karen looks surprised at Amanda.

"Yeh! I met him a couple of weeks ago."

"What are you two girls up to then?" he asks.

"Nothing much," Amanda replies.

"Is Ian here?" Karen jumps in.

He looks around. "He's somewhere about, we're off to Saltburn fancy coming?."

"I don't know your name," Amanda replies.

"I'm Ricky and your Karen aren't you?"

"Kaz."

"And you're?"

"Amanda," she replies.

"Now we know each other are you coming?"

"Come on it'll be fun." Karen tries to persuade her.

"I don't know," Amanda, replies unsure.

"She means yes," Karen interprets putting on her jacket.

"OK! But I must be back for ten," Amanda says

reluctantly.

The girls follow Ricky out of the amusements down the road to the bikers parked outside the Ritz.

"Here… Mand, I want you to understand something right, Ian is a biker I met the other night, I know he's ugly but I'm after the lad on the Yamaha 250 over there," she points him out. "He's called Dave, OK!"

"You don't have to explain to me, you know what they say, start with the ugliest you can only get better," Amanda and Karen laugh as they run across the road to Ian and Ricky. "CB 250 nice bike!" Amanda comments to Ricky.

"You've ridden bikes before?" He asks as he helps Amanda on with her helmet.

"Yeh! My dad rides a Harley Davidson around London, I sometimes…well used to go out with him on weekends."

"Nice bike," Ricky's impressed.

"What are you waiting for?" Karen yells to them. "Come on let's go." They zoom off heading for the coast road.

Winding down a steep bank they join bikers congregating around Saltburn Pier. Others have already gathered around the bonfires on the beach.

"All right Amanda?" Ricky asks.

"Yeah! You went a bit slow."

"That wasn't slow I hit seventy," Ricky laughs.

"You'll have to go faster than that for me."

"Yeeee Haaaa," Karen jumps off the bike.

"Yeeee Haaaa, we're not cowboys!" Ian states.

"That was great, I'm tingling all over! Do you think there's a biker in me?" Karen asks Ian.

"There might be later," Ian winks at her.

"I might not need one… I think I've just come in my pants."

Ian laughs. "Hey everyone, Karen's just come in her pants," He shouts to the bikers around the fire, they all laugh.

"Oye! I don't want everyone to know what I say to you," Karen snaps at Ian.

"Get used to it we share everything here… Get us a beer from over there," Ian tells Karen.

"Get it yourself," Karen walks off annoyed and sits by the fire joining Amanda.

"Karen, they were only joking with you."

"I don't like being laughed at, and I don't like being called Karen."

Ricky strolls over and sits with them. "Here's a beer for you girls."

"No thanks," Amanda politely refuses.

"I'll have yours then," Karen grabs both cans.

"Thanks for asking me to come," Amanda smiles

at Ricky.

"That's all right, I can understand you not wanting to come, but we're not as bad as people think you know."

"So what's the set up?" Karen asks Ricky.

"What do you mean?" he asks.

"Every gang has a leader, is Dave your leader?"

Ricky laughs. "Leader, no, but he looks out for us all."

"And Ian where does he fit in, in this leaderless gang?" Karen asks sarcastically.

"Ian… he's Dave's mate but they haven't been getting on great with each other lately."

"Amanda, that's Jenny she's with Nick her boy friend," Karen points them out.

"Yeah she's a right cracker," Ricky stares at Jenny.

Amanda looks annoyed at Ricky's lack of polite-ness while he entertains her.

"You won't get anywhere with her," Ian says as he walks up.

"What do you all get up to?" Amanda asks.

"Just ride around the place and meet up with other bikers," Ricky replies.

"Do you get into fights," Karen dribbles beer down her shirt. "SHIT!"

"Sometimes, if they start it we'll finish it," Ian brags.

"Hey there's Dave, I'm going to talk to him… if

he likes it or not," Karen jumps up and walks over to him.

"Hey I thought you came with me?" Ian shouts to her.

Ricky turns to Amanda. "You're quite a good looking girl." Amanda blushes. "Can I see you again?" he asks.

Amanda looks at him, "Close your eyes?" she asks.

"What?"

"Close your eyes," she asks again.

Ricky closes them and puckers up his lips slightly ready for a kiss.

"Open them again?" she asks, he opens his eyes looking puzzled. "There you go you can see me again."

"Oh very funny," he takes a drink from his beer.

"Dave isn't it?" Dave sits on his bike looking out over the sea, he gives Karen a blank look. "You don't like me do you?" Karen asks.

"What makes you think that?"

"You don't talk to me."

"Talk then," he takes a drink from his can.

She stands awkwardly looking at him, and then looks at the ground, then the sea.

"You'll run out of things to look at in a minute."

She stands embarrassed. "I got a croggi off Ian."

"Pillion!" Dave corrects her.

"What?" Karen looks at him getting frustrated with the lack of communication.

"I said pillion. You ride pillion, we don't call it croggi unless you're on a pushbike."

"I knew that," she says embarrassed.

"So you're sticking around with us then?" he asks.

"Might do."

"I'd better introduce you to some of the lads then."

"Yeh," she gets excited. "I mean thanks."

They walk over to a group of bikers around a small bonfire. "Listen up everyone, this is Karen."

"Hi! Kaz to my friends."

"All right," the bikers greet her.

"This is Mark we call him Pagan because that's what he's into."

"Hello."

"And Steve we call him Soldier because he's always dressed in combat gear, Phil's just Phil."

"All right Kaz," Phil waves his beer at her.

"That's Simon, Nick, Andy, Eddy and Peter he's just Pete because he smells like dirt."

"Thanks mate," he laughs.

"And there's Brett, forget about him."

"Hi."

"Now the girls," they walk over to them. "Jenny

I guess you've already met, Julie, Babs, Sue, Janine, Hayley and Alison."

"I've got a friend called Alison." There's a silence as they look at Karen waiting for her to finish.

"Yeh well, thanks for sharing that with us." Dave goes back over to the lads and sits down, Karen follows him.

"Kaz come and sit over here with us," Jenny calls to her.

"No I'm all right over here," she sits down next to Dave.

"Go sit with them," Dave tells her.

"I'll sit here!"

"Go sit with them!" Dave tells her again.

"Come here Kaz!" Jenny calls and waves her over; she gets up and walks to the girl's fire looking back at Dave.

"Here have another can," Jenny offers. "Don't think anything of it, us girls stick together."

Karen sits and has a drink from her third can. "Is he always like that?"

"What Dave, take no notice of him he's just broke off with his girlfriend."

Karen drinks up interested in this new piece of information. She asks. "I thought you said he doesn't have girlfriends?"

"He doesn't, but he really liked this girl, Beatrice was her name."

"Where's she now?"

"She's gone to London."

"Is he seeing anyone else?" Karen asks subtly.

"You're determined to get in there aren't ya?" Jenny laughs.

Karen says nothing as she takes another drink looking over to Dave.

"Let me tell you, he's not interested in girls like you."

"And why's that?"

"You're still a virgin."

"I'm not!" Karen lies.

Jenny takes a drink and looks at her. "I'm a girl I can spot a virgin a mile off... you've never been laid."

"So what if I am?" Karen confesses.

"Well just take it from me, Dave doesn't shag virgins."

After a few beers Karen relaxes and laughs along with the girls feeling a part of the group, every now and then she sneaks a look at Dave.

At the same time Ian is keeping an eye on her. "I see you're having a good time Kaz?" Ian approaches her.

"I might be," Karen slurs, finishing off her fourth can of newie.

"So you like to have fun?" Ian asks.

"Depends who with," Karen and the girls laugh.

"Go away Ian," Jenny tells him.

"OK! I get the message, you don't want a lift home then?" Ian leaves them to it.

Karen jumps up and chases after him. "Hey if you don't give me a lift how am I supposed to get home?"

"Don't worry, I'll take you home…here roll me a joint." He holds out his backie tin as they walk further along the beach towards the dunes.

"I've never rolled a joint before," she says.

"I'll show you." They sit on the sand away from the others.

"What about the police?" She hands back the tin.

"What about them?" Ian looks around checking. "They don't bother us as long as we don't bother them, here hold this." He pulls out from his top pocket a small bag of grass and hands her the Rizla pack. "Get out two papers," he instructs. She hands them to him; he licks and joins them to make one large paper, taking some of the backie from his tin he blends it with the grass from the bag and rolls a splif. "Now I'll show you how to smoke one." He looks at her as he tears off the twisted end and lights it, then inhales deeply holding it in for around ten seconds, then exhales. "Now you try."

She holds the joint between her thumb and fore-finger copying as much as possible what Ian did, Karen a smoker herself tries to look confident as she quickly takes a drag and coughs it out.

Ian laughs out loudly. "Try again but this time slowly," he tells her.

She does, then exhales. "Oooooh, what is this stuff?"

"Its just grass."

"Grass! I didn't think you could smoke it."

"It's a leaf, we call it grass...it looks like dry grass when it's ready to smoke." They share the joint

"Oh it makes you feel…"

"Lay back and look at the stars," Ian tries to relax her.

Karen lies down looking up at the night sky. "Oh don't the stars look bright… there's thousands up there…I feel…"

"Take another drag," Ian tells her, after she has another he takes it from her to have a smoke himself. He leans over her to kiss her.

"What you doing?" she asks.

"You're so beautiful," Ian kisses her again.

"I feel funny."

"Take another drag," Ian holds the splif to her lips. "Take a big one this time." Karen takes in another. "Hold it," he leans over and kisses her stopping her from exhaling. She coughs; smoke shoots out the sides of her mouth as Ian snogs her hard.

She pushes him back. "What are you doing I can't breath?" Karen coughs.

He slides his hand up her leg and under her skirt.

"Oh…I feel… am I your biker girl?" she asks finding herself feeling tired and zonked out with the beer and now the wacky backy.

"You can be if you want," Ian kisses her moving his hand over her legs.

"You're not going to shag me." Karen informs him, her head spinning, knowing what Ian's up to but still thinking she's in control.

He runs his hand up inbetween her legs and lifts her skirt.

"That tickles," Karen giggles.

"Just relax Kaz," he pulls her leg towards him, snogging her, he slips his hand into her knickers.

"Can I be in your gang?" she mumbles between kisses.

Ian says nothing as he moves over on top of her, his hand pulls away to unfasten his belt and unzip his flies. He lies between her legs using his legs to keep her from closing hers; pulling her knickers aside he holds his knob and guides it towards her fanny lips and starts to push at her mound.

"Ow, that hurts," she cries out.

He pulls his hand away and spits on it rubbing it in, to wet her vagina. "Let's see if it will go in now," again he pushes. Suddenly he feels a boot on his shoulder kicking him off. "What the fuck…" Rolling on to his side he grabs his trousers.

"Oh hello Dave, I'm gonna be a biker girl." Karen giggles.

"No you're not, get up," Dave grabs Karen's arm and lifts her to her feet. She falls about as Dave struggles to keep her up.

"Will you make me your biker girl?" Karen throws her arms around Dave.

"What's your game?" Ian shouts at Dave as he fastens his pants.

"I think you've had enough."

"Dave why don't you like me?" Karen asks.

"You're just fucking jealous," Ian picks up his backie tin and leaves.

"What's happening?" Amanda and Ricky run up to them.

"I feel sick," Karen bends over.

"I think she'd better go home," Amanda suggests.

"She can't ride pillion in that state, she'll fall off," Ricky points out.

"I'll be all right in a min…ute," Karen throws up.

"Jenny," Dave calls to her. "She'll have to sleep it off here, she can share a tent with you," Dave hands her over to the girls.

"I'd better go home now, will Karen be all right?" Amanda asks.

"Don't worry, Jenny will look after her, I'll take you home, she'll be all right."

Ian walks back to the fire and sits on his own,

pissed off with Dave.

The morning sun rises over the calm sea; small waves break on to the sand next to the tents, Karen emerges from one.

"You're awake then?" Dave asks stoking up last night's fire boiling some water.

"I might be dead for all I know… where am I?" she crawls out of the tent.

"Here, I've made a cup of coffee, you have it I'll make another."

She walks over to the fire sitting down shielding her eyes from the bright sunlight. Dave hands her the coffee.

"Thanks, this sun's hurting my eyes."

"Here." Dave gives her his sunglasses.

"Ta."

"What were you thinking of," he asks her.

"What do you mean?" she replies.

"Last night, Ian of all people, he's the last to trust."

"Why! What happened, he didn't shag me did he?" She asks worried.

"No… but you were lucky I arrived in the nick of time."

"Thanks!"

"Don't thank me, next time I won't be there to help you."

She takes a drink of coffee then spits it out. "Err

it hasn't got any sugar in it?"

"Shut up out there!" a voice shouts from a tent, "people are trying to sleep."

"Forget it! I'll take you home."

"Thanks again," Karen says climbing off Dave's bike outside her house.

"Look Karen," Dave takes his helmet off.

"What?" she asks.

He looks at her. "Nothing," he straps the spare helmet to his bike.

"I'll see you again?" Karen asks.

"We'll see," he rides off.

Karen watches him. "I'll see you Dave."

Hair Today Goon Tomorrow

Settled into their new Saturday hairdressing jobs Sally sweeps the floor while Sue sorts out the towels. A young lad with red hair, freckles and some facial acne enters the salon.

"Sally can you see to the young man?"

"Yes Mr Wilcox," Sally walks over to the reception desk. "Hello, can I help you?"

"I want a hair cut!" he tells her looking round the salon.

"We can fit you in, in fifteen minutes would you

like to wait?"

"If I have to like," the young lad takes a look at Sally and changes his attitude. "Err… yeh ta."

"Sally wash his hair now, I'll cut his next."

"Yes Mr Wilcox," Sally walks over to Sue. "I haven't washed anyone's hair before."

"There's nothing to it, just wash it." Sue tells her.

Sally walks back to the lad. "Would you like to come this way sir?" she asks nervously. The young lad follows her and sits in the chair. "I'll just pop this towel round your shoulders," she runs the water and sets the temperature. "Can you lean back please?"

He leans his head back into the basin as Sally runs the shower over his hair.

"Ow! That's hot," he shouts.

"Sorry I'll turn it down," Sally quickly adjusts the taps.

"Be careful Sally."

"Yes Mr Wilcox."

"Now that's cold!" The lad complains.

"Sorry," Sally apologises again.

"You're new at this aren't you?" he asks looking up into her eyes.

"Can you tell?" Sally replies with a nervous laugh and smiles back to him.

"My head can like," the lad states.

"Sorry I'll get it right in a minute," she fumbles

with the taps.

"That's it! Don't touch any more taps," he calls out.

"OK!" Sally takes some shampoo and starts to wash his hair.

"Virgil's the name," he introduces himself.

"Sorry?" Sally asks as she rubs the shampoo into his scalp.

"My name's Virgil."

"Oh! Hello."

"What's yours?"

"Sally."

"Make sure you wash it well like," he instructs.

"Are you going somewhere special tonight?"

"No! Why's that?" Virgil asks.

"Because you've come for a haircut, I thought you might be going somewhere special."

"Just a regular night out with the lads like, I've just got a new car."

Sally rinses the shampoo out. "Do you want conditioner?"

"Go on then."

As Sally pours the conditioner on to his hair it spills out too much. "Oh err," she says worried.

"What have you done?" Virgil turns his head trying to see.

"Oh nothing," Sally rubs it in at the same time fiddling with the tap wanting to rinse some of it off.

"Ow! It's hot again, you're not going to cut my hair are you?" he snaps at her worried.

"Oh no, Mr Wilcox will be cutting it."

"I'm glad," he settles back in the chair. "Phoenix orange it is."

"What, I mean sorry?" Sally half listens to his conversation.

"My car it's a Ford Escort, the colour's Phoenix orange."

"Oh that's nice," she starts to rinse his hair. "Is that better?"

"It'll do like."

"Is it new?" she tries to take his attention off what she's doing.

"No seventy-four model I can't afford a new one, I'll take you for a spin if you want?" he offers.

"Thanks... but I'm a bit busy these days."

"Pity...you're rinsing my hair a lot."

Time To Go Home Girls

"Good-bye Mr Wilcox," Sally shouts.

"Good-bye, see you next week girls, you've done a good job today Sally," Mr Wilcox calls from the back of the shop.

"Thank you...bye." Sally and Sue link arms and head for home. "Didn't today go quickly?" Sally comments.

"Yeh! Look at the tips we got," Sue counts the money in her hand.

"How much did you get?" Sally asks.

"I got two pounds… thirty-five pence," Sue counts.

"I got one pound seventy-eight."

"Here," Sue hands Sally thirty pence. "It'll make us nearly equal."

"Thanks Sue, you don't have to you know."

"Its OK, we'll share the tips from now on shall we?"

"Yeh OK." They both walk on home with a spring in their step pleased with their day's work.

They don't get far from the salon before a car pulls alongside them, the window winds down and a voice calls to them. "Want a lift girls?" Sally looks at the driver.

"Don't stop Sall! Ignore him," Sue tells her sister.

"It's Virgil, I washed his hair today… that's his new car."

"You like my car?" Virgil asks.

"It's all right," Sally looks but Sue ignores him.

"Hop in I'll give you a spin."

"No ta," Sue refuses and quickens her pace.

"You can give us a lift home if you like," Sally requests.

"Sall, what yer doing?"

"Same thing like," Virgil stops to let them in.

"Come on Sue it'll be all right," Sue stands looking at Sally as she approaches the car then reluctantly joins her.

"Let them in," Virgil tells his mate in the passenger seat. "This is Ali my mate," Virgil introduces him to Sue.

"Hi girls! Climb aboard." Ali lets them into the back.

Before Ali has a chance to shut the door, Virgil shouts. "Hold on to your knickers," spinning his back wheels he speeds off down Park Avenue.

"Slow down," Sue shouts as they both hold on to the back of the front seats.

"I'm only doing forty like."

"It says thirty on the sign back there," Sue tells him.

"Ah, forget the signs they're only there for learners," Ali says laughing.

"We'll see what the police say then, there's one behind you," Sally informs him.

"Shit!" Virgil pulls over.

"That'll teach you for speeding," Sue tells him smirking to Sall.

The policeman approaches the car. "Hello sir do you know the speed limit along this road?"

"Yes officer its thirty miles per hour," Virgil says politely.

"And what speed were you doing?" the police

officer asks.

"I'm sure I was only doing thirty like, it was thirty wasn't it Al?" He looks at his mate who smiles to the officer nodding his head in agreement.

"I think sir, you were doing more than that."

"My speedo said thirty," Virgil lies.

"Where are you going?" the officer asks.

"I'm dropping our girlfriends home."

The policeman looks through the window. "Are you all right girls?" he asks them.

"Yes," Sally looks at Sue.

The officer's radio calls him. "OK I'm on my way," he replies to his station. "Keep a check on your speed, if I have to stop you again I will book you. OK you can carry on."

"Thank you officer I will," Virgil drives off. "Pig! Should be out catching murderers."

"That was close," Ali comments. "Couldn't do anything anyway our word against his," he laughs.

"Thank you officer I will... like," Sue says sarcastically. "Anyway what do you mean we're your girlfriends?" Sue questions.

Virgil says nothing as he drives on feeling embarrassed.

The car screeches to a halt outside the twins' house, Ali lets the girls out. "See yer around girls," Alistair says winking at Sue.

"I'll pop in next week like, for a trim?" Sally turns and smiles at Virgil as he speeds off down the street.

"I don't like them much… like," Sue tells her.

"They gave us a lift home," Sally sticks up for them.

"Nearly got us arrested more like… now I'm doing it…like," Sue walks into the house. "Hi mam we're home," she calls out.

"Who was that in the car?" their mam asks coming out of the front room.

"Just some lads giving us a lift home from work," Sally answers.

"You've just started work and you're getting lifts home from strangers," their mam shakes her head disapprovingly.

Sally sits down at the table. "Where's Adi Mam?" she asks.

"He's upstairs asleep go and wake him it's time for tea."

Sue runs upstairs and creeps into Adi's bedroom and sees him sitting up in his cot. "Hi Adi, you're awake, look what I've earned today," she shows him her money. "I'll put 10p in your piggy bank yeh!"

"Piggy," Adi tries to say.

"I'm going to have a bath now, I'll take you down for tea first shall I?"

"Tea," Adi calls out. Sue brings Adi down to the table and sits him on her lap. "Can I have a bath before tea Mam?" Sue asks calling to her in the kitchen.

"No, your father's coming home any minute now, you know he likes to have his bath after working at the racetrack."

"Oh! I feel dirty," Sue moans.

"We're covered in hair more like," Sally backs her up.

"Sit down and wait for your tea," mam tells them.

Just then their father enters from the back door. "Is my tea ready yet!" he shouts entering the dining room throwing his coat over the armchair.

"It'll be ready in a minute."

"Hurry up with it…I want to have my bath."

"Is it all right if I jump in the bath first dad?" Sue asks.

"I'm not bathing in dirty water, no you can't," he shouts back to her.

"Thanks," she mutters under her breath.

"You'll have to wait until the fire warms the tank up again," mam calls from the kitchen.

"That'll take ages," Sue complains.

"You can use my bath water when I've finished," dad tells her.

"No ta," Sue sits at the table and starts to read the TV Times, pointing out the pictures to Adi.

"You can go and run my bath now!" he orders.

"I don't want to dad," she says burying her head

in the mag.

Mam enters bringing dad a mug of tea. "Oh go on Suzie you know how your dad likes you to set out his towels and things ready for his bath."

He looks at Sue at the same time pulling his pipe out from his jacket pocket tapping it in the ashtray. "Just do it," he says sitting back grabbing his tobacco off the TV set. Sue puts down the magazine, settling Adi on to the chair. She goes up stairs as she's told. "Put my food in the oven woman I'll have my bath first."

Mam walks into the room holding two plates of food. "It's ready now," she puts Sally's dinner in front of her.

"Did you hear what I said?" he shouts.

Mam walks back into the kitchen with his food. "Sometimes I don't know if I'm coming or going."

"Stop yer whingeing," dad tells her. He sits filling his pipe with backie watching Sally while she eats. "Well what do they pay you down there," her father asks her.

"55p an hour plus tips."

"I suppose that's OK... I'm off down the local later, I don't suppose you'll treat your dad to a pint."

"Of course dad, here, here's 80p," she takes the money out of her purse. "I earnt a lot of tips today is that how much it costs?" She hands it to him. He looks at it. "It'll do." Leaning to one side he puts the money in his trouser pocket. "I saw you getting out of a car when you came home, whose car was it?"

"I got a lift home from work," Sally explains.

"I could see that, I asked whose car?"

"It's a lads, I met him doing his hair."

Mam enters again. "Is your sister having something to eat? I thought you were going to have your bath?"

"Put her's in the oven with mine," dad orders. "I don't want boys giving you lifts home right?"

"It's not like that dad," she carries on eating.

"I don't like boys with cars picking up my daughters, see it doesn't happen again."

"Yes dad," Sally sulks.

"I'm going for my bath." He leaves the room and makes his way upstairs.

"It's not fair, why can't I meet a boy without dad stopping me or scaring them away."

Mam walks back in and puts Adrian's food in front of him handing him a spoon. "You're too young to be worrying about boys, he's only looking out for your safety…there's too many girls coming home pregnant these days."

"I'm not going to get pregnant," Sally raises her voice.

"Just make sure you don't, I'm not going to be straddled with another child." Adi plays with his food mam smacks his hand making his food spill on to the table. He smiles at mam. "Now look what you've done," mam returns to the kitchen to fetch a cloth.

"I'll see to him mam," Sally picks up his spoon. "Look at this lovely mince and gravy," she feeds him a spoonful. "Who's a good boy? You'll grow to be a big boy one day… I hope you don't meet dads like ours or you'll be a bachelor for the rest of your life."

Mam comes back in. "Here's a dishcloth… what's taking your sister so long?" she opens the dining room door and calls up the stairs. "Susan your tea's ready, come down and get it now!" Mam heads back into the kitchen.

"Mmm, that's a big mouthful," Sally wipes Adi's chin.

"Yum, yum," Adi speaks; his food dribbles on to his T-shirt.

"Oh you're a messy bugger," Sally laughs.

Mam enters again. "Now look at him, I'll clean him up, you go and fetch your sister before I throw her tea in the dustbin."

Sally walks into the hall and shouts upstairs. "Sue your tea's ready," she hears nothing but the bath water running and goes upstairs, her father crosses the hallway from the girls' bedroom his trousers over his arm with just a shirt and Y-fronts on. "Err dad," Sally jokes. "Can't you get undressed in the bathroom?"

Saying nothing he walks into the bathroom, closing and locking the door behind him.

Sally walks into their bedroom, she sees Sue lying on the bed. "Your tea's ready Sue!"

"I'm tired, I'll eat it later," she says with her head buried in the pillow.

"Mam will throw it out if you don't come now."

"Let her, I'm tired, leave me alone," she shouts rolling over to face the wall.

"She won't be happy." Sally closes the door and leaves Sue alone.

Time For Bed

Wendy lays on the settee her head resting on Paul's lap watching the film credits. "I hope you haven't just popped Paul."

"No! It must be the dog."

"Buster get out you smelly dog, go to your basket," Wendy commands. "Oh Paul it is you, I can tell," she jumps up. "I can tell your…"

"Go on say the word," Paul looks at her laughing.

"Wind!"

"I can't smell anything," Wendy's sister sits the other side of the room curled up in the armchair.

"It's time you went to bed Crystal," Wendy tells her.

"Farts," Paul laughs. "Go on say farts."

"Paul! Don't talk like that in front of Crystal."

"I call them farts as well," Crystal says giggling.

"1, 2, 3," Paul counts.

"Farts," Paul and Crystal say together.

"Paul don't encourage her, come on Crystal the film's finished now, mam and dad will be home soon," she looks at her watch. "In half an hour."

"Orr, it's only half ten, can't I stay up another fifteen minutes?" Crystal moans.

"No! Come on, I shouldn't have let Paul talk me into letting you stay up in the first place, you know mam will kill me if she caught you up at this time."

"Why do I have to go to bed early? It is Saturday night." Crystal still protests.

Paul jumps up. "Come here," he runs over to Crystal's chair, Crystal holds a cushion up and hides behind it as Paul grabs her waist and tickles her.

"Stop it, stop it," Crystal laughs.

"Paul leave her alone she's only fourteen."

"I'll be 15 soon." Crystal screams as she gets tickled.

"I don't care, stop it Paul…I said STOP IT!" Wendy stands shouting annoyed at their antics.

Crystal wriggles free. "I'm off to bed," and runs out stopping at the door. "And if you're going to be doing that kissing thing I'm telling on you."

"Just get to bed!" Wendy slumps on the settee.

"Or I'll tell about cousin Andrew and what I caught you doing in the garden shed last week."

"I'll see you in the morning Paul," Crystal runs upstairs giggling, the bedroom door slams behind her.

Paul sits next to her. "You didn't have to shout, we heard you the first time," he puts his arm around her.

"Don't tickle my sister," Wendy tells him sitting back into the settee with her arms folded feeling jealous.

"Why? We're only playing," Paul cuddles her.

"Well don't, please, I've asked you now," she gets up. "Buster come boy, in your basket," she walks into the kitchen and puts Buster in his basket.

"Do you want a drink Paul?" she calls through.

"No ta," he lays back watching the adverts on telly. "So what happened in the garden shed last week?" Paul asks shouting through to the kitchen.

Wendy walks in with a glass of milk. "I heard noises coming from the shed and when I looked through the window, Andrew my 16 year old cousin was kissing her."

"That's where it all starts," Paul jokes.

"What does?" she puts her milk down.

Paul grabs her and pulls her on to his lap. "This!" They kiss.

"Since you saw that sex education film you

haven't stopped have you?" Wendy sighs.

"Come on, give us a kiss or I'll slobber all over your neck."

"No you won't," she fights back.

"Arrr slobber, slobber."

"Err! Get off you're dribbling all over me."

"Sorry I didn't realise my zip was undone."

"Paul stop it," they make themselves comfy on the settee lying side-by-side looking up at the ceiling.

"Wend," Paul speaks softly.

"Yes."

"I was thinking."

"I thought I could smell something burning," she jokes.

"No, I'm being serious now."

"OK."

"Have you ever wondered what it's like?"

"What?" Wendy looks at him.

"You know, sexual intercourse."

"You can wait until we get married, I'm going to walk up the aisle in white," she rests her head on his chest.

"That wasn't the question... well?" Paul asks. "It would be nice to know wouldn't it?"

"I suppose... what are you trying to say?" Wendy asks him.

"Well we already do more than kissing."

"That's different...anyway you're the only boy

I've let touch me."

"And you're the only girl that's touched me." Paul kisses her on her hair.

"I have thought about it," Wendy admits. "What if we don't like it? I mean after we're married, say it hurts you or me and one of us doesn't want to do it anymore," she glances at him. "If I didn't like it would you go off me?" she asks.

"No of course not, I love you for being Wend not a sex slave," he tickles her.

"Stop it," she slaps his hand.

"Yes miss," Paul replies stretching to attention and saluting.

"We're not getting married until I'm twenty-one… it's a long time isn't it?" She looks up to Paul.

"A bit… I'll be drawing my pension by then."

"But a proper girl doesn't do stuff like that, what happens if we do it and you finish with me…how could I marry someone else if I've already done it with a boy… its all right for you lads you can sleep with as many girls as you like and still be all right to marry."

"Is it?" Paul jokes.

"Be serious Paul," she slaps him on his belly

"I'm not going to finish with you! How long have we been going out with each other now?"

"Since first year," Wendy replies.

"That's four and half years, why should I finish

with you?" he gives her a reassuring cuddle.

"I remember the first time I saw you," Wendy reminisces. "You were lining up for school dinner and you looked over at me, you were with Geoff."

"You were with Sam, we still haven't got those two together," Paul laughs. "Maybe we should try blackmail."

"I pretended it was my birthday the next day and you bought me a box of mint flavoured match makers remember?"

"Remember! Do I? They cost me 67 pence," Paul moans.

"Well… it started the matchmakers craze didn't it, nearly everyone ended up getting a box."

Paul shuffles on to his side. "And then I had to buy you another box because you lied about your birthday."

They lay together not saying anything for a minute. "I'm not trying to push you into doing anything you don't want to, I just wondered if you'd ever thought about it?"

"If you love me you'll wait," Wendy looks at Paul.

"I'll wait until your sure," he kisses her. "I love you Wend."

"I love you too Paul," Wendy says as they lay together kissing and cuddling. "Who knows I might only wait until we get engaged." Wendy smiles at him.

The front door opens. "Hello! We're home!" Paul and Wendy jump up and sit straight, her mam and dad come in.

"You're early mam, dad," Wendy questions.

"Your mother's got a headache so as it's church tomorrow we didn't want a late night... so you'll be going home now Paul?" Wendy's dad hints.

Paul stands up. "Yes Mr Stokes, I'll see you tomorrow then?"

Wendy gets up and walks Paul to the door, they step outside.

"I don't see why when they come home, you have to go," she complains to Paul.

"They want to go to bed," Paul puts his hand around Wendy's waist and smooches with her. "What's that about waiting until we get engaged?" Paul asks.

She smiles at him and steps into the hall, blowing him a kiss goodnight. "See ya, love ya."

"Love you too," Paul turns to walk home.

Party Time But Not At School

There's talk of a party, Wendy and her friends gather round a large table in the form room.

"So who are we inviting to your party?" Sam asks Wendy.

"When is it?" Jackie enquires.

"The Friday after 'wits' holiday, come round it starts at seven o'clock."

"Can we come?" Sally asks.

"Of course," Wendy replies.

"What kind of party are you having?" Jackie asks.

"Oh just a normal one, a small marquee in the garden, a DJ with disco and lights.

"Normal! That'll be great, can I bring my boyfriend?" Jackie asks.

"I was only going to invite girls to my party."

"You've got to let boys come!" Jackie tells her.

"I'm only allowed thirty people," she explains.

That's enough," Jackie rubs her hands together.

"You've got a boyfriend, you've just asked if he can come," Sue queries.

"I know but it's still nice to have other lads look at you," the girl's laugh.

"I suppose Paul's invited Geoff along?" Sam asks.

"Well, yes… I suppose boys can come," Wendy backs down and agrees.

"Not all of us have boyfriends," Sally states.

"What about Virgil?" Sue suggests.

"Shut up," Sally interrupts her.

"Whose Virgil when he's at home?" Sam asks.

"No one!" The girls turn and look at Sally.

"He's got a car and fancies her," Sue tells them.

"He doesn't!" Sally replies.

"Doesn't what! Have a car, or fancy you?" Sam looks around at everyone.

"Tell us," Jackie insists.

"Stop it… both, I mean car, oh…" Sally gets flustered.

"You can invite him round if you want to, then we can see if he fancies you and of course what car he's got!" Wendy mocks Sally.

Amanda pulls up a chair. "Hi! What have I missed?"

"Wendy's having a party," Jackie informs Amanda. "And there'll be boys there."

"Can I come?" Amanda asks.

"I didn't think you'd want to come now you're pals with Karen!" Sue announces sarcastically.

"Does that mean I can't come?" Amanda asks Wendy.

"Of course it doesn't, just don't bring Karen or her friends," Wendy demands. "So I take it you'll all be coming to my party?"

"Yesss!" they all agree in unison.

"Has anyone applied for any jobs yet?" Sam asks.

"I've got an interview for Newboulds Butchers," Jackie announces excitedly.

"I've applied for sixth form, I'm going to become a midwife," Wendy tells them confidently.

"I don't know what I want to do yet," Sam replies.

"I might join the R. A. F." Amanda ponders.

"I'm sticking with hairdressing, its great fun," Sally pipes up.

"Yeh, especially when boys ask you out," Sue quips.

"Jealousy doesn't become you," Sally tells her sister.

"I'm not jealous!" Sue snaps at her.

"Are you all right?" Amanda asks.

"Course I'm all right," Sue snaps again, picks up her bag and leaves.

"I don't think she likes me because I'm friends with Karen," Amanda whispers to Sam.

"Can you blame her," Sam has a dig.

"I can choose my own friends if I want," Amanda sticks up for her rights.

"It doesn't matter anyway, we'll all be finishing school in six weeks," Sam points out.

"Can't wait," Jackie says enthusiastically.

"Wait on Sue," Sally puts her coat on. "Where you going?"

"To the library, I want to be on my own," Sue walks on without her.

"Wait I'll come with you," Sally follows.

"Didn't you hear me? I want to be on my own!" Sue shouts as she walks off leaving Sally standing in the corridor perplexed.

At The School Gates

Karen, Sharon and Alison hang around the school gates. "What is it five, six weeks and we're free?" Karen asks.

"Six I think," Sharon sits on the curb throwing bits of gravel into the road.

"That's when I start my new job at Woolworths," Alison, announces standing, chewing gum and combing her hair. "What about you Kaz?"

"I don't care what I do," Karen replies.

"You'd better start looking Kaz or all the good jobs will be gone and you'll end up on the dole," Sharon informs her.

"So! Sixteen pound a week on the dole ain't bad... beats working," Karen declares.

Sharon looks at her watch. "It's nearly time for English." Just then Dave and Ricky ride up to the gates.

"Hey it's Dave!" Karen dashes to the curb excited to see him.

"All right Kaz," Dave takes off his helmet.

"Hi! How did you know this was my school?" she

asks.

"You told Jenny, I was passing so I thought I'd see if you're about."

"Hi Kaz! Is Amanda around?" Ricky asks.

"She's somewhere in school."

"Can you get her for me?"

"She could be anywhere."

"I'm going Kaz," Sharon gets up and makes her way back to the school building.

"Wait up, I'm coming as well," Alison follows.

"Go and get Amanda Shaz," Karen orders.

"OK, if I must," Sharon says feeling left out.

"Where are you off to then?" Karen asks Dave.

"Thought we would take a spin to Roseberry Topping."

"Can I come?" Karen asks excited.

"You've got school."

"Sod school, anyway we're only hanging around for exams, can I come?" she strokes his arm. "Please."

"You go Dave… I'll stick around here for Amanda, I'll catch up with you later."

"Oh! Go on Dave it'll be fun," Karen pleads with him.

"Climb on then."

Karen grabs the spare helmet and hops on the bike.

"OK Rick, see yer later." Dave tries to start his

bike with the electric ignition but it fails to work.

"What's wrong Dave?" Karen asks raring to go.

"Oh the bloody electric starter is faulty," he kick starts the bike and speeds off towards the country-side.

Ricky climbs off his bike and stands leaning against the wall waiting to see if Amanda comes out.

"OK dinner break's over settle down, we are doing some revision today for your English literature exam," the teacher settles them down for the after-noon's lesson.

Sharon enters and sits down across from Amanda. "Sorry I'm late sir."

"Now class, who can name me any Shakespeare play?"

"Pssst," Sharon calls to Amanda.

Amanda turns pointing to herself. "Who me?"

"Who else, there's a lad on a motorbike outside waiting for you."

"Where?" Amanda asks.

"With Kaz at the gates."

The teacher catches Sharon talking. "Sharon would you like to share that with the rest of the class?"

"Sir," Amanda interrupts.

"Yes Amanda."

"Can I go to the toilet please?"

"No! You had all dinner break to go."

"It's a girl's thing sir."

The teacher pauses. "OK then, but be quick about it," Amanda hurries out. Racing down the corridor she bursts through the main entrance and sees Ricky riding off down the road.

"God! Shit!" she curses.

Father Ellis walks past her. "Just in time to save you my child, the toilets are through the doors and on the left," he jokes to her.

"Sorry sir, er... father," Amanda returns back to her class disappointed she's missed Ricky.

Topping Roseberry Topping

Karen out of breath climbs the last rock. "Beat you to the top."

"You weren't playing fair... you had a head start," Dave says trailing behind almost on his knees with exhaustion.

"I'm knackered," Karen slumps on to the rocky top. "Let's sit here and rest a minute."

"Let's rest an hour you mean," Dave clambers to the top collapsing in a heap; lying on his back he turns his head to one side.

"Look at the view," he says sitting up. "You know it's the first time I've ever climbed Roseberry

Topping.

"It's great from where I'm looking," Karen stares at Dave.

"You don't give up do you, I meant over there," he points out over the valley.

"Can you blame me?" Karen looks around throwing small stones over the cliff's edge not taking much notice of the view. There's a silence between them. "When can I join your gang?"

"We're not a gang," Dave tries to explain. "We're just mates who like doing stuff."

Karen moves closer to him. "But I want to hang around with you Dave."

"Don't talk rubbish, anyway I don't hang around with kids."

"You brought me here!"

"You asked!"

There's another silence between them. "It's not rubbish," she turns away sulking. "I'm not a kid, I'll be eighteen in two years," she turns back to him. "What kind of stuff?"

Dave looks around out over the Cleveland hills and thinks for a second. "Well…" he leans forward to Karen and whispers. "Secret stuff."

She grabs his arm excited as her heart thumps, is she about to learn how to become a gang member.

"What secret stuff?"

"It's not as simple as that," he pulls back.

"What isn't?" Karen looks puzzled.

"Well first.... You have to meet a biker."

"Yeah, that's you," she says looking intensely at him.

He looks around again; her heart thumps faster as he stares back into her eyes.

"You ride naked...on the back of his bike...down Redcar High Street," Dave pauses. Karen's eyes widen. "Through Boots the Chemist."

"You're joking!" she gasps.

Dave looks at her and winks.

"You're not joking are you?" Karen thinks for a second, Dave looks around smiling to himself.

"I'll do it!" Karen agrees.

"I'm only joking," he explains.

"God...I thought you were serious then." She looks away sighing with relief.

"I meant Woolworths." She looks at him. "Yes Woollies," Dave repeats.

Karen pauses. "OK! When?" she says with apprehension in her voice.

"No you won't," Dave lays back.

"Yes... just name the day, I'll be there."

"OK! I'll let you know... look Kaz," he turns on his side to face her. "Some guys will take advantage of girls like you."

"Not me, I won't let them," she looks at him directly. "Anyway I've got you to take care of me."

"There, you're talking rubbish again," he stands up. "I think we'd better go before I do something I'll regret, Come on I'll race you down the hill and this time I'll have the head start." He jumps off the rocks and starts running down.

"Dave you cheat…wait…that's not fair!"

Nearly at the bottom Dave is just ahead of Karen. "Wait Dave…wait…catch me, I can't stop, aaar-rrgh," she stumbles, Dave catches her in his arms, they swing round and tumble landing together in the thick bracken.

"Ow, my bloody back," Dave, cries out. "I think I fell on a rock, get off," Dave tries to push Karen off him.

"Shhhh."

"What?"

"Listen," Karen looks around.

"I can't hear anything."

"Did you see anyone?" she giggles.

"No! I think we're on our own." Karen steels a kiss, but Dave stops her.

"Now I've told you," Dave rolls Karen on to her back.

Karen smiles at him. "Go on you know you want to." She kisses him again. Dave hesitates, and then gives into her pleas. "Dave!" Karen moans as he moves over her neck biting into it. "Give me your mark Dave, let them see I'm yours." He sucks on her tan coloured soft skin. "I want to be your biker girl," she says looking to the bright blue sky closing her eyes in triumph, as she knows she always gets the lads she wants, in this case, a biker.

She feels his hands roam her waistline moving over to her firm breasts, popping a button as he pulls her school shirt and bra to the side revealing her dark nipple, he licks and sucks on it feeling the shape with his lips as it hardens in his mouth from the pleasure Karen is experiencing, Dave slides his hand between her legs, her body twists and moves as his fingers push into her pants. "God you're wet." He says slipping a finger in, panting as if he'd just climbed Roseberry Topping again.

Karen gasps, her body jerks as she feels it enter with such ease. "Fuck me Dave! I've never been fucked before," she cries out.

Just as sudden as his uncontrolled passion was aroused, it stops.

Karen opens her eyes. "What's wrong?"

Dave jumps up, "Get up."

"Dave? Don't you want to fuck me?" she asks.

"I'll decide when to fuck you if I fuck you! Anyhow I don't fuck virgins!" He walks off back to his bike.

"What do you mean you don't fuck virgins?"

"Get up, we're going," he shouts back to her.

"Dave stop! Why don't you fuck virgins?" Karen shouts clambering out of the bracken. Dave says nothing. "All right! All right! You don't have to get all grumpy about it…wait for me then!" She runs after him hopping from one leg to the other straightening her knickers and skirt, confused at his last remark. "Dave!" she grabs his arm. "Why don't you fuck virgins?"

He stops, turns and stares at her. "Because Virgins don't know how to fuck!"

She stands looking at him for a moment composing herself. "Virgins don't know how to fuck?" She repeats. "Oh! I get it! Well teach me then?" she smiles at him. He walks on shaking his head. Angry and embarrassed Karen makes her way down the lane. "Anyhow," she mumbles to herself. "I'll decide when you fuck me, not you!"

Happy Birthday Wendy And Paul

"Sam! I thought you weren't coming, where have you been?" Wendy gives Samantha a big hug.

"Sorry I'm late the bus broke down, I was coming home from Middlesbrough after getting you this," Sam hands her a decorative little paper bag with a small teddy bear stuck on the front.

Wendy peeps into the bag. "Oh Sam! What is it?"

She opens a ring box. "Sam it's beautiful, a lickle charm bear, orr thanks, you're my bestest friend ever," They hug each other.

"I'm glad you like it, I know you like collecting them, I hope you haven't already got that one."

"No, it's lovely, I'll get the jewellers to solder it on my bracelet next week."

"What did Paul get you?" Sam asks as they walk into the garden to join the other partygoers.

"I don't know he hasn't given me it yet."

"The birthday present I hope you mean," Sam laughs.

"Sam! What do you take me for… do you know what it is?" Wendy asks.

"No he hasn't told me, anyway I wouldn't tell you if he had," she laughs. "Did he like your present?"

"I won't give it to him not until he gives me mine…I think he's got me that necklace we were looking at last week."

"I thought you were looking at rings?" Sam asks.

"Well we were, but I'm not getting engaged until I'm 18… no! It's the chain with the locket on, I bet," Wendy guesses.

"Sounds expensive?" Sam questions.

"Hi Samantha! Are you coming for a dance in the tent?" Geoff shouts from the marquee.

"Not with you I'm not," Sam yells back. The girls wander around. Sam spies Paul dancing. "Paul is having a good time."

"Yeh, he prefers to dance with my sister rather than me."

"Haven't you had a dance with him yet?" Sam asks.

"No!"

"Well no wonder, come on it's time you had a dance with your boyfriend." Sam grabs Wendy's arm and pulls her on to the dance floor.

They all dance to Mike's mighty music sounds, the DJ Wendy's parents hired for the party. Geoff, as usual jumps around like an idiot. "Come on every-body it's time to do the birdie dance," the DJ announces.

"Yeah," they all scream and start to flap their arms around like hens with their heads chopped off.

"Hey… guess who I met today?" Sam yells to Wendy who's flapping her arms out of sink with the others.

"No who? I can't get this," she struggles to dance.

"Chris."

"Who's Chris when he's at home?"

"You know… Christian, the lad who did the school discos two years ago," Sam reminds her.

"No I can't say… Oh yes! Not the one you had a crush on."

"I didn't!"

"Yes you did… anyway what did he have to say?"

Wendy asks.

"He's working in the empty houses down our road, he started to chat me up," Sam smiles.

"No, really?"

"Well… we talked a bit, then I went down town."

"Are you going to see him again then?" Wendy asks at the same time suggesting the idea.

"I don't know, I'm going to walk past and see if I can see him tomorrow." The girls carry on dancing, all legs and elbows trying to follow the others doing the birdie dance.

Sally, Sue, Ali and Virgil pull up outside.

"Is this it?" Virgil looks through the windscreen.

"Yes, number fifteen," Sue pushes on Al's seat. "Come on let us out then."

"Hang on," Virgil snaps. "Al, get the beer by your feet."

"Yeh, stop pushing the seat," Al snaps at Sue.

They clamber out of the car, Sally straightens her clothes. "You are going to stick around aren't you?" Sally asks.

"For a bit, I promised to meet me mates down the pub later."

"I thought you wanted to come?" Sue questions Virgil.

"I'm here aren't I?" He snaps back at her. "But I'm not staying if it's trifle and jellies."

"Let's go round the back, I can see the tent," Sue suggests grabbing Sally by her arm leading the way. The boys follow them hiding the four cans of Newcastle under their jackets.

Entering the marquee Virgil straight away eyes up the talent. "She's a cracker."

"Nice legs shame about the face," Ali comments.

"It could be worse I suppose," Virgil opens his first can and sneaks a mouthful.

"Hi Wend... happy birthday," Sally shouts waving to her over the dancers.

"Happy birthday," Sue jumps up and down to see her.

"Hi yeh! I'm glad you could make it, where's your new boyfriend then, have you brought him?" Wendy asks squeezing past the dancers to reach them.

"He's over there," Sally sees Virgil chatting to a girl.

"Here's a little something from Sal and me, hope you like it." Sue hands Wendy a small present. Excited she opens it.

"Another ring box, seems to be the craze today."

"We bought one each," Sally helps her open the gift.

"Oh! Earrings," Wendy holds them up so they dangle in the box.

"Since you've had your ears pierced we thought

they'd be a good present."

"You two," she hugs them both. "Are my bestest friends."

"Is Amanda coming?" Sally asks.

"No, she's had to go to see her uncle.

"Shame, looks like she's missing a great party." Virgil joins the girls. "Wendy, meet Virgil and his mate Ali."

"Hi! Thanks for coming," Wendy greets them.

"Where's the grub like?" Virgil asks rudely.

"Yeah, I'm starving," Al rubs his belly.

Wendy looks at the lads then Sally and Sue, the girls shrug their shoulders as if to say sorry. "In the kitchen, it's nearly all gone," Wendy, points the way.

"Ta," the lads wander off in search of food.

"They won't cause any trouble will they?" Wendy asks.

"No they're just like that," Sally, explains.

"Paul, stop Geoff acting the goat with Sam!" Wendy yells.

"Geoff put her down, you don't know where she's been," Paul shouts.

"Thanks," Sam shouts in the background.

The party goes on into the evening. Wendy's mam runs around with food for her friends and relatives, hitting the odd boy over the head if they get out of hand. All seem to be having a great time except for Sally.

"I'll come and pick you up around ten," Virgil argues.

"Or! Stay a little longer, I thought you wanted to be with me?"

Wendy's dad steps up behind them both. "Sally isn't it, are you enjoying yourself?"

"Yes Mr Stokes."

Virgil takes a drink from his can looking away.

"What's that your drinking son?" he asks Virgil.

"Beer, what's it look like?" forgetting it's a sixteen year olds party.

"Where did you get it from?"

"I bought it myself, I'm not pinching yours if that's what your thinking."

"I'll take that!" Wendy's dad tries to take the can from him.

"Fuck off! I paid for it." Sally panics and looks around for Sue and Ali.

Wendy's dad grabs Virgil's collar. "All right lad out you go,.

"Get off me…who do you think you are?" Virgil spills his beer over partygoers as he struggles with Wendy's dad.

"You can leave this party, I don't allow drinking let alone foul mouthing in my house," he pushes Virgil out of the tent.

"Get off me you sad bastard."

Sally finds Sue. "Where's Ali? Virgil's been

thrown out of the party by Wendy's dad."

"I knew there'd be trouble," Sue looks around. "I'll find him, you stay there."

Sally spots Al. "There he is chatting up Wendy's sister, I'll meet you out the front."

"OK," Sue goes to fetch Ali while Sally runs round to the front to find Wendy's father pushing Virgil out into the road.

"Where's my mate?" Virgil yells trying to push by him.

"No you don't I'll find your friend," Wendy's dad blocks his path.

"Don't fucking tell me what to do like," Virgil faces up to him.

Wendy runs out followed by Paul, Sam and Geoff.

"Are you all right Mr Stokes?" Paul asks.

"Go inside all of you, there's nothing to interest you here."

"Dad! What's happening?" Wendy starts to get upset.

"That includes you love."

"Yeh, go inside little girl, to your kiddies' party," Virgil shouts out.

Ali and Sue run round the corner. "What's up Virgil?"

"You take your mate home, I don't want to see the likes of you around here again," Wendy's dad warns them.

Ali says nothing and jumps in the car. "Are you coming like?" Virgil shouts to Sally as he climbs in.

"Is this your car?" Wendy's dad asks.

Virgil winds his window down and starts the engine. "What if it is like?"

"How much have you had to drink son?"

"None of your fucking business, and you're not my dad."

"If you don't leave in thirty seconds, I'll phone the police," he threatens.

"Fuck off you wanker, come on get in," Al yells to the girls.

Sally starts to walk towards the car but Sue grabs her arm. "Don't be stupid they've been drinking," she says.

"You're not coming then?" Sally asks releasing her arm from Sue's hand.

Sue thinks for a second, concerned for her sister's safety. "I suppose I'll have to." She follows her to the car. "I'm sorry Mr Stokes," Sue apologises walking past him.

"You girls take care."

"You decided to come then," Virgil says sarcastically to her as she climbs in the car.

"I'm not leaving you alone with my sister."

With some speed Virgil reverses down the cul-de-sac and hand-brake turns at the end on to the main road, the girls scream with fright, then with a loud wheel spin they speed away down the road.

Wendy approaches her father upset. "I'm sorry dad, I've never met those lads before."

"It's not your fault you go back and enjoy your party."

Her mother runs around the corner. "What's happening? Wendy get inside now."

Dad turns to her mam. "It's OK love, Wendy go and enjoy your party."

The party carries on as before, some kids get excited as talk about the punch up around the front gets exaggerated giving the party a buzz.

The birthday cake arrives, mam proudly carries it into the marquee. Thirty-two candles burn brightly while the kids all join in a chorus of happy birthday.

Mam places the cake on a speaker, the DJ looks on at the fire risk. "Now both of you blow out your candles," her mother insists. Wendy looks around embarrassed, Paul takes hold of her hand and kisses her then together they blow out the candles in one breath.

"Hurray!" everyone cheers.

"Hip, hip, hurray. Hip, Hip, Hurray," Geoff calls out, a silence falls in the marquee as no one joins in, Geoff tuts. "Oh forget it," they all laugh.

"Make a wish," Sam calls out to them.

Wendy looks at the cake amazed, little sparks

from the candles spit as they relight one by one. The DJ now approaches the cake with a small but important looking fire extinguisher.

"Blow them out again," Wendy's dad instructs. "They're new trick candles."

Laughing Paul and Wendy blow the candles out again, and once more they light up, both now laughing too much to blow anymore. Paul wets his fingers and starts to snuff them out.

"I'll go cut the cake pet and wrap a piece for everyone to take home with them," her mam and dad collect the cake and head for the kitchen.

Wendy stops them. "Thanks mam, dad it's been the bestest party I've ever had," she kisses them both.

"Oh you're growing up so fast," dad gives her a big squeeze.

Paul grabs the microphone. "Hold up everyone, I've got another present for Wendy." Everyone looks at Paul. Wendy's mam stops and turns at the marquee entrance, holding the cake she smiles proudly.

"Last week we were shopping for some ideas for presents, she's wearing one now." He holds the chain around her neck to show them; it has a large heart shaped locket attached. "And boy isn't she hard to shop for… just like all girls," The lads laugh and the girl's groan a protest whilst giggling. "But unbeknown to her," Wendy nudges him. "I mean Wend, yesterday I broke into my piggy bank," they all laugh. "Well actually I borrowed some money from my granny to buy you this," turning he holds out a small box.

"Paul!" Wendy gasps putting her hand over her mouth, tears swell up in her eyes. Her mother looks on puzzled; lowering the cake she walks through the crowd to see Paul bending down on to one knee. Wendy's dad stands and smiles.

"Wendy…will you marry me?" Paul removes the ring from the box and places it on her finger.

"I don't know what to say."

"NO!" her mother shouts as the cake slides off its tray crashing on to the floor splattering over the guests shoes that happen to be in its line of fire. "Give that back right now," she grabs Wendy's hand and removes the ring and slaps it back into Paul's. "You upstairs," she tells Wendy.

"Paul you can take that back to the shop and give your gran her money back."

"No honey," dad steps in. "they're not kids any more, don't ruin their moment."

"I'm not discussing it in front of everyone."

Wendy runs out of the marquee back to the house upset and embarrassed, her mother follows.

"Mr Stokes, I didn't mean to…"

"Don't worry Paul, come with me. OK everybody the party's over, thanks for coming," Wendy's dad announces walking with his arm around Paul's shoulder back to the house.

The guests start to leave whispering amongst each other, some rating it to have been the best party they've ever been to.

Wendy's mam re-enters the marquee. "Dad!"

"Yes love."

"Pay the DJ," she walks back to the house.

"Yes love."

Wendy lies on her bed crying into her pillow, picturing in her head the moment Paul asked to marry her, ruined by her mother. The bedroom door bursts open, her mam walks in shutting the door behind her.

"Now miss! What's this all about?" she demands to know.

"Do you realise what you've just done." Wendy cries.

"You, miss, are far too young to be thinking about getting married."

"Who's getting married, I'm not getting married... not until I'm twenty-one."

"Get engaged I meant," her mam corrects herself.

"I didn't know Paul was going to ask me... what did you want me to do, tell him to wait a minute while I just consult my mother to see if it's all right to do what I want to do with my life?" Wendy becomes more upset.

"Don't get all sarcastic with me young lady, you must have discussed it at some time with him."

"Go away, just go away, it doesn't matter what I say you won't believe me, well you can't tell me what to do any more I'm sixteen now."

Wendy's mam approaches the bed. "Is that the thanks I get for raising you as my own… now I'm going down stairs to have a talk with Paul, I just hope he can get his money back for that ring, because you are not getting engaged, right!" She opens the door to leave. "And don't you come down unless you apologise to me and your father for that last remark, OK… do you hear me…"

Wendy cries into her pillow as her mam slams the door.

Sitting at the kitchen table, Paul fights back the tears. Wendy's dad sits with his hand on Paul's shoulder reassuring him he's done nothing wrong in his eyes. Wendy's sister Crystal leans against the fridge looking at Paul with a hint of a smile on her face.

"I didn't mean…to upset…anyone…I love Wend," Paul sobs.

"Don't worry Paul, it was just a shock to Wendy's mam, I must admit it did knock me back a bit… we'll put things to right again."

"Thanks… Mr Stokes" Paul wipes his eyes.

"Call me John or shall I say dad," Wendy's dad thumps Paul on his arm in a man-to-man gesture as he jokes. Paul looks at him, he smiles and bursts into a single laugh then cries again.

Mam enters the kitchen. She stops and looks at Crystal. "Upstairs to your room please."

"Orr mam," she protests.

"Just do as I say, now!"

"I never get to see the good parts." She leaves slamming the door behind her.

Mam walks to the table and leans over it looking at Paul.

"Now, when did you get this ridiculous idea about getting engaged?"

Dad stands. "Now love calm down, it's only a ring."

"No it's not! It's sneaking behind our backs, the pair of them," she yells at dad.

"No it's not," Paul stands. "I love Wendy and I'm going to marry her one day… if you like it or not."

"I think you had better go home now," he tells Paul, "we will talk about this tomorrow."

"Can I say goodbye to Wend first?"

"No, I think it's best if you leave now."

Paul splutters out a cry, turns and leaves by the back door.

Dad walks over to mam and puts his arm around her. "Now Doreen sit down, that was a bit over the top wasn't it?"

Mam lowers her head into her hands. "I don't know love," she cries.

"She's a young lady not a child any more," dad says resting his head against hers.

"I don't want them to grow up John, they're still my babies."

Outside Paul walks round to the front of the house, at the gate he pauses and looks up to Wendy's bedroom. He sees Wendy at the window, she presses her hand on to the glass. Paul with tears running down his face blows her a kiss, turns and makes his way home.

Sally Waits In The Car Park

Sally and Sue sit waiting for Virgil on the back seat of his car in the Cleveland Bay car park.

"I'm bored of this, why didn't we stay at the party?" Sue asks Sally.

"You didn't have to come with me, I'm old enough to look after myself you know," Sally points out. Virgil and Al stumble out of the pub laughing to themselves.

"At last," Sue says relieved as the lads climb in the car. "What took you so long?"

"Sue!" Sally nudges her to shut up.

"We've been sitting here waiting for nearly an

hour," she complains.

"It's not our fault you don't look eighteen like," Virgil slurs, "What do you expect?"

"Where are we going now?" Sally asks.

"I want to go home," Sue demands.

"Are you all right to drive Virgil," Sally asks.

"Yeh, of course, I've got a drink licence, I mean driving licence," Virgil and Al laugh sillily to themselves.

"Leave him, he's OK," Al says a bit drunk himself.

"Anyhow, I concentrate more when I've had something to drink, it makes me more…aware." Virgil starts the engine and reverses the car.

"Mind the bin," Al points out.

"What bin?" Virgil looks around driving into it. "Oops! Oh that bin," then wheel spins out of the car park.

The car pulls up on to the stray between Redcar and Marske the lights turn off leaving them in total darkness, Virgil switches the interior light on while Al lights up two cigarettes passing one to him.

"Coming for a walk Sue?" Al asks.

"Anything to get out of this car," she pushes on to the passenger seat. "Let us out then!" Al gets out and falls over. "Get up you're drunk," Sue says climbing out. She shuts the door leaving Sally in the back and Virgil puffing on his cigarette behind the driver's wheel.

"What's wrong with you?" Virgil asks.

"Nothing!"

"Well why don't you get up front." She climbs over the passenger seat, Virgil looks at her legs as her skirt lifts revealing her knickers. She sits down and pulls her skirt straight, Virgil throws his cigarette out of the window and then closes it. He leans over to Sally and puts his arm around her to kiss her.

"No!" she pushes him away. "You're drunk, you smell of fags and you've been horrible all night."

"Thanks, here I'll eat some mints, there's some in the glove compartment, I keep them in case the coppers stop me like, anyway you're the one who talked me into going to that cruddy party."

"Why did you have to bring drink, I told you Wendy's dad wouldn't be happy." Sally passes back the blame.

"Oh, I'd forgotten about that, forget it, it was a crap party anyway."

"It was my friend's party," Sally looks out of the passenger window wiping the condensation off the glass looking into the darkness to see if she can see Sue.

"Look Sal, I'm sorry," he puts his arm around her again.

"That bloke got up my nose… I wasn't doing any

harm until he stuck his oar in like." There's a silence between them.

Sally hears Sue outside laughing in the darkness, shouting.

"Stop it, stop it."

"They're having fun," Virgil peers through the windscreen then looks at Sally. "You look lovely tonight like," he tells her. "I was proud to have you as my girlfriend."

"It didn't seem that way," she turns to him. "You spent most of the time looking at other girls." There's another silence between them.

"I can't believe I'm going out with you," he leans over and kisses her.

"Why?" she asks.

"Why what?" Virgil slips his hand under her jacket.

"Why can't you believe it?" she shuffles in her seat.

"I've never had a girl as lovely as you," he kisses her neck. "Me… I'm just an ugly plug."

"No you're not, I wouldn't go out with you if you were," Sally kisses him back.

They kiss and cuddle for a couple of minutes. Virgil tries to undo her shirt but struggles with the buttons. "Help me out like," he instructs.

Sally unfastens the top three buttons. Virgil slips his hand inside her shirt and pulls her bra down. He lowers his head to kiss her breast.

"Sometimes I think you're only nice to me when you want something," she says as he pulls her bra down further revealing her nipple.

"Rubbish," he says as he sucks on it. "Mmm, I love your tits."

"Yeh! All two of them, I know," Sally remarks repeating his favourite phrase.

Virgil slides his hand between her legs. "Stop it… it tickles," she giggles. "No! Don't," she orders grabbing his hand.

"What's up?" Virgil looks at her.

"Not your hand, its staying here," she puts his hand around her waist. "I've only known you a few weeks."

"That's long enough to know each other," he says. "Away you'll like it."

"Like what! A hand all over my pants."

"You mean you've never let anyone touch your cunt like."

"Don't call it that," she snaps angrily.

"You don't know what it's like then… when someone touches your cu… fanny."

"No!" Sally says embarrassed.

"Let me show you then," he lowers his hand and lifts her skirt.

"No I said," she goes to grab his hand. Virgil thrusts his hand up her skirt and pushes his fingers between her legs over her knickers. She stretches her legs to sit up and tries to pull his hand away. "Ow! Virgil you're hurting me."

"Listen, do you wanna go out with me?" Virgil stares at her. Sally says nothing. "Well don't fanny about, you're gonna let me sometime, so it might as well be now." He pushes his hand harder. She jumps in her seat. She stares at him then looks out of the window wanting Sue to return. Virgil kisses her neck releasing his hold on her. "I just want you to experience the feelings you'll get from me touching you like." He massages his hand over her knickers. She relaxes her legs and opens them slowly. "That's better, now give us a kiss." She turns to him and submits to his demands. Virgil rubs with his hand, now gently, feeling her soft mound through the material with his fingers.

"Mmm! You feel lovely," he says with a smirk on his face as they kiss again, Sally feels a tingle and shudders in her seat.

"You felt something then?" he asks. Sally says nothing they carry on kissing. She jumps again as she feels another tingle inside her. She moans quietly. Suddenly there's a tap at Virgil's window.

"Virgil!" Ali shouts through the glass, Sally pushes his hand away.

"Shit! What do you want can't you see I'm busy," Virgil lowers the window.

"Give us a fag, I'm freezing me balls off out

here," Ali asks.

"Let me back in, I'm not standing out here all night," Sue demands.

"Your fucking sister," Virgil moans getting out to let them in.

"It's freezing out there," Sue clambers in the back.

"Come on give us a fag Virgie," Al asks again.

"Don't call me that," Virgil snaps.

"Sorry," Al apologises. "What have you two been talking about?"

"I want to go home now if you don't mind," Sue insists.

"Yeh! It's getting late," Sally agrees.

"Great like, fucking great."

Karen Joins The Party

Motorbikes, more than usual, gather round the slipway. The beams from the headlights shine in all directions in the cold midnight air. Karen stands next to Jenny avoiding Ian, but keeping an eye on Dave. Dave stands on a bin and announces, "OK the party's on." Karen walks over to him.

"Can I come to the party?"

He jumps down. "It's not the type of party you'd like, I think tonight you'd better go home."

"I'm not going home, if you won't take me I'll go

with Ian."

"Please yourself, but keep out of the way."

Karen walks off annoyed at his attitude, arms folded to keep warm with just a small fur jacket and red leather skirt on, she decides to talk to Ian.

"All right Ian?"

Ian looks at her. "Boyfriend dumped ya?"

"He's not my boyfriend."

"Not what I'm hearing."

"Can I come with you tonight," she asks putting her hand on his thigh.

"Why?"

"Well we didn't exactly finish what we started last time."

"Oh yeh," Ian takes no notice.

Karen walks away looking back over her shoulder. "Next time you won't need to drug me."

"Where you going?" He asks.

"To find a real biker."

"Come on then," he calls her back.

Karen stands looking at him. "I don't know now!" she teases him.

"Don't fuck me about, do you want to come with me or not?"

"OK," she quickly walks back to him in case he changes his mind. "Where's your helmet?"

"Where it always is," he hands her it.

"Cheeky." She pulls up her skirt, Ian stares at her

crotch as she climbs on.

Dave climbs on his bike glancing at Ian and Karen and roars off down the sea front, the rest of the bikers follow. Taking up the full width of the road, they drive towards the town clock, within minutes the bikes are parked and the riders have dismounted. There is an eerie silence in the town centre. They sit and wait.

"What are we waiting for? I thought we were going to a party?" Karen asks Ian.

"The party's here."

"What! Redcar clock?" she looks around. "There's no music."

"Shhh! Listen," Ian tells her.

In the distance a roar can be heard, then from the roundabout on Corporation Road a mass of grebo's on their motorbikes turn on to West Dyke Road and ride towards the clock.

"Oh! We're waiting for more of your friends," Karen watches the bikes approach.

"Not quite," Ian remarks.

"Right," Dave calls out. "Get ready."

Just then, Dave and the bikers pull out from under their jackets pickaxe handles, chains, bike chains, knuckle-dusters and other items that can be used as weapons.

"What's going on Ian?" Karen starts to panic.

Ian pulls out an iron bar from his sleeve. "We're

going to have a party."

"I'm off." Karen runs across the road towards the clock tower, under the archway she sees a metal ladder leading up to the clock's workings. She climbs up out of sight.

The grebos pull up fifty yards from Dave, they too draw their weapons. The leader looks around. "I fancy a bit of window shopping, what do you say lads?" Laughs of agreement mingle among the grebos. The leader looks back and nods to one holding a baseball bat, he lashes out against the window of the, 'anything for a pound,' shop.

"You've just cost that shop a lot of money," Dave points out.

The biker looks at the window as shards of glass fall to the floor. "I'll pay for it, what is it? Anything for a pound... Mike throw a pound note in, you know what they say in for a pound in for a penny."

Dave stands shaking his head thinking, 'what a thick bastard'.

"The other way round Spike," a grebo shouts to his leader.

"What?"

"In for a penny in for a pound," he corrects Spike.

"I know that, that's what I said."

"You said..."

"OK! OK!" Spike interrupts trying not to look stupid. There's a silence, then. "Charge!" The grebos lunge forward at Dave and his friends.

"OK then!" Dave shouts. "Let's get the bastards." The grebos smash windows and doors, Spike runs at Dave, Dave whips out a long chain and hurls it around his feet Spike is sent flying. Dave's gang go into battle, there are bats bashing heads and backs, chains wrapping legs and arms, knuckle dusters denting jaws and smashing teeth. Dave gets a blow on his back; he slumps to the ground winded, Ian runs to his aide with his iron bar and lashes out at the culprit, saving Dave from further injury.

This is no pub brawl, this is a biker's war that's been brewing for months. Some of the grebos retreat to their bikes riding off in defeat; others lay on the floor injured. Spike gets his leg stamped on by Dave; he feels it break through the sole of his boot, Spike yells out in agony, Dave grabs his collar lifting him off the ground and head butts him. "Don't even think about coming back," Dave threatens.

Karen nervously climbs down to check what's happening, she stares shocked. Except the odd school rivalry, she's never seen a fight like this before. "Dave, behind you," she shouts. "Jenny look out… smash him Phil." Blue lights flash reflecting off the shop windows. "Pigs," she shouts. Karen runs from her hiding place. "The police Dave."

He turns and runs to his bike. "That'll do lads come on let's get the hell out of here."

Karen runs up to Dave as he tries to start his bike. "Come on, come on, bloody electrics."

Karen shouts to him. "Don't leave me!" Looking round she sees Spike trying to get up on his hands and knees. "Wait a minute," Karen runs over. "Take that yer fat bastard," and kicks him in the bollocks. He collapses to the floor screaming clasping his balls.

Dave kick starts his bike. "Come on then Kaz," he calls her.

Karen runs and jumps on the back of his bike, quickly fastening her helmet she grabs him around the waist just in time when the front wheel lifts as Dave wheelies down West Dyke Road to escape.

The other bikers scatter in all directions, a police paddy wagon pulls up, coppers pile out the back doors just as one of the grebos crashes out of control, throwing the rider into the back of the wagon. The police pile in, to arrest him.

Dave speeds up West Dyke Road reaching sixty, seventy mph. The level crossing gates start to close, other bikers follow him but only Dave manages to ride between the gates before they shut.

"Yee hah!" Karen screams.

Following behind, Ian knows he can't make it and skids a ninety into the warehouse car park. Speeding to the end and through a gap in the fence, he escapes along the railway line but rides into the path of an oncoming Boulby potash train. Bouncing over the track he narrowly misses the locomotive and heads for the Redcar Lane crossing, the gates raise allowing him to turn on to Redcar Lane and make towards Saltburn.

Five other grebos speed towards the level crossing, with the gates shut and the police following behind, they're trapped. One notices a sloping wall by the closed gates and takes a gamble attempting to use it as a ramp to jump the lines.

At top speed he hits the slope clearing the first gate, his mates skid to a halt and look on in awe as they see him fly just missing the locomotive to land safely on the other side making his getaway.

Cornered with two jam sarnies heading towards them on each side of the road and no alternative, they about turn and ride back, head on, to play chicken with the cops. Bunching together certain that the cops would bottle out, they ride full throttle towards the two cars. As expected one splits from the other and careers out of control hitting the curb sending it rolling on to its roof into a car park, wiping out two other cars and crashing through a wall sliding to halt.

The other car nineties into Railway Terrace, losing control it bounces off a wall into the back of a United bus rupturing the petrol tank causing it to explode.

Racing through the back alleys, Queen Street,

Redcar High Street, Coatham Road and Lord Street, Dave's friends knowing the area escape the police.

But for five maybe six grebos, all got away. The final few top a tonne and race along no man's land to Saltburn, leaving the police chasing them hopelessly in their Granadas down the coast road.

What a night, within minutes the quiet town of Redcar, some people would call 'a dead town' was awakened by the battle of the bikers and for the summer of nineteen eighty it was a battle that will always be remembered.

Is It Worth It?

Dave and Karen sit on the grass bank at Errington woods overlooking the rooftops of New Marske. On their left the lights from British Steel and ICI illuminate the night sky, in contrast over to their right, only the speckled tiny lights can be seen from the tankers awaiting clearance to enter Tees dock, breaking the darkness of the North Sea.

"Let me look at your eye, you got a good whack from that lad," Karen shuffles close to Dave.

"It's OK leave it," Dave pushes her hand away.

"It's not, you have a cut above your eyebrow, here." She gathers the cuff of her shirt and wipes the blood from the wound.

"Ow! You bitch," Dave grabs her arm.

"Sorry! I think you'll need stitches."

"What are you a doctor now," Dave says sarcastically. She hits him on his arm. "Ow! That arm's injured," he shouts.

"Fuck off! Fuck off will you," Karen yells. "I'm trying to help after you dragged me into that blood bath."

"I dragged you?" he questions.

"And all I get is, what are you a doctor now," she mocks Dave.

"OK, OK..." Dave submits. "I'll let you look at me eye."

"As long as you don't beat me up," Karen laughs. "Now let's have a closer look." Karen wipes his forehead, he flinches. She moves closer to him. "That's nasty," she spits on the cuff of her shirt. Dave watches her and reels back in disgust.

"What are you doing?"

"It's only spit, my mam does it to me, it won't kill yer," she wipes blood from around his mouth, leaning forward to take a closer look she kisses him.

"That'll do." He lies on his back taking a deep breath and relaxes. "That was some fight, I don't think we'll see those Borough bummers again."

Disappointed at his rejection, Karen sits looking out over the sea as she listens to him ramble on about the fight. Looking down at her shirt she casually and discreetly unfastens two buttons parting it slightly, then laying back raising one leg she slides her skirt up just enough to reveal some silk and closes her eyes wishing he would shut up and notice her for once. Dave falls silent, Karen opens her eyes and turns her head to him, he lays staring at her chest then reaches out and slips his hand under her shirt to fondle her breast. Karen looks to the sky and closes her eyes, a little smile breaks her frustration. Dave leans over and kisses her full and hard on her lips. Karen clasps a handful of grass as her body feels a wave of sexual excitement race through it.

Dave's lips quickly slide round to her neck, with a sharp intake of breath Karen bites her bottom lip as he bites hard and sucks on her neck.

"Dave…" she sighs. He returns to her lips, they kiss for what seems like ages, his hand moving over her body and down between her legs. Karen's body trembles gently as his fingers slide up and down over her knickers, roughly he pulls at her silk panties, his fingers slip inside her, Karen gasps as they open her more than she's experienced before, he kisses her harder. "Dave…" she mumbles between his kisses "Make me your… do me… Dave, do me now," Dave releases his hand from her pants and unfastens the belt of his leathers, rolling on top of her as if time was the essence, never parting from her lips he pulls at his shorts releasing his full erection.

"Dave… now…please now…" she begs. Lifting her legs and drawing aside the silk, with one thrust Dave pushes his cock in. Karen's eyes shut tightly as she feels a sharp pain, grasping at his hair with both hands she pulls his head from her lips to take a deep breath. Silently she cries out as he thrusts again, deeper he penetrates. "Orr Dave," she cries out as he bangs her hard, she pants and blows taking deep breaths trying not to show him the pain she is taking. "Yeh Dave…Yeh you know you want me." Dave pants as he bangs away ripping at her bra, Karen quickly pulls her straps down to help him as he sucks on her tits. She pulls his head closer to her.

"Do me...Dave" Her squirming mouth turns to a smile as the pain starts to give and a new sensation she's never felt before grows inside her. "Oh Dave…yer…yer that's it, that's it I can feel… oh Dave…Dave," Karen responds. "Don't stop, don't stop."

He suddenly lets out a cry of pleasure and collapses on to her. Karen pauses for a moment looking down at his head resting on her chest. She releases her grip. "Is that it?" she asks as he rolls off her pulling up his pants.

"Dave!"

"Come on we'd better get back," he jumps to his feet and walks towards his bike.

"Fuck off!" she shouts. "I was just getting into

it... is that all I get the first time I let you shag me...."

"What were you expecting? Come on." He carries on walking.

She pulls her knickers and bra straight, plucking the grass out from her hair as she follows him mumbling under her breath. "I've snogged for longer," Karen stops and watches him climb on to the bike, she thinks to herself, 'I told you I'd decide when you'd fuck me.'

Dave starts up the bike. "Now the electric ignition works! Are you coming then?" he shouts over the roar of the engine.

Winding down Grew Grass Lane they ride towards Redcar, Karen holds on to Dave, angry at his selfish act but at the same time smiling to herself. She got what she wanted. This is her new life, now a true biker girl and in the end for her it was worth using her virginity to get it.

Last Day At School

"Can you get a copy for me?" Jackie asks Samantha.

"Yes OK, smile everyone... and another for luck," Sam snaps photos as the girls clown around.

"Has everyone signed my t-shirt?" Wendy calls out.

"Frilly knickers," Sam shouts.

"Frilly knickers," the girls say in unison.

"Argh," Wendy falls off her chair.

"Got it, that should look good are you all right Wend?" Sam asks.

"Yeh, I'll survive," Wendy gets up and sits back in the chair embarrassed, all the girls laugh.

"Hey it's three o'clock, half an hour left and it's all over," Jackie announces.

"I'll miss school," Sam sighs.

A silence falls over them, then in unison again. "No!" they burst out laughing hugging each other.

"I'll miss you."

"Orr I'll miss you too!"

"We must all stay in touch."

"I haven't signed your shirt yet Sue," Sam scribbles her name on her back.

"I've only been here about three months," Amanda makes a speech. "But I've got to know you all as lovely people, you've become such good friends to me so I've got you each a present to say thank you."

"Orr Mand, you didn't have to," Wendy says receiving her gift.

"It's a pen with my name engraved on it!" Sally calls out surprised.

"This must have cost you a bomb," Sam admires the pen.

"No, not really I got them on bulk order."

"Thanks Amanda," Wendy and the other girls give her big hugs.

Karen walks in sporting her new hair cut, short black hair tinged with red tips. Sharon trails behind. "Are you coming Alison?" she calls to her.

Alison is sitting at her desk putting the last of her books into her rucksack. "Coming where," she asks.

"Home, where else."

Alison looks at the clock above the blackboard. "It's only five past three."

"What can they do, give us detention," Karen laughs.

"Never thought of that." Alison grabs her things and heads for the door.

"Hey girls!" Karen yells across the classroom. Sam, Wendy and the girls look over.

"Fuck off for the last time."

"Oh fuck off yourself," Wendy says bravely.

Amanda looks at Karen puzzled.

"See you in twenty years loser," Sue calls out with her back to Karen.

Karen, Sharon and Alison leave laughing, a silence falls in the room.

"She's right for once," Sally comments.

"Who is," Sue asks.

"Karen! Why don't we go home now we don't have anything to stay here for?"

Mr Evans strolls in. "What's that? Going home already girls?"

"Can we sir?" Sally asks. "What's there to wait for?"

Mr Evans stands looking at the girls. "The rest of your lives I think… go on and I wish you all well in your futures."

"Thanks sir," the girls jump up grabbing their bags.

"I'll miss you."

"I'm going to cry."

"I'm going to miss you too." The girls hug each other and start to cry.

"Come on Sam I'm looking for Paul," Wendy grabs Sam's arm.

"Goodbye sir," Sam shouts.

"Thank you sir, you're the bestest teacher ever." Wendy and Sam leave.

"Go on get out the lot of you, before I change my mind," he turns to wipe the blackboard as the rest of the girls leave. The classroom falls silent, he looks around then packs his things into his case as his eyes glaze over, "Stupid me, every year the same."

Wendy with Sam in tow, races down the corridor giggling.

"What class is he in?" Sam asks.

"Five B, down here I think." The girls stick their heads around the classroom door. The lads are sitting in a group throwing paper and pens at Geoff, laughing at one of his silly jokes.

"Paul!" Wendy calls. "We can go early are you coming."

"I was waiting for you," Paul jumps off the desk and grabs his bag. "Are you coming Geoff?"

Outside Paul unlocks his bike; Geoff swings from the bike-shed roof. "Remember Sam, this is where I first kissed you on the first day we started here."

"And it was the first and only kiss," she reminds him.

"Pity… we could have gone places Sam, you know, you and me babe."

Sam walks up to him and grabs his face with both hands. She kisses him.

"Ooohhh! What was that for?" He drops to his knees.

"Just for old times sake, and that is definitely the last kiss," Paul and Wendy laugh.

"I'll never wash these lips again."

They all walk to the school gates, Geoff stops and turns back "This is it guys and girls."

"What?" Wendy asks.

"The last time we cross these school gates, let's

never forget we spent five years of our lives here as class mates and friends, friendships have been forged here to be remembered from this day forward for the rest of our lives till death do us part. So let us stand here for one last moment and remember those friendships and memories least not forgetting the happy times we've had at Redcar High," Geoff turns to them. "What do you say guys?" Paul, Wendy and Sam have walked on ahead chuckling to themselves. "Hey you lot, wait for me," he runs after them turning back for the last time to look at the school. "No sense of nostalgia, bye school, thanks," he runs and catches up with them.

At the East Halt on Borough Road they separate to go home.

"I'll see you tomorrow Sam."

"OK Wend, bye Paul."

"I'll walk with you Sam, if you want," Geoff tags along with her.

"If you must."

"Hey Sam, now we've left school can we start afresh," Geoff asks.

"Yeh OK," she says agreeing.

"Great will you go out with me?"

"Get lost."

"OK, I get the hint."

"It's only taken you five years," Sam sighs.

Paul and Wendy walk home. "Are you sure your mam won't mind me coming round tonight to baby-sit with you?" Paul asks.

"I've told you, it's all right, it's taken her a couple of weeks to calm down and come to terms with what you did but she's OK now."

"I know," Paul says. "But I wanted it to be a surprise not a planned date," he explains.

"Well it certainly was a surprise, at least dad's started calling you son."

Paul walks Wendy home for the last time from school, one arm around her shoulders the other steering his bike, as they have done for the past four and three quarter years.

Sam's Home Early

"I'm home mam," Sam shuts the front door.

"You're home early," mam calls from the lounge.

"Yes, the teacher let us out, there was nothing doing," she hangs her coat and enters the lounge "what are you doing?" she asks her mam.

"I thought I'd get some knitting done while tea's cooking, it'll be ready by five for when your dad gets home."

"I'll quickly jump in the bath then, is there plenty

of hot water?"

"Yes," her mam gets up. "Oh! A letter came for you this morning, I left it on the TV."

"I wonder if it's about that new job I applied for at the newspaper office," Sam picks it up and opens it; a big smile spreads over her face. "Oh mam, I've got an interview, Tuesday next week."

"That's good news pet, let's keep our fingers crossed shall we," her mam goes into the kitchen. "I'll make us a nice cake for supper shall I…oh Samantha can you nip down the shops for me I'm out of sugar?" she calls from the kitchen.

"OK… is that all you want?" Sam asks putting her coat back on.

Mam re-enters the room with her purse and hands her fifty pence. "I think that's all you need,"

"OK I won't be long." Sam leaves walking down the garden path with a bounce in her step.

Just up the street Sam walks past the house she knows Christian works in, she slows down and approaches looking in to see if he's there.

"Hello!" A man pops up from behind the garden fence; Sam jumps out of her skin. "Can I help you?" he asks.

"No… erm… well yes, I was wondering if Christian is working today," she asks nervously.

"Yes, he's inside, hang on there I'll see if I can get

him for you," he walks into the house before Sam could stop him yelling. "Chris there's a young lady outside to see you," Sam stands at the gate looking around blushing. Suddenly she hears clonking of work boots as Christian runs down the bare wooden staircase inside, he appears at the front door. Sam looks at him his overalls covered in dust and paint with holes in the knees and his hands are dirty.

He wanders over to the gate. "Hi! How are you?" he asks smiling.

"OK," Sam replies blushing.

"Where you off to then?" he asks.

"Oh just to the shops, I haven't seen you here for a while?"

"No I've been on another contract, I've just started back here today… isn't this the week you finish school?" he asks.

"Yes we finished today," she looks at her watch. "Thirty-six minutes fifteen seconds ago," she laughs. "Guess what?"

"What?" Chris asks.

"I've got my first job interview."

"Well done, where at?"

"The Evening Gazette, next Tuesday."

"Well I hope you get it, what will you be doing there?"

"Oh I suppose secretarial work or sell advertising, I would like to be a journalist one day… so what time do you finish?"

"Not until five fifteen," he looks at his paint-covered watch. "That's when I go back to the shop to get my wages, then we finish at five thirty, can't wait I'm starving!"

"I'd better go then I've got to get mam some sugar, I'll see you later then," Sam says goodbye.

"Yeh OK, I'll see you again!"

Samantha walks on leaving Chris with a smile beaming on his face. Chris walks back into the house, he sticks his head back out of the door to take another look at her. Samantha turns round and sees him, she waves, he waves back.

Friend Or Foe

Amanda sits in the armchair watching TV, there's a knock at the door. She jumps up and opens it.

"Is it safe then?" Karen stands at the door smiling.

"Karen! I thought you…"

"Kaz if you don't mind, yeh sorry about earlier, I didn't mean you when I told the others to fuck off."

"Are you coming in, mum's gone out to dinner with Norman."

"No, Dave's outside."

"Oh right."

"Ricky's downstairs he wants to see you."

Amanda pops her head over the balcony.

"All right Mand, are you coming?" Ricky calls to her. "We're all going down the South Gare."

"Where's that?"

"Get your coat on, I'll show you."

"OK, wait a minute." Amanda dashes in and grabs her jacket. Slamming the door behind her, they both run down the stairs.

"All right Mand jump on," Ricky tells her.

They ride towards the sea front stopping at the indoor fairground by the boating lake.

Amanda jumps off the bike. "Is this the South Gare?" she looks around puzzled.

"No, we're going there later," Ricky walks with her to the main doors, slipping his arm under her jacket. She looks at his hand appear around her waist then looks at Ricky, she smiles and lets him keep it there. Before Ricky gets a chance to catch up with what Amanda's been up to for the past few weeks, Karen grabs her arm and drags her away from him.

"Come on Mand, let's go on the dodgems."

"Wow! I haven't been on one of them for years are you two coming?" Amanda calls back to the lads.

The girls share a dodgem, Dave and Ricky take one each and after three goes the girls surrender.

"I'm going on the ghost train," Karen jumps off the dodgem. "Are you coming?"

"Not for me," Amanda shouts. "I'm grabbing a bite to eat in the café."

"I'll join you," Ricky runs up behind her.

"Dave, come on," Karen shouts running to the train. "You're not scared are you?"

"No, but you will be when I've finished with you," he runs after her.

"A pepsi, a coke and a slice of fudge cake please," Ricky orders.

"I'll save us a seat over there Rick," Amanda walks over claiming a table next to the window. She sees Kaz and Dave entering the ghost train as it takes them through the tunnels of terror.

"Here we are your favourite," Ricky sits down splashing the drinks on the table. "You'll get fat eating that," Ricky hands her the fudge cake.

"I'll worry about that when it happens," she tucks into the treat.

"I haven't got to see you lately, I'd thought you'd forgotten me."

"I've been busy finishing my exams, helping the old lady next door, decorating with my mam and I've been going to York for the past few weekends to visit my sick uncle."

"You're quite a busy girl, I thought you just didn't want to see me again!"

"What makes you think that?"

"So I can see you a bit more now you've left school?"

"If you want to," she takes a big mouthful of cake. "As long as you keep buying me fudge cake.

"It's a deal then," Ricky slides closer to Amanda.

As Ricky and Amanda finish their drinks, Karen runs into the café and over to the table laughing.

"What's funny?" Amanda asks.

"One of the dummies in the ghost train fell off its stand and landed on Dave," she laughs. "He shit himself."

Dave approaches. "I should sue for damages, I may never have children again."

"Come on let's go to the Gare," Karen runs out, they all look at each other.

"What's she on?" Dave asks.

Leaving their motorbikes parked beneath the South Gare lighthouse Karen, Dave, Amanda and Ricky walk around the Gare wall, dodging the waves crashing over the sides. Dave grabs Karen around the waist and nearly throws her in. "Tell ya mam I saved your life," he yells.

"Argh! You fucking idiot…I could have fallen in," Karen yells at Dave. He laughs as he dodges her flying fists.

"Now you know what it's like to shit yourself."

"That was different," she runs after him trying to kick him. "Come here you bastard."

"Missed me," Dave runs away.

Ricky and Amanda are left alone; they look out over the sea watching a tanker enter the mouth of the Tees. "Core! It's a bit chilly," Ricky says gently pulling on Amanda's arm turning her towards him. With her hands in her pockets she looks at him and smiles, Ricky slowly moves forward hesitating a moment before kissing her.

It was just the right time and place for their first kiss. His soft slow gentle kissing made Amanda tingle inside, Ricky parts from her lips and looks into her eyes, she leans forward to instigate the next kiss, releasing her hands from her jacket pockets and slipping them into his jacket to pull him closer towards her.

Dave dashes down a small set of stairs under an archway trying to hide from Karen, a steel door blocks his escape. "Shit it's locked," he pulls on the handle.

"Got you now," Karen runs down the stairs and crashes into him.

"Ow! Me arm," Dave grabs his arm protecting it from Karen's onslaught.

"You're not using that excuse," she tries to tickle him.

"Stop it… stop it… I said STOP IT!" he raises his voice. Karen steps back frightened at his response.

"Only kidding," he grabs her waist pinning her against the metal door tickling her.

"No! No!"

"Come here you tart."

"Hey, who you calling a tart and mind your hand!" She grabs his wrist and stops it from going up her skirt.

Dave and Karen snog. "Orr Dave I'm so glad I'm with you," he starts to bite her neck, slipping his hand under her skirt into her knickers pulling at them.

"Dave! What are you doing?" She grabs his wrist again.

"What's it look like?" He kisses her to shut her up.

"Someone…might…see us," she says between kisses. "Go on then who gives a shit." Karen submits, bending down slipping off her knickers.

Dave releases the buckle of his belt; Karen quickly helps him unzip his leathers. "I can't pull them down," Karen struggles.

"Here I'll do it," Dave drops his pants to his knees.

"Orr! Dave, come on I want it good," he pulls her to the side of the stair well pressing her back hard against the wall, lifting her skirt he grabs her right leg and raises it by his side, she stretches out placing her foot behind him on the other side of the stair well so she can lift her left leg to pin herself against the wall.

"Orr that's it!" Dave shouts, Karen groans as he makes his first entry.

"Yes, yes Dave," she wraps her arms around his neck to give her more support, while he hammers her hard. His belt buckle taps against the wall to the rhythm of their heaving bodies. "Screw me, screw me," she turns him on even more with her words as she's learnt he likes to hear her voice when they fuck.

Dave puffs and pants his knees weakening and his hands slipping off her arse cheeks as he becomes tired from the weight of his horny sex toy.

"Yeh, yeh, yeh, yehhh," Karen groans with pleasure.

"Orr...orr yehhh," he moans with pleasure, Karen and Dave's voices echo out from under the archway over the South Gare. One last push by Dave finishes him.

"No another...don't stop!" He accommodates. "Argh! Yes, yeesss," Karen finishes her climax and rests her head back against the wall, looking up to the ceiling she takes a deep breath with a smile on her face. "Argh!" she jumps down.

"Ow! Me bollocks." Dave grabs himself.

"Spider," she shouts tripping over running up the stairs, her arse mooning back at Dave.

Dave stands doing up his trousers. "What are you panicking for?"

"Spiders! I can't stand spiders," she shouts dashing out pulling her skirt down. Dave walks slowly up the stairs laughing.

"Get my knickers?" she points down the stairs. "I left my knickers at the bottom."

"Get them yourself."

"No, there's a big spider down there," she looks in fear as Dave walks off still laughing to himself. "Thanks a lot," she glares at him, then takes a deep breath and scurries down to collect them, screaming as she runs back up.

Hopping on one leg she slips her knickers back on. An elderly couple out for evening stroll watch as she stumbles past, the old man smiling at the view. The old lady looks at Karen with disgust and hits her husband reminding him that she's with him.

Karen runs up to Dave slipping her arm through his. "Save me Dave!"

"You're still alive then?"

"Just…my legs are shaking," she tells him.

"My balls are killing me," he pulls down his trouser crutch to relieve the pain.

"Sorry!" she looks at his crutch. "Can we do it again somewhere else?"

He looks at her and pulls a face. "Later!"

Ricky and Amanda break from their adoring kisses.

"I've never met someone so lovely as you," Ricky tells Amanda.

"I bet," she looks out over the sea embarrassed at the compliment.

"No really, there's something about you that's different."

"Like what?" she looks at him.

"Er… I don't know."

"Well, when you do, let me know," she jokes.

"There! That for a start."

"What?" she asks.

"You come out with what you want to say, you're not like other girls who just stand next to you chewing gum, playing with their hair saying naught. You're more mature than other girls."

"I don't know if I should take that as a compliment."

Ricky kisses her again.

"Rick! Are you coming?" Dave yells over from the top. Rick and Amanda part, staring into each other's eyes.

"No… but it sounded as if you were!" Ricky shouts up.

"Orr that, come on I'm freezing, I want to get round a fire."

"Come on," Amanda pulls Ricky's arm from around her waist and leads him back towards the bikes.

They ride back along the tarmac track that led them to the lighthouse, turning down a slipway taking them on to the sands. A quarter of a mile in the distance they see bonfires burning and bikers congregating for tonight's beach party.

"Wait a min! I've just got to see Pete about something," Ricky dashes off. Amanda sits herself on a log by the fire. Karen jumps next to her. "All right Mand?"

"All right."

"Having fun eh!" Karen nudges her arm.

"Yes you could say that," Amanda smiles. "What about you? Yes, yes, yeesss," she giggles.

"Oh! Did you hear?"

"Put it this way, if it had been foggy they wouldn't have needed the lighthouse fog horn.

"No! I wasn't that bad was I?"

Amanda raises her eyebrows.

"Here Dave, chuck us some beers!" Dave throws Karen a couple of cans. "Do you want one Mand?"

"No thanks, I'll skip the beer tonight."

"Good more for me then," she opens the cans and takes a drink from each. "I always think the first mouthful tastes the best."

Amanda looks sideways as Karen sips away.

"Depends on what you're drinking!"

Karen spits her drink as she laughs uncontrollably wiping her chin with the sleeve of her jacket, she leans into Amanda. "You're tops Mand, I'm glad we got to know each other."

Ricky's motorbike slowly pulls into Amanda's estate. Climbing off the back Amanda removes her helmet and hands it to Ricky.

"Thank you for a fun evening," Amanda smiles at him.

"When can I see you again?" Ricky asks.

"I'll meet you down the amusements tomorrow at 2pm."

"Yeh! OK," Amanda places her hand on Ricky's as he holds the steering column. "Till tomorrow," they kiss a long slow kiss.

"Till tomorrow then," Ricky starts his bike and roars out of the estate. "See yeh," he yells.

"Shhh," she looks back up at the flats to see if any of the lights come on.

Carefully she shuts the front door, so as not to make a sound. The hall light suddenly switches on and the brightness makes Amanda raise her hands over her face.

"You're not starting that game," her mother stands at the bottom of the staircase.

"What game mum?" she lowers her hand.

"Coming in all hours of the night."

"It's only twelve thirty, I've left school now."

"You're still only sixteen and now I find you getting lifts home on the back of motorbikes by some skinhead."

"That's Ricky, he's not a skinhead!"

"He's got a motor bike, what is he a Hells Angel then."

"No! Don't talk rubbish," Amanda pushes past her mam and walks upstairs to her bedroom.

"Amanda! I don't want you out late, I do still worry if anything should happen to you."

She turns at the top of the landing. "Nothing's going to happen mum," she slams her bedroom door behind her.

"I'm getting fed up with your attitude," her mam yells as she switches off the light and quickly climbs the stairs stopping outside Amanda's door. "You can stay in all next week."

Amanda opens her bedroom door the light shines on to her mam. "Yes and do what? There's nothing to do in this dump you brought me to, so I may as well stay in and rot," her mam slaps her around the face.

"Don't talk to me like that young lady," Amanda slams her door again. Standing in the dark her mam for a second goes to call Amanda but stops and returns to her bedroom, leaving her crying in her room.

Sally Goes To Work

Smiling with a spring in her step Sally walks past the houses Christian is helping renovate.

"Hi Sally!" Christian calls to her.

"Hi Chris! Still working on those council houses?" Christian joins her; they walk together along the street.

"Yeh, got a bit left to do yet, where are you going this sunny Saturday morning?" Chris asks.

"Off to the hair salon, did I tell you I start full time next week."

"Very good, you can do my hair any day."

"Everyone's saying that, I could start my own business if I was qualified," she laughs.

"How's life treating you then?" Chris asks.

"All right," Sally replies.

"Got a boyfriend yet," he smiles at her. "If not I'm available."

"I've got one thanks."

"Shame, what's his name then?"

"Virgil."

"Oh… isn't he in Thunderbirds."

She looks at him. "Not funny."

"Sorry… where does he work?"

"At British Steel, he's got a car."

"Ooooo! What type?"

"Er… Escort I think, well it's Orange."

"I know the type," Chris says. "I hope he looks after you, if not send him to me I'll sort him out." They walk on a bit in silence, Christian contemplating what to say next. "What's your ambition in life then?"

She looks at him puzzled. "To be a hairdresser?" she replies.

"I know that, but have you got a dream, a goal in life, put it this way if I was your fairy godmother and granted you a wish what would you like to be?"

"I don't know… a hairdresser," she says again.

"You have a beautiful face… you should consider taking up a modelling career."

"My boyfriend wouldn't like that."

"What? It's not for him to say, it's your life, you do as you think, don't let anyone tell you what to do."

"I'm not that pretty," she says embarrassed.

"Believe me Sally, you are beautiful and don't forget it."

"What's your ambition then?" she asks.

"I'd like to write."

"Oh yes! What?"

"I'd like to write films, so keep going to the pictures, one day you might see my name in the credits."

"But you're a joiner," she says laughing.

"Well, I've got to do something to fill my time."

"I have to get to work now," Sally walks on.

"Say hello to your mam, I'll pop round one night for a cup of tea."

"I'll tell her, bye Chris."

Christian stands outside the gate of another house he's renovating and watches Sally, this petite, long blonde haired girl with a face of an angel.

"I wish," he sighs.

Sally arrives for work. "Hi everyone!"

"Hello Sally, could you make a start by making a cup of tea for us all," the boss asks.

"Yes OK!" she walks through to the back of the salon.

"No Sue today?" he asks.

"Er… no, she's not well," Sally makes an excuse.

"Can you tell her if she doesn't want her Saturday job can she let me know?"

"Yes Mr Wilcox, I'll tell her."

Virgil pulls up outside the salon, he jumps out of

his car and dashes in. "Is Sally at work yet?" he shouts across the shop.

Sally pops her head around the door, her boss looks at her disapprovingly. "Sorry Mr Wilcox."

"One minute and back in OK," he tells her.

Outside by the front door, Virgil stamps his fag out on the pavement.

"What is it?" Sally asks, looking back into the salon, some customers sit watching her.

"I've got to go to the dentist," he opens his mouth and shows her his bad tooth. "See the back one," he talks with his finger in his mouth.

Sally looks back into the salon again seeing customers turning their heads in horror. "I'd rather not if you don't mind." She walks with him to his car. "What do you want? I've got to get back in," Sally tells him.

Virgil climbs into his car. "Look Sal I'm sorry about last night."

"That's all right."

"It's just your sister's always with you."

"Well… you're always with Al."

"Fair point," he shrugs his shoulders. "Look tonight, we'll go out on our own… deal."

"I'm babysitting."

"I'll babysit with you."

"I don't think they'll allow me to have my boyfriend round."

"I'll come round when they've gone and I'll go before they get back."

"I don't know," she hesitates.

"Don't you want to be with me?"

"Yeh... you know I do." Her boss taps on the shop window mouthing the words, 'Tea please.'

"Look I've got to go Virgil."

"What about tonight then?" he asks.

She thinks for a second. "OK... come around... about seven thirty, they'll be gone by then, thirteen Windsor Gardens."

"Great, I'll see you tonight then, I'll bring some drink round."

"No! No drink," she tells him.

"Give's a kiss then," Virgil asks.

Sally leans over and gives him a quick peck.

"You're breath stinks."

"It's the tooth," Virgil mumbles sticking his finger back in his mouth.

Sally runs back to the salon as Virgil starts his car. He pulls away sounding his horn to the tune of charge-of-the-light-brigade. Sally stands at the door, her eyes closed. 'Do you have to,' she thinks.

When she opens them she sees the customers looking at her and Mr Wilcox standing with a box of tea bags in his hand.

From Me To You

Christian steps out of the house he's working in and finds Samantha standing by the garden gate. "Hi! What brings you here?"

"I came to give you this," she hands him an apple. "I thought you could have it for your break, so you don't get hungry."

"Oh thanks," he takes it. "I've never had an apple given to me before, especially by someone as beautiful as you."

"It's only an apple," she says embarrassed. "Do you always work Saturdays?"

"Only mornings for some extra overtime…hang on a minute." Christian dashes into the house and through into the back garden, he plucks the last remaining red rose off a bush poking out from beneath the rubble. Running back in he rummages around the corner of the room where all the rubbish from used tea bags, meat pie foil trays and chip papers lay. "There it is," he picks up a Kit Kat wrapper, removes the foil and wraps it around the stem of the rose. Bounding out of the front door and back up the footpath, hiding it behind his back, he stops looks into her eyes and produces the flower. "Here, for you," Christian hands Sam the delicate rose.

Sam laughs as she takes it. "Thank you," she

smiles tilting her head to one side, blushing. "I'll put it in water and when it blooms I'll press it to keep forever," There's a silent pause as they look at each other.

"Listen, do you fancy going out tonight?"

"I might," she says smiling.

"Don't force yourself girl."

"Where then?" Sam asks.

"How about the pictures."

"Only if we pay to get in," Christian looks at her puzzled. "Don't ask," she says giggling to herself. "What time then?"

"How about seven?"

"OK! I'll see you at seven," Sam walks on.

"What's your phone number?"

"Oh yes! Here," she pulls out a little notebook and scribbles her phone number on it, she tears it out and hands to him. "See you tonight then," she says walking off. She stops and turns. "Thanks for the rose," she calls out.

"Thanks for the apple," Chris calls back, taking a bite from it. His face screws up, he turns his head and spits the mouthful out over into the garden next door. "Err! God that's sour," he looks back just as Sam waves to him. Chris smiles. "Thanks," he shouts waving the apple in the air.

A face pops up from next door. "Can you spit your food elsewhere, not in my garden?"

"Oh sorry!" Christian hurries back to work.

Later that night, Chris rushes around the flat he shares with his father.

"Calm down son, you won't get anywhere faster." The phone rings, his dad answers it. "Chris, it's your boss."

Christian enters the hallway. "Have you seen my wallet dad?" he picks up the telephone. "Hello… Mr Gilbert… I was going out tonight… yes, I understand… very well… I'll be ready in ten minutes…bye," he puts the phone down. "Great! That's just great."

"What's up son?" his dad asks.

"The scaffolding around Hutton's carpet shop has collapsed and it's all hands on deck to dismantle it… that means I'll have to cancel Sam and it's our first date." Christian picks up the telephone and pulls the paper with Sam's phone number on from his top pocket and dials it. He waits and waits. "She's not in, she can't be out," he tells his dad. "Hello! Is Samantha there? Hello… is Sam there… Samantha… is this four eight four ... I'm looking for Samantha," Christian raises his voice. "I said Samantha, forget it," he puts the phone down. "I'll try again," he redials. "Hello… oh! You again, sorry bye."

Later at Samantha's house she sits quietly watching TV with Bobby and Ann.

"He's not coming is he mam?"

"He should have at least phoned to let you know," her mam says calling from the kitchen.

"I don't understand it, I thought he wanted to take me out," Sam looks at the time, fifteen minutes past seven.

"Give him another five minutes, boys are always late," her mam laughs trying to be positive.

"The picture will be starting soon."

"He might have another girlfriend," Ann suggests.

"Shut up Ann."

"Well he's not here is he?"

Sam gets out of her chair and takes off her coat making her way upstairs.

Her mam steps out from the kitchen. "I'll have words with that boy next time I pass those houses he's working in."

Upstairs Sam looks out through her bedroom window, still no sign of him coming.

Virgil Comes To Baby Sit

Sally opens the front door. "Is it clear like?" Virgil stands asking looking over her shoulder.

"Yeh! Come in." He pushes his way past her

walking quickly into the lounge.

"Hey nice pad, look at the stereo system," he walks over to it and lifts the lid.

"Don't touch it, you might break it." Virgil switches it on and the music blasts out loud. "Turn it off, you'll wake the baby." Sally dashes over seeing Virgil fumbling with the buttons, she flicks a switch and all goes quiet.

"Sorry!" he closes the lid.

"Do you want a cup of tea?" she asks.

"No, I pinched a bottle of wine from me dad's garage, he's got a new batch from Germany, Liebfraumilch," he looks at the label. "He has loads, he won't miss one."

"I said no drink."

Virgil hands her the bottle. "Find a cork screw."

She looks at the bottle. "It's a screw top."

He takes it back. "Just testing, go and get two glasses." She does as she's told and goes into the kitchen to hunt for some glasses. Virgil looks around unscrewing the bottle top and drinks a mouthful. He spots three one-pound notes on the mantelpiece.

"It's not strong alcohol is it?" Sally asks walking back into the room with the glasses.

"No it's..." he looks at the label again, it reads 12%. "It's only 4% alcohol." He lies.

"I don't want to be drunk when they get home," she stands next to him and hands him a glass, Virgil sits and fills it.

"Give us your glass." Virgil pours the wine.

"I don't want a lot," she pulls the glass away spilling some on the settee. "Mind you'll stain the cushions!"

"Oh stop your moaning, you haven't stopped since I got here," he takes a big swig from the bottle, then places it on the floor. "Now sit down like."

Sally sits and takes a small mouthful. "Mmm it's nice, I don't often get to drink wine."

"Get used to it, you girls always drink it."

"Do we?" Sally looks at him suspiciously.

"So I'm told like," he lays back drinking from his glass.

"I hope your not trying to get me drunk."

"Don't talk rubbish, give it back, then you won't get drunk will you?" he holds out his hand.

"I can handle it," she pulls her glass towards her chest.

"OK! Don't blame me if you get tipsy then… what's on the box?" He grabs the TV Times.

"A film's about to start," she gets up and switches on the TV.

"What film's that like?"

"Herby rides again."

"Lucky him… that's the beetle car isn't it?" he asks.

"Yeh," she sits back, Virgil puts his arm around

her.

"I was thinking of putting a stripe on my car, you know like Starsky and Hutch."

"That'll look brill," she agrees with his idea.

"Yeh, I thought that," he takes another drink.

"Your car's a nice car," she takes a sip of wine.

"Nice! Leave it out, it's the dog's bollocks and when I can afford it I'm going to get alloys from that new car shop in town, Dixon Tuning, it sells high performance car parts."

"You like your car a lot don't you?" she asks.

"Like it, love it, I live for my car, it's everything to me, I'd be lost without it. It's a babe magnet.

"I hope not," she sips her wine looking at the TV.

"Well not any more, now I've got you like," he takes her glass and with his he places them both on the carpet next to the bottle. "Come here," he kisses her pushing her back into the cushions.

"Lift your legs up then, let's get comfortable," raising his legs off the floor he lays beside her and pulls her legs up to his, they kiss and his hand quickly goes over her jumper feeling the shape of her breasts through the thick wool.

"The film's about to start," she says turning her head to the TV. "Let's watch it."

"Yeh… OK," he leans over grabbing the bottle of wine and takes a drink while Sally rolls her back to him and settles down to watch the film.

Virgil shuffles behind her. "Do you feel that? That's what you do to me."

Sally shuffles again trying not to feel his bulge pressing against her.

The film finishes. Now laying on his back, his right arm tucked behind his neck and his left hand resting on top of the bottle. Sally lies with her head now resting on his chest wedged between him and the sofa.

"What did you think of the film?" she asks.

"Wasn't bad, it was clever how they got the car to drive on its back wheels to do a wheelie, I'll have to fix my car to do that." He turns on to his side trapping her between him and the back of the sofa. "It's time I gave you some attention," Sally giggles. "What are you laughing at?" he asks.

"Does it always get hard?"

"Only when I'm with you like," he kisses her and rubs himself against her leg. Sally says nothing. He slips his knee between her legs and starts to kiss her on the neck. "Move over a bit." She shuffles letting him climb between her legs. They kiss for a minute or two then he lifts her jumper revealing her bra. "Let's see those lovely tits of yours… you've got a front fastener on!" he notices smiling.

"I bought it today, to make it easy for you."

"You do love me," Virgil unfastens her bra and

moves his mouth over her nipples.

"Ow! Don't bite," she tells him.

"Open your legs a bit," he moves his hand and slides it down her bare leg slowly slipping it under her skirt.

"That tickles," she grabs his hand.

"Just relax, you'll like it when I get started."

She giggles again. "Don't you touch yourself up?" he asks her slobbering over her tits.

"No!"

He looks up at her face. "You mean you don't wank off!" She says nothing. "Well watch what I do, I'll teach you how."

She looks down between herself and Virgil, as he lifts her skirt and pulls aside her white cotton panties fumbling pushing his finger into her.

"Ow! That hurts you could have cut your nails first." He takes his hand away and spits on his fingers then rubs the spit into Sally slowly pushing and pulling two fingers in her. Sally lifts her body up the settee trying to make herself comfortable as he continues. She closes her eyes and lets him carry on.

"Like that do you?" She says nothing. "This is how you do it," Virgil kisses her neck and starts to bite into her.

"Don't!" she pushes his head away.

He works on her for a minute or two while Sally just lays there unsure of what she should be getting out of this, she takes a sharp intake of breath as he hurts her again forcing his fingers further inside her.

"You felt that then, trust me I know what I'm doing, I've read all the mags."

"No! Stop it, it's hurting too much," she pulls his hand out of her and straightens her panties.

Virgil kneels between her legs and unfastens his trouser belt.

"What are you doing?" she asks.

"What do you think like?"

"I don't want to go any further," she says concerned.

"No… but I've got urges too," he lays on top of her pulling his trousers down over his backside. "Don't worry! Give us another kiss," he kisses her for about a minute then takes Sally's hand and pulls it down towards his underpants.

"What are you doing now?" she asks pulling it back.

"Just relax," he pulls her hand again. Her shoulder bends downwards as her arm is stretched. He places her hand over the erection in his pants. "Well grab it then!"

"I've never…"

"Just grab it!" he orders, she presses her hand over the material of his pants feeling his bulge.

"What do you want me to do now?"

"Rub your hand up and down."

"What… Like this," she tries to accommodate.

"Yeh! Yeh that's good," he starts to kiss her more vigorously as he gets worked up, now and then their teeth clash against each other making Sally cringe. Virgil takes a breather looking down at what Sally's doing to him. "Now slip your hand in my pants," she struggles, stretching her arm even more taking hold unsure what to do next. "Move your hand up and down then." She does as he orders "Ow! Don't pull so fucking hard."

"Sorry!"

"That's better, don't stop."

She leans her head back on to the arm of the sofa looking at the ceiling while she wanks him.

"My arm's aching…how much longer do I have to do this?"

"Orr let go then."

She breathes a sigh of relief. "Phew I thought my arm was going to drop off."

He kneels up again this time to pull her pants down.

"No! I don't want to," she grabs her pants to pull them back up.

"I'm not going to," he says pulling on them more. "I just want to feel my self against you."

"No!" she pulls them back up.

"OK," he lies on top of her pulling the front of his underpants down and starts to rub against her.

"Stop it! Stop it," she struggles pushing him off her and jumps to her feet, she pulls down her skirt and fastens her bra pulling straight her jumper.

"What the fuck's wrong with yer?"

"I don't mind doing the other stuff but I'm not going all the way."

"You don't trust me do you?" he says angrily getting dressed. "You don't really love me!"

"Of course I do."

"So why don't you trust me?"

"I do, keep quiet you'll wake the baby," she stares at him.

"Well, you do want to have fun don't you?" he whispers.

"I just don't want to… you know."

"You know what?"

"You know… make love."

"Will you get off that make love shit," he pulls her back on to the settee. "Listen I'm not going to screw you, OK."

"OK!" she starts to get upset.

"I'm just trying to show you some fun, it's called foreplay, it's what girlfriends and boyfriends do. Now do you want me to teach you… you know… the guy that loves you?"

Sally thinks for a second. "I suppose so," she looks down into her lap picking at her nails nervously.

"OK let's start again, lay back!" he instructs her. She lays back and puts her legs up keeping her arms down by her side.

He unfastens his trousers and lies between her legs, lowering his head next to hers, he lifts her skirt.

"Please don't take my knickers down," she asks.

"All right! I'll leave your knickers up," he mumbles into the cushion, knowing he can't push his luck any further. "Just lay there, let's have some fun," he slips his brown Y-fronts down again over past his buttocks. "That's the stuff, just relax enjoy it," he rubs his cock over her knickers, she closes her eyes more tense than relaxed. "Orr! I love you Sal, you're Great, put your arms around me." She struggles to free her arms and folds them around his back, Virgil grabs her leg and raises it. "Open your legs a bit more," he slides his hips up and down using her knickers to rub himself off. "Ooooo you feel good."

"Ow! You're rubbing too hard," she cries.

"Yeh! Just relax I'm nearly finished."

"Ow! Stop it your rubbing to hard, it's burning me." She moves her hands down to his waist trying push him and ease the pressure.

"Orr yes! Orr yes! Don't move," Virgil cries out. "Arghhh SALLY," Virgil cries out and collapses on top of her, he pauses for a second. "Oh that felt good."

"Can you get up now?" she insists.

"Hang on," he gathers his trousers and rolls off the sofa falling on to his backside, then gets up and leaves the room.

"Or what's this mess? It's all over my knickers."

"It's just spunk," he shouts from the kitchen.

She gets some on her fingers. "Err!" she sniffs it, "Err! It smells awful."

Virgil walks back in from the kitchen zipping up his trousers. "Does a bit, you ought to taste it," he laughs.

"Err no thanks," she cringes.

"Here use this kitchen roll." She tears some from the roll and wipes it off.

"It feels cold," she tears off another strip and stuffs it down her knickers straightening her clothes.

Virgil drops on to the settee and picks up Sally's half empty glass of wine. "Do you want this like?" He drinks it.

"No you have it," she gets up and takes the used paper and roll into the kitchen.

"What time do the owners come back?"

She re-enters the lounge. "In about an hour, I'll clean these glasses."

"When can I see you again?" Virgil stands and walks around the room looking at the photos on the wall, he looks back to Sally through into the kitchen standing at the sink.

"Don't phone me you know dad doesn't like boys

phoning me," she calls to him.

Virgil spots the three one pound notes again and takes one. "Tell me about it."

Sally comes back in. "You can pick me up as usual at work."

"OK! I'll shoot off now."

"What now! Can't you stay another half hour!" she asks.

"I've gotta start work tomorrow, early like, you know it's my turn to do the Sunday shift."

"OK then," she picks up the wine bottle and hands it to him.

"Take this with you I can't let them find it here."

Virgil walks into the hall, Sally follows. "I'll pick you up after work on Monday then."

"Yeh OK,"

He steps out on to the path and walks towards the gate. "Haven't you forgotten something?" Sally calls.

"No! What?" he says looking at the bottle in his hand.

"Don't I get a goodbye kiss?"

"Oh yeh!" he hops back up the step and gives her a kiss. "Close the door, you don't want to get cold," Virgil tells her. "And I'll see you Monday."

Sally closes the door. Virgil struts down the path, looks at the bottle and throws it on to next door's garden. He dashes to his car, unlocks it and jumps in.

Starting the engine, he takes a look in his rear view mirror fixing his hair. Smiling to himself as he drives away.

Karen's Stuck In The Bathroom

It is morning and Karen's mam can hear a noise in the bathroom. She sees the door ajar and pushes it open revealing Karen on her knees throwing up into the toilet. Her mother stands and looks at her. Karen turns her head, tears run down her cheeks. "What are you looking at?" she says quickly turning back to be sick again.

"If you want to come home drunk every night don't expect sympathy from me," scolds her mam walking away.

"Piss off!" Karen curses under her breath and heaves again.

Sunday Walks On The Beach

"Next Friday, I'll pick up my first wage, twenty-five quid," Paul tells Wendy as he picks up a stick and throws it across the sand for Buster to fetch. It is a misty Sunday morning, Paul and Wendy walk together along the beach towards Marske.

"That's great, just think when you've finished your apprenticeship you can build us a big house."

"Hang on! I haven't sawn a piece of wood yet, I don't know how long it will be before I can build a house."

"I'm glad you're going to be a joiner."

"Why's that?" Paul asks.

"Well I wouldn't like you to be a mechanic, all that horrible dirty oil or a bricklayer, sand and cement everywhere."

"I'll be coming home covered in sawdust."

"Oh that's all right, I won't notice the sawdust, it'll blend in with the stuff in your head," Wendy laughs running away from him.

"Come here you," Paul chases her almost falling over Buster. He grabs her by the arm swinging her around, they stop and look at each other giggling, arms wrapped around each other's thick coats. They kiss.

"I love you Wend."

"How much?" Wendy asks.

Paul holds his forefinger and thumb in front of Wendy's face with a tiny gap between. "Oh this much."

"What?" she hits him on the arm insulted.

"From this finger," Paul points. "All the way round the world back to this thumb."

"Oh Paul, I do love you," She cuddles him as they

walk on.

"I'll build you a house, it will have a big garden, nice kitchen and a dozen bedrooms."

"A dozen?" Wendy interrupts. "What would we want with twelve bedrooms?"

"So we can have lots of children."

"I'm not giving birth to the next Boro team." Paul wraps his arm around Wendy's neck snuggling her head into his chest. "I'm only having two children," she says, her voice muffled by his coat.

Paul whispers in her ear. "Shall we start practising now," he jokes.

Wendy straightens up and looks out over the sea. "I don't know!" she says quietly.

Paul steps in front of her, but she still looks past him at the sea. He gently turns her head and looks into her eyes. "You know I wouldn't ask you to do anything you didn't want to do."

"I know," Wendy sighs.

"My dad talked to me, you know after the party, he said when he and mam got together they did it after they got engaged, mam got pregnant with Alex my older brother."

"Didn't they use condoms?" Wendy asks.

"Dad told me they weren't easy to come by and the pill wasn't invented."

"I'm not going on the pill!" Wendy says adamantly.

"I'm not suggesting that."

"What then?"

"Well you're sixteen now and I'm sixteen and we'll be getting married one day... when your mother allows us," there's a silence between them.

"What are you trying to say Paul?"

Paul looks at her. "I'd like us to sleep together."

Wendy thinks for a second, "As long as you really love me, stop! What am I saying, I know you love me, but it's got to be right." They walk on together. "Is it legal?" Wendy asks.

"Yeh we're over sixteen."

"We'll have to get some condoms."

"I'll pinch some off my dad."

"No you won't, I'm not using second hand ones." Paul laughs. "Stop laughing, anyway he's older than you, won't they be too big?" she asks.

"Condoms fit all sizes," Paul replies confidently.

"Even yours?" Wendy makes her escape.

"Come here you."

"You'll have to catch me first...Buster here boy, come on boy."

Sorry Sam

"Samantha, Samantha," Chris runs across the road and catches up with her. She walks on past the house he's working at, not saying anything or even looking at him. "Wait!" Chris jumps in front of her. "I'm sorry about Saturday but I was called into work, the scaffolding at Hutton's carpets had collapsed, it was a mess it fell on three cars, luckily no one got hurt."

"Yes! I believe you," she walks on past him.

"It's true, you'll read about it in tonight's Gazette," she walks on not interested, "I tried to phone," he shouts. "But got this deaf old woman."

Sam stops and turns. "What phone number did I give you?"

Chris pulls out his wallet and rummages for the slip of paper she gave him. "Here," he hands her it. She looks at it and smiles.

"Oops!" she giggles raising her hand to her mouth.

"I just got this deaf woman who just kept saying get off me, get off me."

"That's my gran," she tells him laughing. "She's got seven cats that are always jumping on her lap, I've given you her number by mistake, I sometimes stay there, I am sorry."

"Thank goodness for that, so I'm forgiven?" Chris asks.

"Well let's see what the newspapers print tonight," Sam replies.

"It's true, I wouldn't lie to you."

"No I'm only kidding, so where are you going to take me this time," Sam enquires.

"What if I was to take you out, Wednesday night seven thirty… for dinner."

"Hi Chris!" Sally walks by on her way to work.

"Hi Sal, all right?" Chris waves to her.

Sam looks at him. "You know her?" she asks.

"Yeh… I've done work for her mam, I pop round for tea sometimes."

"Don't you have a home to go to?"

"Yeh, I share a flat with my dad."

"Oh," she says eyeing him up suspiciously.

"Well! How about Wednesday?" Chris asks.

"OK then," she turns and walks on.

"Sam," Chris calls to her.

She stops and turns. "Yes!"

"Can I have the paper back with your proper number this time and to be safe your address?"

She holds it up looking at it. "Oh yes sorry," she laughs.

On The Back Seat

"You're elbow's sticking in my side," Sally grabs it and tries to get comfortable.

"Move over then," Virgil tells her as they both struggle on the back seat.

"That's better," she relaxes.

"You smell so sweet." He kisses her neck.

"Don't get it on my skirt it leaves a stain."

"It washes out," he mumbles as he moves his lips over her tits.

"So my mam told me when she washed my knickers yesterday," Sally looks up to the window, "it's gonna rain I think."

"Open your legs!"

"Hey! You nearly pushed it in," Sally pushes his hips away from her. "If you don't stop, I'll pull my knickers back up," Virgil says nothing and just keeps sucking on her nipples. "No! Stop it, get off," she tries to push him off.

"Don't Sal, don't move," he tells her.

"Do it again and I'm stopping," she warns him. The weight of Virgil's body forces her head between the seat and door panel. Sally moans with discomfort as she listens to Virgil's heavy breathing. She lays thinking to herself 'How long's this going to last?' When suddenly Virgil grunts with pleasure. "Are you done now?" she looks down at his head resting on her chest as he grunts his last grunt. "Orr you got it on my leg, you're determined to cover every inch of my body," Virgil climbs over into the front and out of the passenger door.

"Shut the door it's freezing," Sally shouts.

"Wait a minute, I've dropped me hanky," he

shouts.

Sally tries to pull her knickers up, not wanting to move as she feels his spunk start to run around her leg dripping on to the vinyl seat. "Give us your hanky," she shouts. He throws it to her. "Orr you've already used it," she holds the handkerchief between her fingers wiping herself trying not to get any on her fingers. "Err!" she sits up and throws it out of the passenger window.

Virgil gets back in the driver's seat, "what yer doing like, that's a good handkerchief?" She looks at him in disgust. "Oh! Never mind," he gets out his cigarettes and lights one.

There's a silence between them as Sally climbs into the front passenger seat.

"Where shall we go now?" she asks.

"I'll take you home."

She looks at her watch. "It's only half past eight!"

"Well what do you expect like," he raises his voice and looks straight at her.

"Don't yell," she looks out of the window.

"Why won't you do it with me?" Virgil snaps.

"I'm not like other girls… I don't want to be an easy lay."

"Trust me, you're not." Again there's a silence. Taking a drag of his fag, he turns in his seat to face her. "Don't you fancy me like?"

Sally looks down at her lap picking her nails

nervously.

"Cause if you don't, just tell me... there's no point in having a relationship if we don't do it sometime... it's the way people show they love each other."

"I will... but not just yet," Sally looks at him slowly. "Why won't you wait until I'm ready?"

"Wait...for how long?"

"Soon."

"When soon?"

"Soon, soon."

"Listen Sal," he sweetens her up. "It'll mean a lot to me, it'll prove you love me."

"I do love you," she looks down twiddling with her fingers again.

"We're gonna do it one day, so why not enjoy it now?" He takes another drag of his fag then throws the butt out of the window. "You like it when I touch your fanny up." Sally says nothing. "You wouldn't let me do it unless you liked it!"

She looks out of the window again thinking to herself, 'I won't do it if you keep pestering me.'

"That's just a smidging of what it's really like."

She closes her eyes, "How do you know?" she asks.

"I...I don't know, but that makes it even better for us... I've never slept with anyone before and you haven't, so we'll be each other's first. It's not like

I've slept with loads of lasses, if I had it would be like sleeping with someone who's… like, you know, dirty, that's why I want you to be my first and me be yours, then no one's touched us but each other."

Sally thinks for a minute. "I'll think about it," she says hesitantly.

"You've been saying that for the past week," Virgil slumps back into his seat with a thud. "It's up to you now Sal, if you want to, let me know…I'm not waiting for ever, I want a proper girlfriend not a schoolgirl virgin," he starts the car.

"I'm not a schoolgirl any more!" she says looking at him upset.

"You're acting like one," Virgil drives off skidding over the grass on to the coast road towards Redcar.

The car pulls up at the end of Sally's street. "I'll see you Saturday after work then," Virgil sits looking through the windscreen.

"OK then… but that's five days away!" Sally looks at him.

"Listen Sal," he turns to her, leans over her and opens her door. "I think it's time to call it a day." Tears swell up in her eyes at the sudden announcement. "I love you Sal but if you're honest with yourself you don't really love me."

"But I do," turning she grabs his arm with both

hands. "Don't finish me Virgil, I need you, I just want to be sure."

"Sure of what?" Virgil looks out through the windscreen, again there's a silence between them. Sally sits holding his arm, a tear runs down her cheek.

"Don't finish me, I love you," she cries.

"Well prove it!" Virgil leans over and pushes open the door. "I'll see you Saturday," she reluctantly climbs out of the car. Without closing the door he wheel spins away, leaving Sally standing in the road crying.

Second Time Lucky For Sam

Samantha wanders into the lounge her dad lies back on the sofa watching TV, Bobby lays next to him and Ann kneels on the floor in front of the fire.

"Are you sure I look all right?" Sam asks fastening her silver belt around the white long flowing dress she has chosen to wear this evening.

Her mam steps over Ann with a mug of tea for dad. "Yes of course, you look lovely pet, now calm down you don't want to look nervous in front of him," she tells her.

"Going to the pictures is one thing mam, but dinner... I don't think I can eat anything," Samantha rubs her belly hoping the butterflies will go away.

"I'll get you a glass of sherry that'll help settle your tummy," she walks over to the glass cabinet. "I can't have sherry that's an old fogies drink," she objects.

"You're an old fogie now you've left school," Ann butts in.

"Shut up Ann, I'm still sixteen, nearly seventeen, I'm not claiming my bus pass yet."

Dad gets up to go to the toilet. "Has he got lots of money?" he asks.

"Dad I don't go out with boys for their money."

"What are you going out with him for, eh?" he laughs as he steps through the kitchen to the outside toilet.

"Shut up dad, you have a one track mind," mam tells him with a giggle.

"Sometimes I wonder if dad's right in the head," Sam jokes.

"Your dad's never been right in the head… do you want this sherry?"

"No mam, I'll skip it," Sam goes into the hall to fetch her coat.

"I'll have it then," mam drinks it and tops up another.

Sam dashes back in. "Oh! He's here."

Bobby jumps up to the window and Ann follows. "Let me look," Bobby pulls back the nets.

"Get away from the window, I don't want him seeing you," Sam tries to drag them away.

Ann plonks herself back down by the fire. "Away from the window." Sam, orders Bobby pulling him away,

"He can't see me looking," he says as he flaps the curtains to get a better look. "He's got a Rover mk II." Bobby knows his cars.

"He's most probably borrowed it from his dad," Sam snaps pulling Bobby away for the third time, dropping him on to the settee out of harm's way. "Now stay there," she tells him. "I'll see you all later," she turns to leave.

"Aren't you going to bring him in so we can meet him?" her mother asks.

"Do I have to?" Sam looks worried.

"Let us meet him, it won't do any harm," mam turns off the TV.

"Orr mam I was watching that," Ann complains. Bobby sits up looking forward to meeting him, thinking it might be fun to have another boy around, it might even things up a little with having two sisters picking on him all the time. There's a knock at the door, Sam stands looking at her mam.

"Well fetch him in then," mam instructs her.

Sam nervously walks into the hall and opens the front door. "Hello, you made it this time?" she laughs.

"I wasn't going to mess this one up, even if it cost me my job," Chris jokes.

"Come on in… I'm sorry the family wants to meet you." Sam whispers closing the front door behind him.

Chris pokes his head around the door. "Is it safe?"

"What do you mean is it safe?" mam calls to him, with her usual happy giggle in her voice. "Course it's safe, come on in."

"Hello everyone," Christian nervously greets them.

"This is my mam, Bobby my younger brother."

"Hello" Chris shakes their hands.

"And Ann my sister."

"Hi," she giggles.

The sound of the outside loo flushing echoes through the adjoining house wall. Sam looks at Chris, there's a silence as dad slams the back door and enters fastening his belt. "Bye heck I needed that," he sighs not noticing Christian standing there. Ann puts her hand to her mouth as she spurts out a giggle. Bobby watches Chris's face for any reaction.

"Dad… this is Christian," Sam introduces him.

He turns and looks. "Hello!" then slumps back into the sofa.

"Are you going anywhere nice?" her mam enquires.

"Yes, I thought I would take Samantha to the

Voyager at Guisborough for a meal."

"That's a bit of a journey!" her mam points out.

"Only a fifteen minute drive, I've borrowed a friend's car," he looks at Sam. "It's a lovely drive especially on a summer evening."

"Well, we'd better be going, we don't want to be late," Sam says eager to escape her family.

Christian walks Sam down the garden path to the car. "You look lovely tonight Sam."

"Thank you," she blushes.

"Here, let me open your door," Sam puts one leg in and turns to sit down, she sees her mam, dad, Bobby and Ann staring through the lounge window. She sits down, Christian shuts the door and walks round to the driver's side.

"No! Go away," Sam mouths, waving her hand to them from inside the car.

"What's wrong?" Christian asks as he sits behind the wheel.

"Nothing, hurry we don't want to be late...mind that cat!" Sam points forward, drawing his attention away from the house.

Chris looks through the windscreen. "Where?"

"Oh it's gone, drive on, I can't wait to see this restaurant."

"Very good," he starts the engine, puts it into gear, checks his mirrors and looks behind him to see if it's safe to drive away. "Aren't you going to wave to your family then," Sam turns to Chris then looks back to her family who are now smiling and waving, she grins and waves goodbye. Christian leans forward over her shoulder and waves too as he pulls away.

"Would you like to order drinks sir, what would you like madam," the waitress asks.

Sam hesitates. "I'll have a coke please."

"Could I have a whisky and lemonade?"

"Certainly sir, I'll leave you the menus to choose your meal whilst I get your drinks."

"Thanks Janette."

Sam looks at Chris across the table. 'He knows the waitress' she thinks to herself.

"I'm starving how about you?" Chris says glancing down the menu.

"Oh, I'm not that hungry," Sam reads the menu noticing the prices. "It's not cheap here."

"Oh don't worry about that, it's my treat for last Saturday's fiasco… you look a bit pale, do you feel all right?"

"Yes… I'm just not used to eating in posh restaurants."

"It sometimes helps to have a glass of sherry before a meal, to settle…"

"Your tummy!" Sam finishes his sentence. "So mam tells me," she laughs.

"It does, that's why they serve it at weddings," Chris explains.

"No, it's all right I'll manage."

"I'm having the prawn cocktail then the rack of lamb, it's absolutely gorgeous, I highly recommend it."

"How come I get the feeling I'm not the first girl you have brought here?"

"You are, what makes you think that?" Chris asks.

"Oh just it's that you know the waitress Janette and now you're recommending the food!" she says suspiciously.

"Oh Janet, she's normally behind the bar, I come here regularly for a drink with my friends, I also came here last Christmas for the works do."

She's not sure if she should believe him.

"Here are your drinks sir, madam, are you ready to order?"

Chris pulls up outside Samantha's house, he turns off the engine and they sit for a moment in the quiet.

"Would you like me to walk you to your door?" Christian asks.

"No it's all right," she collects her handbag by her feet.

"Oh! I forgot, how did your interview go?"

"I'll find out next week I think," she replies.

"Do you think you're in with a chance?"

"I don't know there were about a dozen people being interviewed the same day." A silence falls between them.

"I don't want this evening to end," Christian takes her hand.

"Thanks! It's been a lovely night," she replies, her hand trembles gently.

"With you it has," Christian looks deep into her eyes, she smiles back, her heart beats fast as Christian leans forward to kiss her.

Two years ago she first saw Christian on stage playing records for the school discos and had what could have been, a schoolgirl crush on him, tonight she can't believe she is going to kiss him for the first time. She closes her eyes as his lips press gently against hers then pull away, she panics thinking to herself, 'What's wrong didn't he like it? Oh no have I got bad breath,' He leans forward to kiss her again. Sam not wanting him to stop kisses him back. He places his hand on to her pale soft warm cheek sliding it down around her neck pulling her head gently towards his, to kiss her more intensely. Sam raises her arm nervously placing it around his wide shoulders, her fingers spread out over his back, to pull herself closer. He kisses her for what seems like ages to Sam, then they part. Sam looks down shyly.

"Till tomorrow," he whispers in her ear as he kisses her on her cheek.

Sam turns and looks at him, her body now trembling with excitement as she kisses him once more not wanting this moment to end, but it must. "Thank you for a lovely evening," she opens the door and turns to leave.

"See you tomorrow?" Christian requests.

Sam smiles, shuts the car door, and he drives away. Smiling, feeling as if she's walking on air, she makes her way up the garden path to her front door taking one last look back to see his car turn out of the end of the road.

Fumbling with her keys she notices a movement out of the corner of her eye and turns her head to find mam, dad, Bobby and Ann looking around the net curtain, through the window, smiling, and waving to her.

A Shoulder To Cry On

"Sally, hey I missed our daily walk yesterday," Christian runs up to her.

"Oh hi Chris... I didn't feel like going to work," she says feeling down.

"You weren't sick were you?" Chris asks.

"No I didn't feel like working," Sally replies.

"I've had that feeling since my first day at work," Chris jokes. Sally walks on silently. "Are you all right Sal?" He looks at her noticing tears swelling up in her eyes, he puts his arm around her. "What's up?" She says nothing as she wipes a tear away. "Come on Sal, here sit down for a minute, it can't be that bad." She stops and sits on the wall looking down the road away from Christian embarrassed. "Is it your job, are things all right at home?"

"I'll be all right," she stands to walk on.

"No don't go, sit down for a minute, and tell me what's wrong." Christian looks at her, thinking to himself. 'What can I do to cheer this pretty little thing up, what can I say,' "It can't be that bad… you haven't cut someone's hair off by mistake have you," Chris tries to make her laugh.

"No!" she giggles.

"It's not your boyfriend is it?" he asks concerned. She lowers her head and cries. "Oh dear you are in a mess, has he hurt you?"

"No."

"Come on, a problem shared is a problem halved... What's wrong?"

"Virgil's finishing with me," she cries.

"I am sorry, you liked him a lot didn't you?" She says nothing. "What do you mean finishing with you?" Chris asks puzzled.

"He… he thinks I don't love him," she cries.

"But you do don't you?"

"Yes," she cries a bit more.

"So what makes him think you don't love him?"

"Because I won't sleep with him."

"Oh...that old ploy!" Christian thinks again. "Have you talked to your mam?" he asks. "No! Forget I said that, your mam would have a chastity belt welded to you before you could say, er mam I was wondering?" Sally laughs between her sniffles. "What about your sister, you're close to her."

"Sue and me have fallen out!"

"Oh dear you are having a bad time of it, listen Sal," Christian turns to her. "I'm just a lad but if you have a problem it's good to talk it out with someone. Find an aunt, a teacher, oh no! You're not at school any more are you? What about an older friend, someone you know you can talk to, there's someone out there who can help."

"What do you think I should do?" Sally asks Chris.

"Well... do you want to... sleep with him that is?"

"I don't know," she wipes the tears from her face.

"Sally... if you're not sure... it means you're not ready."

"But he says he'll finish me if I don't."

"So he'll finish you, what's the worst thing that can happen? There's plenty more lads out there that would die to have a girlfriend like you."

"He says if I do it, it will prove I love him."

Christian gets angry. "That is one of the most selfish things a lad can say to a girl, it's virtually blackmail, you'd do it if you loved me?" Christian repeats sarcastically climbing off the wall, he crouches in front of her. "Sally...you are one of the most beautiful girls I have ever met and if your boyfriend threatens to finish you because you won't sleep with him, it tells me he's not worth keeping, I know it hurts but if he really loves you, he'll wait until you're ready. It should be a precious moment in your life, don't listen to his blackmail because that's what it is," Christian stands up becoming more angry. "It doesn't matter how much you love him, if you don't feel ready, listen to what your body is telling you, because now it's telling you he's not the one."

"I'd better get going," Sally jumps down off the wall and walks on. Christian walks with her.

"Sally... I don't know what to say but I don't want to see you get used, it happens to so many girls."

"Thanks for listening, you won't say anything to anyone about this will you," she asks.

"Of course not Sal, but please, please don't do anything you don't want to do."

"I'll see you then," she walks on to work by herself.

"Yeh, bye Sal, take care," Christian stands

watching her as she quickens her pace to get to work.

Strip Poker

Amanda opens the door to her flat. "Hi Mand are you coming out? We're going down the Hydro pub for a head banging session, then there's a party round Stuart's place," Karen jumps up and down like she's on hot coals, trying to talk Amanda into coming.

"I don't know, I promised to help Betty next door put up some net curtains."

Ricky walks along the balcony. "Hi Mand are you coming with us?" he asks.

"Where's your mam?" Karen looks over Amanda's shoulders into the flat.

"She's gone to York to visit my uncle this weekend, with Norman," her voice drops a little as she mentions his name. "She's just left."

"So… she won't be coming back till tomorrow?"

"No, why?"

Karen runs to the edge of the balcony. "Hey everyone Amanda's mam's out come on up."

"What are you doing Kaz?" Karen turns and walks past her into the flat. "Kaz!" Amanda follows her.

"It'll be all right, we'll have a drink first and then we'll all go down the pub and meet up with the others." Karen plonks herself on the settee. Amanda stands looking at her.

"Karen, I don't want this place messed up." Ricky walks up behind.

"Don't worry Mand, I'll keep them in check," he sits on a chair.

Amanda stands in the lounge doorway as Dave, Jenny, Nick, Mark, Jackie and Pete pile into the flat.

"Hi Amanda," Jenny kisses her on the cheek.

"All right love," Nick passes by.

Mark raises his hand and gives her a nod.

"Cool pad Mand," Pete sits himself on the floor in front of the TV and turns it off.

"I don't want anything broken," Amanda pleads.

"Have you got some music we can put on?" Jenny looks through the records. "Johnny Mathis...Andy Williams... The Beatles," Jenny calls out as she fumbles through the collection.

"Put the Beatles on, it's better than naught," Pete yells.

"Gotta pack of cards?" Dave asks.

"I think I've got some in the kitchen drawer," Amanda replies.

"Go and get them then," Dave orders.

Amanda walks out of the room looking back to check all is OK, then dashes into the kitchen and searches through the drawers, she pulls one out too far spilling the contents over the floor. She sees the cards and grabs them dashing back. At the lounge door she calmly walks in. "Here they are," she chucks them to Dave.

"Give's a beer Dave," Karen asks. He throws a can to her. "The flat looks good Mand, I see your mam's nearly finished the decorating," Karen opens the can of beer it sprays on to the wallpaper. "Oops," she looks at it then at Amanda.

"I'll get a tea towel," Amanda runs back into the kitchen and grabs a tea towel off the worktop. A bowl of sugar resting on the corner of the towel is dragged off and smashes over the lino. "Shit!" she curses and starts to pick up the broken bowl. She hears Ricky in the lounge.

"Don't spill it on the carpet," Amanda drops the sugar bowl and rushes back in.

"You haven't spilt it on the carpet have you?"

"Only joking Mand, come on sit here with me," Amanda chucks Karen the towel and drops on to Ricky's lap giving up. "Here give us a kiss,"

"Stop it!" she pulls away from him.

Karen wipes the beer off the wall. "There… doesn't show," she says as she looks at the stain and slides a small table with a vase of flowers on so it hides the mark.

"What card game shall we play?" Dave calls out. "Fifty-two card pick up."

"Yeh, that sounds cool," Pete says eager to play.

"Pick them up then," Dave throws the cards in the air over Pete, everyone laughs.

"Very funny," Pete starts to pick them up.

"Let's play twos and eights," Jenny shouts. "Penny a point!"

"What about threes and fours?" Mark asks.

"I like seven sevens," Amanda suggests. Everyone goes quiet and looks at her puzzled. "The first person to collect seven seven's by adding your cards up to seven… wins." There's a silence in the room as they all look at her strangely. "We play it down south."

"Strip poker it is then," Dave announces. "Come on Pete deal the cards then."

"No thanks," Jenny says. "I'd hate to see you naked."

"Who said I'd be naked?" Dave replies.

"Kaz… can I have a word," Amanda gets up off Ricky's lap and they both walk into the hall. "Your friends… OK," Amanda, states.

"Your friends too," Karen replies.

"Drinks… OK, but strip poker that's going too far."

"Oh, lighten up Mand," Karen walks back into the lounge.

Within one hour Karen is down to her knickers. "This is not fair," folding her arms around her chest holding her cards complaining.

"What!" Dave says, "I've only got two pieces of clothes left so stop yer moaning."

Jenny sits fully clothed. "I'm glad I'm not playing, I'd have lost by now."

Pete sits in his boxers, with Mark and Jackie still fully dressed. Amanda has her trousers on but is down to her bra.

"OK! My cards first," Dave turns over the ten of hearts. "Karen?" Karen turns over the eight of clubs. "Oooooh," Dave laughs. "Ricky?" he turns the jack of clubs. "Lucky, lucky, Jackie your turn."

"King of diamonds," Jackie screams with relief.

"No!" Pete throws in the five of diamonds. Amanda hesitates. "Come on Mand," Karen tells her. She turns the card slowly revealing the two of spades. "Oh!" she stands to take off her trousers. "No highest card chooses," Dave stops her.

"What do you mean highest card chooses? You keep changing the rules," Amanda questions.

"Just split the pack," she slumps to the floor and cuts the cards pulling the Ace of clubs. "Yeh!" she jumps up running on the spot. "You can't beat that, so I'm taking off my trousers."

"Wait!" Dave stops her again. "You split the pack, I'll find the jack." Dave cuts the pack and draws the Jack of Hearts.

Amanda yells. "Yes! You lose."

"No!" everyone looks at Jenny.

"No! What do you mean?" Amanda asks.

"Ace is low when picture shows."

"You're not playing," Amanda protests.

"Dave has the pick!" Karen shouts.

"Now let me see which item of clothing is it going to be the trousers or the bra… It's the bra, get it off."

"Off off, off off," they all chant.

The front door opens and Amanda's mam walks in followed by Norman. "It only passed its MOT a few months ago," she stops and listens. "What's all that racket?" She walks past the kitchen and sees the mess all over the kitchen floor. "What's going on?" She opens the door to the lounge and sees Amanda standing in the middle waving her bra in the air with everyone cheering. Then a silence descends. "Amanda!" her mam yells.

There's a mad dash as everyone tries to grab their clothes, beer, cigs and shoes making for the front door. Amanda sits quickly putting her bra back on, the room empties but for Pete who casually puts his clothes on. Amanda's mam and Norman stand watching him.

Pete walks past them. "Hey chill, don't get stressed, life's too short," and shuts the front door behind him.

Amanda puts on her jumper and starts to tidy up. "Sorry mum, they just…"

"I don't fucking want to hear it."

Amanda looks at her mam shocked, hearing her swear for the first time. "Mum!"

"Norma," Norman approaches her to keep her calm.

"Get up those stairs I've had enough," her mother points.

"It's not my fault, they just invited themselves in," Amanda explains.

"Just get up them stairs NOW!" Her mam grabs her by her arm and drags her to the stairs.

"Get off me," Amanda shouts.

Norman stands looking embarrassed.

"I go away for one weekend… lucky my car broke down or I don't know what I would've found when I got back." Amanda falls on the stairs. "Get up," her mother pulls her up and takes a swipe at her.

Norman intervenes. "Don't hit her, let her get up."

"Go please Norman just go, it's got nothing to do with you," she yells at him. Norman makes a hasty retreat and exits out of the front door. "Get up you selfish little…"

"Mum, stop it!" Amanda cries as the blows rain down on her.

"Get off me," Amanda struggles free and makes for the front door dashing out on to the balcony. "It's all right for you to go for a dirty weekend with Norman, but me I have to sit and watch TV for the rest of my life, well fuck you mum, I'm doing what I want to do for a change!" Amanda turns and runs down the stairs and across the car park.

"Amanda come back," her mam calls to her over the balcony. "Amanda sorry... I didn't mean... Amanda," her mam cries. "Amanda come back please," she watches as Amanda disappears around the flats.

She slams the front door behind her and runs upstairs into her bedroom crying. Slumping on the bed, she pulls a photo from her bedside cabinet next to a bottle of sleeping pills and looks at it. It is a photo of herself holding Amanda as a newborn baby in hospital. "I'm sorry, don't make the same mistake I did, I didn't want it to be like this," she reaches for the pills and lies down holding the picture against herself sobbing.

Hydro Electric

Karen head bangs on the dance floor to the Stranglers latest hit, Mark's long hair wafts about in all directions and the others join in. Ricky holds Amanda's waist jumping up and down with her. Dave sits in the corner of the pub with Pete chilling out on a joint,

Karen runs over to them and jumps in the seat

next to Dave. "Come on dance, why don't you join us?" He says nothing just picks up his pint and drinks. "What about you Pete, are you coming with me for a head bang?"

"Not my scene man," he lays back.

"Oh, you party poopers," she jumps up and rejoins the gang on the dance floor.

"My legs are going to drop off," Ricky shouts to Amanda.

"What!" she shouts back.

"I want you to pull my cock off," he yells to her knowing she can't hear him.

"OK!" she yells back and walks with him back to the table. "Oh that was great," Amanda takes a drink from her glass. "I'll have a rest though, before you get your dick out."

Ricky looks at her embarrassed. "Sorry I didn't think you could hear me."

"That's OK, lighten up Rick, you're too…"

"Too what?" Ricky asks.

"Too nice," she snogs him.

"Oh yeh! OK," he smiles at her and grabs her for another snog.

"Don't get any ideas though…come on let's have another dance." Ricky follows her to the floor, puzzled at the hot and cold messages Amanda keeps giving out.

On the balcony Ian stands looking down over the

dance floor, with a drink in his hand and a lot more in him, he stares across the room at Karen head banging. She looks up noticing him and waves to him to join them. He turns back and carries on drinking. "Slag," he speaks into his glass before taking another drink.

The Party

Later that evening they are all well into Stuart's house party. Karen stands on the coffee table donning a quilted settee cushion over her head, acting out her authority on the other bikers. They kneel before her around the table, wearing plain cushions over their heads.

"We are not worthy," Ricky bows before her.

"Oh great one we adore you," Stuart calls out.

Mark raises his head. "What is your wish oh quilted one."

Karen laughs an evil laugh as if she is the ruler of all. "I wish you to streak majestically down the north road, towards the great north star, with your anointed cushion of brown velvet."

"You mean to the Yorkshire Coble?" Mark asks.

"Yes," she calls out. "And pick up a pack of fags while your there, oh and don't forget the salted peanuts." She smiles at him.

"Your wish is my command," Mark stands and drops his kegs, strips off his t-shirt and makes for the front door kicking off his Y-fronts.

Karen jumps down from the table. "I was only joking," she laughs.

"Too late," Stuart sings, "he's a dedicated follower of cushions."

Karen catches Jenny in the hallway talking with Nick and Ian. "Have you seen Dave, Jenny?" she asks.

"He's in the kitchen."

"Ta," Karen pushes past partygoers to find him.

"That'll put the cat amongst the pigeons," Ian smiles sitting on the stairs.

Karen spots Dave in the kitchen, she stops for a second and sees him leaning against the worktop with an unknown girl opposite him laughing, her hands straightening the chain around his neck. Karen approaches. "All right Dave?" She slips her arm through his not looking at the girl, but making it obvious he's with her. "Are you coming for a dance Dave?"

"Yeh in a minute." She stands looking at him. "I said in a minute!" he repeats himself sharply staring at her.

Karen pulls away and glares at the unknown girl. "In a minute then," she reminds him and walks back into the dining room.

"Come on Kaz," Amanda calls to her. "Let's dance."

"OK!" she dances with Ricky and Amanda watching Dave through the kitchen door and sees the girl run her hand through his hair.

"Is everything all right Kaz?" Amanda asks.

She storms off into the hall, pushing past Ian as she climbs the stairs.

"Find Dave then?" Ian laughs.

Amanda enters the hall. Seeing Karen run upstairs she follows.

"Oh leave the slag," Ian tells Amanda.

Amanda carries on upstairs and sees Karen vanish into the toilet, she knocks on the door. "Karen are you all right?"

The door opens. "Come into my office and call me Kaz!"

"Yeh sorry," Amanda squeezes in. "What's up?"

"Nothing!" Karen removes the toilet cistern lid. "Here hold this." She passes it to Amanda and lowers the toilet seat to sit down. "Give's it here." Amanda passes her the lid, Karen places it on her lap and takes out from her jacket a backie tin, she opens it and pulls out some wacky backy.

"What are you doing?" Amanda looks at her. "What's that? It's not..."

"Yeh, so," Karen empties some of the packet on to the cistern lid, takes two Rizla papers and starts to make up a joint.

"How long have you been doing that for?" Amanda asks.

"A while… Jenny gets it for us… do you want one?"

"Course not, I don't do drugs…you're only sixteen you shouldn't be doing it."

"Why not? I want to live life," Karen stands and replaces the lid. "You sit I'll stand," Karen orders.

"There are better things in life than doing drugs," Amanda informs Karen.

"And I'll get round to them later…you haven't even had a shag yet! So don't go round preaching life to others," Karen lights up. "Here try it."

"I don't smoke," Amanda refuses.

"Have you tried smoking yet?"

"Yes, but I didn't like it."

"You haven't tried one of mine," she takes a drag and holds it in passing the splif to Amanda. "Go on try it or are you just gonna be a prude all your life?"

Amanda reluctantly takes the joint and drags on it.

"Take it down… hold it," Karen instructs her.

Amanda holds it for about five seconds then coughs it out and hands it back.

"Take another."

"No, I don't like it."

"What do you want Mand?"

"What do you mean?"

"Do you want to enjoy yourself, have fun or just exist doing what everyone else does, living their boring lives." Karen takes another drag and holds it out to her again. Amanda takes the splif, drags on it again, holding it in for as long as she can then coughs it out. "So why haven't you shagged Ricky yet?"

"I haven't known him long enough," Amanda puts her hand to her head as the effects of the drug take hold.

"Don't worry your head will feel better in a minute... Ricky's all right, he'll show you what it's all about."

"Maybe I don't want to do it with him, I've told you before I'm waiting for the right guy to come along."

"And when your thirty you'll be wishing you started at thirteen... don't you fancy Ricky?"

"Yeh... he's OK, oh God I feel a bit... light headed."

"Here have another drag," Karen holds it to her mouth.

"No more please, I'll try it another day."

"Please yourself," Karen takes a long drag, holds it and sighs with pleasure as she exhales. "This is good stuff, it's the second best thing to an orgasm."

"What's the first?" Amanda asks.

"Having your back scratched."

"Yeh! I guess that's good," Amanda laughs, "What's it feel like?"

"What? Having your back scratched," Karen giggles.

"No!" Amanda giggles with the effects of the splif now taking hold. "An orgasm."

"You haven't had one yet?" Karen laughs.

"I haven't made love yet!" Amanda giggles.

"You mean you don't masturbate?"

"Don't what!" Amanda bursts out laughing.

"You need to start to live Mand, I twat myself at least twice a week." Amanda looks at her and cracks up laughing.

"What are you laughing at?" Karen sniggers.

"I… I found a dildo in my mum's box when we were unpacking."

"Get away! Well done to you mam, mind you she won't be needing it now she's got Noorrmmaan!" Karen collapses on to Amanda laughing.

There's a knock at the door. "Are you finished in there Kaz?" Jenny asks.

"In a minute, I'm having a smelly crap!" Laughing hysterically the girls find it hard to talk.

"Tell me," Karen looks Amanda in the face "What's it like kissing Ricky?"

"It's not bad… it makes me tingle inside."

"Is that all?"

"I suppose," she laughs. "I feel horny," Amanda

confesses.

"Does it feel a bit like this," Karen grabs her head and kisses her full on the lips.

Amanda tries to pull away, her feet kicking, her arms pushing at Karen's neck.

There's another knock at the door. "I'll piss my knickers in a minute," Jenny shouts.

Karen lets go. "How does that feel?" she asks giggling.

"It doesn't!" Amanda stands up wiping her lips.

"I'll do it again," she grabs her head and pins her against the wall.

"No… I… stop it!" Amanda fights her off, wiping her lips again.

"Tell me it doesn't feel any different?" Karen looks her in the eyes.

Amanda says nothing, giggles and then bursts out laughing shaking her head.

"And I only kissed you," Karen sits on the bog seat smiling to her.

Amanda unlocks the door to leave. "We'd better get back to the party."

"Thank God for that," Jenny squeezes past pulling her knickers down. "Away Kaz let us on," Karen lifts the seat and Jenny plonks herself on the loo. "Argh that feels good!"

"Hey Mand," Karen calls to her from the toilet door. "You've only got one life, use it."

Amanda smiles at her then goes back downstairs, leaving Karen in the toilet with Jenny.

Amanda strolls into the lounge. "Hey Amanda I wondered where you'd got to," Ricky grabs her hand. "Here I've saved you a can, come and sit with me," she sits taking a drink of beer. "You all right Mand," he asks.

"Yes," she drinks a long drink.

"Wooh, it's the only can I could find, better make it last," he pulls the can away. "How's about a kiss?"

She looks at him. "Can we go somewhere else where it's quiet?" she asks.

"There are only the bedrooms."

"That'll do," she gets up taking Ricky by the hand and walks him upstairs. As they pass the toilet they hear groans of pleasure from inside.

"Sounds like someone's getting off in there," Ricky laughs. Amanda pulls on Ricky's hand and leads him into the bedroom. She closes the door behind them.

Amanda sits on the bed while Ricky stands in front of her.

"Well are you going to join me?" she asks tapping the bed beside her.

Ricky sits next to her and kisses her. Amanda lays back and looks at him. "Have you done it with anyone before?" she asks as he takes off his jacket.

He looks at her. "Yeh! One girl." He lays beside her, they kiss again.

"What was it like?"

"Where are you going with this?" Ricky questions.

"I'm only asking, don't get any ideas."

"Well... it was awkward the first time I didn't really know what I was doing, but after a few goes, it got better."

"Was it her first time?"

"No, she was older than me, anyway less about her," he kisses her on the lips, their heads roll from side to side as their kissing becomes more and more passionate. She folds her arms around his shoulders pulling him towards her.

Ricky pulls back. "You've changed," he looks at her.

"Do you like me," Amanda asks him.

"I've liked you from the first time I saw you Mand, here let's get up on the bed properly, I can't lean over you with my legs dangling off the bed." They shuffle up getting more comfortable and lay together looking into each other's eyes. "That's better."

Ricky slides his hand over her waist, he leans over and kisses her neck whispering into her ear, "Mand you're one rare chick," she lays her head to one side closing her eyes, letting him bite her. She sighs as she relaxes.

Karen leaves the toilet with Jenny sitting smoking a joint, she wanders down the stairs having to step over Ian, deliberately kicking his shoulder.

"Watch it bitch!" Ian shouts.

"Don't hog the stairs then," she retaliates.

"Dyke," Ian slates her as she walks into the lounge.

She heads for the kitchen seeing the girl now standing next to Dave laughing and joking with him. Dave leaves her and walks into the dining room searching for some drink, not noticing Karen standing there. Karen strides into the kitchen taking the opportunity to have a go at the girl who's moving in on her man. "What's your game?" Karen stands in front of her.

The girl stops talking to her friend and looks at her. "Sorry?" she asks.

"What do you think you're doing?" Karen asks again.

"Run along little girl," she's told.

"Leave Dave alone, or I'll smash your face in," Karen threatens.

The girls laugh "You and who's…"

Before she could finish her sentence, with her left hand, Karen smashes her fist into her face sending the girl crashing into her friend and out the back door on to the garden patio.

"There's a cat fight in the kitchen," someone shouts and the partygoers congregate around the door.

"Do you want some more?" Karen threatens with her fists clenched ready to lay into her again. Suddenly Karen is grabbed by her arm and hustled down the garden. Stumbling over the girls, she's dragged shouting. "Hey get your hands off me."

Dave swings her round slamming her against the shed. "What the fuck's going on?"

"You, that's what," she looks at him angrily. "You've ignored me all night and spent all of it with that slut down there."

"So what!" Dave looks at her. "I'll talk to who I want."

"I want to go," Karen insists.

"Go where?"

"I don't know, somewhere, away from here."

"Go then," he pushes her aside and walks off.

"Dave! Don't go I want you."

He turns and walks back to her. "Listen, you change your attitude OK, I'm fed up with your miserable little face, all week I've had to put up with it."

"Fuck me Dave." Karen grabs his arm.

"What!"

"I want you now," she pulls at his trousers trying

to undo his belt. "You never used to refuse it."

"God what's got into you?" Dave complains.

"Come on you know what I like."

"I wish I'd never shagged you from the start," he tells her.

"Don't say that," Karen's voice breaks. "You don't mean that."

"Look Kaz we'd better call it a day." There's a silence between them as Dave looks around. "It's been fun, now it's time to move on," he looks at her straight in the eyes. "See you around," he walks away.

"Dave… don't do this, Dave… I'm pregnant!"

He stops and turns to her, rushing back he pushes her hard against the shed. "What did you just say?"

"I think I'm pregnant," she starts to cry.

"You think you're pregnant, what the fuck does that mean?" he grabs her arm twisting it.

"Ow! Dave you're hurting me."

"I don't want a kid… right," he bangs her against the shed again.

"Dave stop it you're hurting me."

"Get rid of it, right."

"Dave, I want to be with you always, I need you."

"Just get rid of it." He storms off up the garden path into the house.

Karen leans against the shed crying, "Dave."

The girl Karen hit appears, friend in tow, "There's

the little cow."

Karen thumps the girl smack in the face again sending her flying, her friend stands aside letting Karen past to chase after Dave.

Pushing through the crowd, Dave storms through the hall and outside to his bike.

Ian sits on the stairs watching as Karen runs after him crying. "Trouble at mill then?" Ian laughs.

"Dave stop don't leave me… wait! I'll come with you," she tries to grab him as he rides off but falls on to the road. "Dave!" she yells clambering to her knees. "Dave come back… Dave I love you."

Shaking and crying she lies on the ground. Jenny runs out of the house. "Karen! Karen are you all right?"

"Jenny!" Karen cries uncontrollably. "Dave doesn't love me, he doesn't want me any more."

"Come on, let's get you back inside."

Running up the street Mark approaches the girls. "Twenty Embassy Number One and a packet of KP nuts as you commanded oh quilted one," the girls look up and see Mark standing naked holding his nuts out.

"Oh grow up!" Jenny yells helping Karen up, she walks her into the house.

Karen kicks the front door as she walks in. "Bastard!" she curses. The girl she hit in the back garden walks into the hallway holding a kitchen towel over her bloodied nose, she sees Karen lash out at the door. "Quick she's coming… out the back," she and her friends hurry out fearing another attack from Karen.

Jenny takes Karen into the lounge. Passing Ian on the stairs she throws him a look sending the message. 'Don't even go there.' They sit on the sofa. Jenny puts her arms around her. "I told you so," she tells Karen.

"What am I going to do?" Karen cries into her arms.

Upstairs Amanda lies on the bed, her jumper off and shirt undone revealing her breasts. Ricky unfastens the button on her trousers and pulls down the zipper, he runs his mouth over her chest at the same time his hand slides over her tummy, his little finger slipping under the elastic of her thin white knickers brushing over her soft fine hair.

His head moves down kissing a pathway to her belly button, she feels his hot breath as his tongue slides around her beautifully shaped naval. She giggles softly as it tickles, looking down for a moment watching him pull on her trousers. His lips slide over kissing the soft smooth material. She lays her head back sighing, enjoying the feelings that race through her body but at the same time thinking to herself, 'do I trust him, shall I let him go further, do

I want to go further, why not? Karen's right, you only have one life.'

"You smell so sweet," Ricky whispers kneeling in front of her. He removes her trousers pulling her legs gently apart revealing to him a thin line of moisture on her panties as if a signature of approval to carry on. His mouth kisses its way back up her legs until it reaches her mound. She reaches down and takes hold of his hair, pulling his head towards her, embarrassed, as she's never had a boy go down on her before. He fights back and she relaxes her grip as his mouth folds around her biting gently into the thin material covering her innocence.

He raises his head and pulls gently on the elastic of her panties, she closes her legs trapping the material. He continues to pull and as they stretch, she gives in and they part from her moist lips revealing her soft brown down. As he removes them he gently pulls her legs aside and kisses her inner thighs.

"No! I don't want you to."

"Ssssh," he carries on. She gasps as a wave of pleasure tingles through her body from the gentle caressing of his lips.

Ricky removes his t-shirt then slips off his trousers and underpants. Amanda sits up removing the last articles of clothing, her shirt and bra, giving Ricky all the signs she's willing to go all the way.

He lays next to her and they kiss, their heads

gently rocking side to side, his hand supporting her neck.

"You know… I've never let a boy go this far before."

"Don't worry, I've never let a boy go this far with me neither," Ricky jokes.

He kisses her and rolls on top, she parts her legs allowing him to move into position.

"Have you got a Clive?" she whispers between kisses.

Ricky looks at her. "A who?"

"Clive… a condom, that's what we call them down south," she explains to Ricky. "Don't ask for a condom ask for a Clive."

"What the hell are you waffling on about?"

"Do you have a condom? Cos I'm not on the pill." She makes it clear to him.

"We don't need one of them," Ricky goes to kiss her.

"Right! Off!" she orders.

"What!" he stops and looks at her.

"Get off please Rick, I don't want to carry on," she tries to sit up moving him aside.

Ricky gently pushes her back down getting back into position. "It'll be all right Mand, I'll be careful," he kisses her as he starts to push.

"No Ricky! I'm not taking any risks," she shoves him to get off.

Ricky says nothing and pushes more.

Amanda feels him entering her. "I said no! Get off me," she struggles managing to keep him out.

He grabs her wrists and holds them above her head. "What's your game Mand? One minute you're up for it and the next your not, just lay there and let's get on with it."

"No get off me!" he puts his weight on to her body and starts to push harder. "Ricky get off me! STOP IT!"

"Shut up Mand, you're ruining the moment."

"No Ricky! No please…don't!" She starts to cry struggling, twisting her body trying to close her legs stopping him from penetrating.

Ricky struggles concentrating more on the act than realising he has now crossed that fine line to 'RAPE.'

"Aaaaaaaaaaaarrrrrrrrrgh!" Amanda screams.

Ricky jumps off. "All right, all right, sorry, I'm sorry, I just thought…"

She quickly climbs off the bed and starts to get dressed. "Is that it to you? When a girl says no, you just think you can carry on and expect them to give in and let you."

"No, Amanda I'm sorry I didn't mean to…"

"Oh yeh!" Amanda yells at him shaking and crying. "I trusted you, I thought you were different than other lads but you're just the same." She grabs her jumper and heads for the door, stopping she turns and looks at him. "I'm glad you didn't have a Clive!" and dashes out of the room running downstairs.

At the bottom of the stairs she bangs into Karen stepping into the hallway from the lounge. "Watch it! Oh Mand it's you, have you shagged Ricky yet?" she laughs in a drunken stooper.

Amanda looks at her with tears running down her cheeks. Frightened she turns and races out of the house and runs home.

Karen reaches the top of the stairs as Ricky exits from the bedroom. "Oh hello Ricky, if you're looking for Amanda, she's gone home I think," Karen slurs.

Ricky doing up his jeans, pushes past her saying nothing and rushes downstairs.

Karen stands looking at the bedroom door. "Am I invisible or has everyone gone deaf Mr Door," she shakes her head. "Yep I'm invisible," she enters the bedroom and closes the door behind her.

Ian steps out of the loo, wiping his jeans with toilet paper where he's dribbled. He walks across the landing looking around throwing the damp tissue paper on the floor. He opens the bedroom door. "Anyone shagging," he calls popping his head round the door, he sees Karen sprawled out on the bed. Ian looks back over the banister, seeing some partygoers spilling out on to the street doing the conga, he sneaks back into the room and closes the door quietly. Slowly he creeps over to the bed. "Kaz … Karen are you awake?" he whispers. She lies still, breathing hard in her unconscious state. "Kaz… guess who's coming to fuck you?" he reaches out his hand and pushes gently on her leg. She snorts as she moves her head to the other side. Ian looks behind him at the door, then at Karen and slides his hand under her skirt between her legs.

He looks at the door again unfastening the belt of his denims.

Home safe

Amanda walks quickly towards home, frightened, also worried about what kind of reception she will receive when she arrives home, but needing the comfort and safety of her bedroom to help her forget the terrible events of the night.

Approaching the council blocks a blue light flashes, bouncing off the walls illuminating the flats. Amanda quickens her pace, puzzled at what's happening. Suddenly a different fear enters her body. "Mum… mum?" She runs around the corner and sees an ambulance in the car park. People are standing on their balconies looking towards Amanda's home. "Mum!" she cries, the ambulance men are outside her front door. She runs up the concrete steps as fast as she can, frightening thoughts going through her head, 'Mum's dead, mum's dead!' She reaches the top step turning on to the balcony pushing past the onlookers. "Mum! Mum!" The ambulance men turn to look at her, she pushes one aside as she dashes into the hallway crashing into her mother.

"Mum you're all right!" She throws her arms around her crying.

"Of course I am love, what makes you think I wasn't?"

"I thought… I… I don't know what I thought with the ambulance and…"

"Now love don't worry."

"But the ambulance?" Amanda looks at her.

"Well after you'd gone I went upstairs and had a sleep, I was woken up by cries from Betty, she'd fallen off her steps trying to hang her net curtains, it's a good job I didn't take a sleeping pill I'd never have heard her."

"Oh mum, it's all my fault, I'm sorry, I'm so sorry," she cries into her mam's arms.

"Come on Amanda, let's see Betty before she goes to hospital," they walk on to the balcony as Betty is wheeled past.

"Betty, Betty I'm sorry, I should have helped you like I said I would."

"Oh no dear, don't be silly, don't blame yourself," Betty takes hold of Amanda's hand. "You're young you have more important things to do."

"I'll come and see you in hospital tomorrow."

"That'll be nice, now run along don't worry about me, I'll be all right." The ambulance men wheel her away down the stairs and into the ambulance.

Amanda's mam walks over to her and puts her arm around her. "Let's go inside love, we have a lot of grown up stuff to talk about." Amanda turns and rests her head on her mam's shoulder as they walk back along the balcony. "I don't want to grow up mum," she says.

"Yes you do."

Leaving Home!

Running out on to the front lawn Karen quickly gathers her clothes.

"Get out and take your things with you," her mam repeatedly appears at her bedroom window throwing her personal belongings out of it, screaming at her. "I won't have a slut of a daughter staying out all hours then comes home to announce she's pregnant."

"Mam let me phone dad... please, I want to talk

to dad."

Her mother appears at the window again. "I'll speak to your father and remind him you were the biggest mistake of my life."

"Mam... don't do this... help me, I need you," Karen cries.

Her mother vanishes from the window.

Sitting on the lawn crying, collecting her things into a plastic bag, she looks across the garden at their neighbour cutting his grass. "What are you fucking looking at?" she shouts. The neighbour briskly walks his lawnmower across his lawn through his pansies up the drive into his garage. The doors close behind him automatically.

Karen reaches for two jumpers beside her when suddenly a pillow lands next to her. She glances up, then closes her eyes knowing what'll be coming next. The quilt lands on top of her submerging her, still reaching out she clasps the jumpers pulling them towards her and cuddles them under the quilt sobbing.

"You made your bed you can lie in it," her mother yells slamming the bedroom window.

"Daddy, daddy," she sobs.

Hearing a motorbike roaring up the road she stops crying and listens.

Dave rides up on to the grass and turns off his engine, he climbs off and walks over to the quivering cover. Grabbing one corner he lifts it up revealing Karen curled up with tears running down her face looking like a lost child.

"Everything all right Kaz?" he asks looking around at all her things spread over the lawn.

"Dave, you've come back!" She jumps up and throws herself into his arms.

"Moving house? Come on pick up yer..."

"I've got everything I need," she interrupts holding up a bin liner and her jumpers. They walk to the bike and climb on.

Her mother storms out of the house. "You Mr, stop right there," she marches across the lawn to the bike. "I'm calling the police you pervert."

Dave climbs off his bike. "Who are you calling a pervert?"

Karen grabs his arm to stop him. "Dave! Forget it, the old bag's not worth it."

Karen's mam looks at him. "If you're the baby's father I will have you prosecuted, for god's sake she's only sixteen," she shouts. Dave climbs back on to his bike and starts it up. "If you think you're old enough to sleep around and get pregnant Karen, then you're old enough to fend for yourself." She turns on Karen not getting a reaction from Dave.

Revving the bike, Karen hangs on, he draws a circle into the grass with the back wheel before speeding down the road, leaving Karen's mam storming back into the house as the neighbours look on.

Stopping at the front door she looks back at the neighbours. "What are you fucking looking at?"

Karen's New Home From Home

Riding down the sloping lane arriving at his flat, Dave parks his bike on the sand covered drive. He lives in a house converted into two flats, his being the upstairs flat has a balcony overlooking the sea and sandy cliffs of Marske. Dave carries Karen's bag and walks up the stairs to his flat. Karen, seeing what a lovely place he lives in, smiles as she follows. The door to the flat opens and Karen steps through looking around. She's amazed by the size and brightness of the room, although untidy.

"You didn't tell me you lived in a house like this?"

"It's a studio flat," Dave corrects her.

"Whatever it is it's great," she runs to the patio door and tries to open it. "How do you open this?" Dave casually walks over and unlocks the handle sliding the door open. The sea breeze flows through the net curtains as Karen steps out on to the balcony. "How long have you lived here?" Karen asks.

"About three years."

"You kept it a secret."

"It's no secret, I just don't like people knowing where I live," he walks back into the flat. Karen follows grabbing him round the waist to give him a big hug.

"Thank you," she says smiling. Dave turns and looks at her. "I knew you'd come back."

"I didn't leave, I needed time to think," releasing her grip he holds her arms. "If you're pregnant, I want to make sure you have it aborted." Karen starts to tremble, her eyes fill. "I'm off out, you can stay here for a few weeks… and that's all." He lets go of her and heads towards the door.

"Where are you going, when will you be back?" she asks as her voice breaks with emotion.

He leaves, slamming the door behind him saying nothing. Karen stands alone looking around the room. It is silent but for the sound of the sea from the open patio door. The roar of Dave's motorbike starting up and riding out on to the beach breaks the silence. Karen runs on to the balcony and watches him riding across the wet sand, heading towards Redcar. "Dave… it's our baby," she says softly as a tear runs down her cheek. She turns and walks back into the flat, seeing the double mattress lying on the floor she walks over to it and lays down curling up closing her eyes. Thunder rumbles in the distance and rain starts to spray in through the patio doors, as she lies crying, feeling so alone.

The Stray Café

"Let's sit here," Wendy shuffles along the seat.

"I'm drenched," Paul plonks himself down next to Wendy dripping from the rain.

"I told you, you should have brought an umbrella, they said there was going to be a summer storm on the weather report."

"It's all right for you, you've got the hood on your duffle coat to keep you dry," Paul pulls out his handkerchief wiping his forehead. A packet of condoms fall out on to the table.

Wendy takes a mouthful of hot chocolate and sees them, nearly choking on her drink, she quickly puts her mug down and grabs the packet, hiding them under the table. "What do you think you're doing?" Wendy stares at him with a face of fury. "How embarrassing."

"Sorry!" Paul says taking them from her.

"How many did you buy?" she asks picking up her chocolate drink and holding it as if nothing has happened.

"There's three in a packet," he looks at them under the table. "I bought three packets."

"How many do you think you're going to need?"

"They were on special offer, buy two get one free."

"Typical, see a bargain and you're in there." She sips her chocolate, looking around as if nothing unusual is happening at her table.

"Well they cost seventy-two pence a pack, so if I get three packs each condom will only cost sixteen pence.

Wendy puts her drink down, leans back in her seat and looks at Paul. "Are you putting a price on what we are, I mean might be doing?"

"No Wend! I didn't mean it like that," Paul puts the condoms away before he upsets her any more.

"You'd better not," they sit in silence for the next minute.

"I was going to get flavoured ones," Paul says sipping his hot chocolate.

"You don't expect me to chew on one while we make love," she whispers to him with her teeth clenched.

Paul spits out his drink and laughs. Wendy looks around the café watching other customers watching them, and then laughs herself. Paul puts his arm around her and gives her a big hug. "That's my Wend, always thinking of new ideas to make our night even more memorable."

Sam joins them. "Hi Wend, Paul, it's raining cats and dogs outside." Christian helps Sam take her coat off.

"Hi Sam," Wendy greets her.

"Shall I get the drinks in, would anyone else like a drink?" Christian offers.

"Oh! Paul this is Christian," Sam introduces him.

"Hi! Chris to my friends," he shakes hands with Paul.

"You've met Wendy, when we walked past the house you were working in the other day."

"Hi Wend! Good to see you again."

"Hello!" Wendy waves her hand to him. "Yes please can I have another hot chocolate with a marshmallow in?"

"Can I have the same Chris please?" Sam requests.

"Two choc-mallows coming up," Chris leaves them to buy the drinks.

Sam sits down opposite Paul and Wendy. "So what's new?" she asks.

Jokingly Paul leans forward and puts his hand in his pocket. "Well, Wendy asked me to buy some…"

Wendy jumps in. "It's going all right then, you and Chris?"

Paul leans back laughing to himself.

"Buy what?" Sam asks looking at them both.

"Oh nothing, it's a surprise, I'll tell you later," Wendy looks at Paul kicking his leg under the table.

"Ow! That hurt."

"I'm glad," Wendy finishes her chocolate.

"Christian's taking me to the Whitby town fair tomorrow for a Sunday drive out, he asked if you would like to come with us?"

"Yes please!" Wendy quickly accepts. "Shall we Paul?"

"Yeh, sounds good," Paul, replies.

Christian returns with their drinks.

"You were quick," Sam comments.

"I know one of the girls behind the counter, she served me first."

Sam looks back to the counter. "Which one?" she asks concerned.

"Say! I'm taking Sam to Whitby tomorrow."

Wendy jumps in. "Sam said! We'd love to come."

"Great!" Christian looks at Sam who's still looking at the counter.

"What is?" she asks.

"Whitby… tomorrow," Chris reminds her.

"Yes."

"We'll have a great time if the sun comes out, I'll pick you up around twelve noon then."

Geoff approaches with his hair wet and covered in paint bits. "Hi guys and girls, it's raining cats and dogs outside, I stood in a poodle."

They all sit looking at Geoff in stunned silence.

"Why have you got paint in your hair?" Sam asks.

"Orr yeh, I've got a job at I.C.I, I'm known as an

industrial painter, I paint all the steel platforms and such like, can't seem to get the stuff out of my hair… hey I want you to meet Vicky my new girlfriend," he looks behind as Vicky walks towards them carrying a tray of drinks and cakes.

"His first girlfriend," Paul whispers to Wendy.

"Paul!" Wendy tries to kick him again.

"Missed me," Paul starts to laugh as he looks at Vicky, a small thin redhead with ponytails hanging over her shoulders, her face covered in freckles.

"Looks like she's been sun bathing under a sieve," Paul jokes.

"She's my boss's daughter," Geoff announces.

"I've heard of getting in with the boss's daughter but Geoff… check out if he has any pets first."

"Paul don't be so cruel," Wendy kicks him really hard.

"Ow! That really hurts Wend."

"Good! I'm glad."

Vicky approaches them. "I have your limeade ice cream floater, that's what you asked for wasn't it?" she smiles looking at him.

"Thanks Vicky," Geoff takes his drink. "This is Paul my mate and Wendy his girlfriend, Sam and… I haven't met you before."

"I'm Christian, Chris to my friends."

"Hello! My name's Vicky." Paul laughs again. "Oh did I miss something funny?" Vicky asks.

"How could she, she's just walked past three mirrors," Paul laughs under his breath.

"I've told you Paul, now stop it," Wendy insists.

"No Vicky," Geoff explains. "Paul was just talking about his clap infection and how the doctors are struggling to clear it up."

"Oh! Er," Vicky looks at Paul. "I'm sorry I hope it clears up soon."

"Come on Vicky, there's a table over there we can sit at." Geoff and Vicky walk off, Geoff looking back at Paul annoyed at his reaction to his new girlfriend.

Sam and Wendy laugh looking at Paul. "How does he know about my clap," Wendy stops laughing but Paul throws his arm around her. "You'd believe anything Wend."

There's A Time And A Place

As Sally washes a client's hair, who's telling her about the big holiday she's about to go on, she looks through the salon window thinking other things to herself. Virgil's Escort skids to a halt outside. Sally quickly glances at her boss who hasn't noticed his arrival until suddenly the sound of Virgil's musical car horn blasts out, 'Yanky doodle dandy.'

Mr Wilcox walks over to the window. "Sally is that who I think it is?"

"Yes Mr Wilcox."

"Ask him to move on please."

"Yes Mr Wilcox," she turns off the water, leaving the lady with her head over the basin, still talking holidays. She grabs an umbrella leaving the salon and slowly walks across the pavement to his car. Virgil blasts his horn again, she looks back to the shop then runs to his car door.

Virgil winds the window down. "Like the new horn?" he smiles proudly.

Sally crouches down. "No! It'll get me the sack."

"Here, I'll play it again."

"No! Please don't," she begs.

"What took yer so long?" he asks.

"Don't come when I'm working," Sally tells him.

"You don't complain when I pick you up to take you home."

"That's different, anyway, what do you want?"

"Aren't you pleased to see me like?" She says nothing. "What are you doing tonight?" Virgil enquires taking hold of Sally's hand.

She looks over at the salon to check what her boss is doing. "I'm staying in with my sister."

"Not your sis again, I haven't seen you for ages," he removes his hand from hers and plays with the car radio.

"I know but Sue's depressed and wants me to spend some time with her."

"Do yer still wanna go out with me like?"

"Yes… you know I do… but my sister needs me now."

"This is stupid, you haven't seen me for five days… you don't even wanna try do yer."

Sally thinks for a second. "All right, I'll see you tonight, I'll just have to make it up to Sue another time."

"Have you thought about it?" he looks at her.

"About what… Oh, I'm still thinking."

"Look Sal… what's the problem… what yer worried about?"

Sally looks at him. "It's just… I don't want… to lose you, my friend said once we've done it, you'll dump me."

"Who's this friend like?" he asks.

"No one, just a friend."

"Well tell them to keep their nose out of other people's business or dump me and let's be done with it," he bangs his radio. "Bloody thing."

There's a silence between them as Virgil looks at her. "Sal I wanna be with you and only you."

"You mean that?"

"Yes, what have I been saying for the last few weeks?"

"Will you wait a bit longer for me?" Sally asks.

"I was thinking tonight, I've got a friend's house we can use."

Sally thinks quickly. "I'm on my period," she lies.

"Great!" Virgil looks away pissed off.

"If we do, do it, will you use a condom?"

"Not on the first time," he says staring at her. "It won't feel right."

"I just don't want to get pregnant."

"You won't, you'll be finished your period by next Saturday, yes." She nods her head. "You don't get pregnant if you do it straight after your period."

"Don't you?" realising her lie has just put her in a fix. "I didn't know that."

"So how about next Saturday then?"

"OK then," she stands ready to leave.

"I'll pick you up usual place tonight?"

"OK!"

"See yer babe... don't I get a kiss?" Virgil requests. Sally bends down and kisses him. "See yer later babe." He starts up the engine and with a screech of his tyres he speeds off, blasting his new horn. Sally walks back into the salon. Her boss approaches her and gives her a ticking off.

Karen's First Night

The evening closes in, plunging the studio flat into semi-darkness. The rain outside continues to pour. Karen lies fully clothed on the mattress, looking up at the ceiling. She hears a motorbike and quickly sits up, 'has Dave finally come home?' she thinks. Jumping up she switches on the light. The flat is now tidy, she even put some flowers in a milk bottle on the coffee table. She switches on the radio low, then runs back to the mattress and pretends to be asleep. The front door opens, seeing Karen asleep, Dave closes it quietly. He takes off his wet covers and goes to throw them over the settee but seeing the room tidy he hangs them up on the peg behind the door.

Pulling out a bag of fish and chips from inside his jacket, he walks quietly over to the bed and sits gently down next to Karen. All the time Karen's ears have been registering his movements and trying not to smile she pretends to stir and wake, opening her eyes slowly. "Dave you're back, what time is it?"

"It's about ten, have you eaten?"

"No I didn't want to take anything without asking."

"I bought you some fish and chips," Dave hands them to her.

"Ta," she sits up and unwraps them quickly diving in for a chip. Starving she fills her mouth with chips as she talks to Dave. "I've tidied up the flat, do you like it?"

"I can see that, I liked it as it was."

She stops feeding herself and looks at him.

"Sorry!" she says slowly carrying on eating. "It was messy, I thought you'd like it cleaned." There's a silence between them. "Do you want some?" she asks holding them out to him. "There's a can of beer in the fridge, I'll get it for you," she jumps up and bounds across the room to get the can from the fridge under the breakfast bar. Skipping back to the bed she plops herself down.

"Mind the chips," Dave puts out his hand to stop them spilling. "Sorry!"

"Don't keep saying sorry," he looks at her as he takes the can and opens it. "Tomorrow," he takes a drink. "You can write a letter to your mam, telling her you're all right."

"Why should I? She doesn't care what happens to me," she picks up the chips. "I'm not telling her where I am." Dave looks at her as he takes another drink from the can, "That's if I have somewhere to live," she says quietly.

"I said you could stay a few weeks, so write to your mam, I don't want charges of kidnapping made against me."

"OK! I'll do it," she says reluctantly as she scoffs a large piece of fish. "Do you like the flat now it's cleaned up?" she asks spitting bits of fish.

"Yeh, I suppose I could get used to it," he carries on drinking from his can.

She puts down the chips and wipes her mouth.

"I'm not hungry any more," she moves up to Dave and kisses him. "Thanks!" she smiles at him.

"For what?" He asks finishing off his beer.

"For looking after me… let me look after you," she kisses him again.

Dave crunches the empty beer can and throws it on the floor, He pushes Karen back into the mattress and climbs on top of her pulling her skirt up.

It's Late I'm Tired

The rain pours down on to the bonnet of Virgil's car, parked at the end of Sally's street.

"You're going to drop me off here, it's pouring down?" Sally protests.

"You're the one who doesn't like being dropped off outside your door!"

Sally sits looking through the windscreen. "I feel so tired tonight, I must be coming down with something… I suppose I'd better go, mam and dad will be back from the Legion soon."

"So next Saturday, when you're babysitting?" Virgil leans over to kiss her. She doesn't respond.

"I'll see you before then won't I?" she asks him.

"Of course, I'll pick you up after work."

"OK then," she opens the door.

"Don't get out Sal, close the door," Virgil orders.

Sally quickly closes the door as he starts the car and drives fast down the road skidding to a halt outside her house.

"You said yer mam and dad were out, so I may as well drop you outside yer door."

"There are no lights on Sue should be in, she's babysitting Adi."

"You'd better jump out, in case your dad sees you," Virgil tells her.

"Thanks, see you Monday then," she jumps out of the car and steps up to her front door. Virgil wheel spins off down the road to the end of the street, sounding off his car horn before turning and driving out of view. Sally smiles to herself, looking up in the air tutting at him as she struggles in the rain to get the key to turn in the lock. Finally she manages to get the lock to open and quickly steps into the house shutting the door.

In the darkness she hears Adi whimpering and calls his name. "Adi… is that you?" She finds the hall light switch and turns it on. Adi sits on the bottom step crying and shaking. "Adi what's wrong, where's Sue? Come here," she picks him up and cuddles him while she walks him upstairs to his bedroom. "Has Sue fallen asleep again? Let's get you into bed, I'll read you a story shall I?" she yawns. "I'm so tired tonight, I don't know why," she tells Adi as she puts him into his bed. "I must be coming down with something, I'll leave the door open for you and be back in a minute OK, I'm just going to see Sue."

Sally leaves Adi still sobbing as she heads downstairs into the dinning room. "Sue!" she calls switching the light on. "Have you fallen asleep again?" she walks into the lounge but there's no Sue. "Sue!" she starts to call her name repeatedly running upstairs to their bedroom.

Worried now Sally dashes back into Adi's room. "Adi! Where's Sue?" She holds his arms as he cries. "Come on Adi tell me, has Sue gone out?"

"No!" Adrian cries.

"Where then? Adi tell me where?"

"Door," he says sniffling. "Bat-room," he cries confused and frightened.

Letting go Sally runs to the bathroom door, at first she can't open it. "Sue are you in there?" she shouts. Shoving hard she breaks the lock on the inside but finds the door hard to push open. She manages to squeeze through, stepping in she slips on the lino, falling on to the floor. "Shit!" she calls out feeling wet on her hands and legs. Reaching up she pulls on the light chord, the fluorescent light in the bathroom flickers and as if in slow motion, Sall looks at her hands covered in blood. Getting up from her knees she sees blood over her legs and on the lino. "Sue!" The bathroom finally lights up, revealing the true horrible picture of Sue lying on the floor blood trailing from her wrists. "Sue!" Sally screams.

Sunday Morning Has Broken At David's Flat

A breeze blows through the patio door as the sun shines over the sea into Dave's flat, lighting up the whole room. Karen quietly cooks him a breakfast of two boiled eggs, toast and a mug of coffee. She accidentally drops the lid off the egg pan. Dave stirs as Karen looks over the breakfast bar picking it up.

"What was that?" Dave mumbles turning and going back to sleep. Karen dishes up the eggs and cuts the toast into soldiers, arranging them neatly on a tray she walks over to Dave and sits beside him. "Dave are you awake?" she looks closely at him. "Dave," he turns over putting his hand to his face and slowly wakes. "Hello!" she says. "I've cooked you some breakfast," she holds up the tray.

"What time is it?" he opens his eyes to look at his watch.

"I don't know you don't have a clock." Karen says looking around.

"Shit... it's only eight-thirty," he rolls over to go back to sleep.

"Dave!" she says sharply. "Your breakfast is ready."

"I don't eat breakfast," he tells her pulling the bed covers over his head. "Leave it on the floor, I'll eat it later."

"But it'll go cold," she insists. He says nothing. Karen bangs the tray down on the floor next to the mattress, the coffee splashes over the mug. "Let it then." She gets up and grabs the cigarettes off the coffee table and steps out on to the balcony to smoke one. Karen watches an elderly couple walk their dog along the cliffs as she puffs away angrily thinking, 'why did I waste my time making breakfast for him?' After a few minutes Dave steps out and joins her biting into a handful of soldiers, he stands in his shorts and t-shirt. "Not a bad morning."

Karen chucks her cigarette over the balcony. "You decided to get up then?"

"Give us a fag."

Karen hands him one and decides to try again, cuddling up to him smiling. "What shall we do today?"

"Don't know!"

"I thought we'd go for a ride somewhere," Karen suggests.

"Where?" Dave asks finishing off the toast.

Karen slips her arm through Dave's. "Let's go to Aysgarth and look at the waterfalls," she asks

"Where are they?"

"About an hour's drive."

"What's great about waterfalls?" he asks lighting up the cigarette.

"Dad used to take me there, come on it's a lovely

day we can make a memory."

"A what?" he asks puffing his cigarette, looking at the sea.

"Dad always told me it's important in life to make as many memories as you can."

"Oh did he," he replies sarcastically.

"Yes!" she snaps going back inside.

Dave looks down over the balcony ignoring Karen's mood.

Karen returns holding a pan of water in her hand. "Dave… look at me… this is a memory," she throws the pan of water into his face.

He stands there, his fag dripping. "You fucking bitch."

Karen runs inside laughing. "No! No!"

"Come here, I'll give you fucking memories," he chases and catches her, throwing her face down on to the bed, kicking over the mug of coffee.

"No!" she laughs. "You've spilt the coffee." He grabs her wrists and lies on top of her lifting her t-shirt. "Dave! No I was only playing."

"How's this for a fucking memory?" He smiles pulling his shorts aside.

With one push Karen gasps and closes her eyes.

"Oh! Dave, do it again."

Dave and Karen ride like the wind through the country roads, speed is what David likes and speed is what David does. Quiet country villages are wakened as Dave roars through them.

They pull up by a kissing gate. Removing her helmet Karen jumps off the bike and runs to it. "Come on Dave, you have to kiss me first."

Dave patiently locks his bike and helmets then walks over to her. "Why?" he asks.

"This is a kissing gate, before you pass through you have to kiss each other," she grabs his head and gives him a full on snog.

"Pity it's not a shagging gate!" he laughs.

Karen runs off towards the falls laughing. "Come on race you there."

Dave walks behind, letting Karen run on. "If you think I'm doing that running thing you're out of your mind."

"Come on!" she shouts, stopping on the rocky edge to look at the torrents of water as they run over the rocks. "Look at it, isn't it great? Look at the river it's high, it must be from yesterday's rain."

Dave joins her and stands looking around. "Yeh! I didn't realise we had waterfalls in this part of the country."

"Down the river there are two more, not as good as this one," Karen walks on.

"So this is what your dad meant about memories then."

"Dad always takes me out for day trips when he

comes home."

"What does your dad do when he's not chasing waterfalls?"

"He works for the UN you know the United Nations."

"That sounds important," Dave says lighting a cigarette. "Do you want one?" He offers Karen one.

"No ta, I like to smell the fresh air when I come here," she takes a deep breath. "I don't know what dad does, it's important though, it keeps him away a lot." She slips her arm around Dave.

"When do you get to see him?"

"He comes home about every three to six months."

"That's a long time to be away."

"I get to see him for four weeks," she falls quiet. "He'll know what to do."

"Do what?" Dave asks puffing on his cigarette.

"Dad will help us."

"Help us!" Dave looks at her. "Help who?"

"You and me… our baby," she looks up at him hoping for a positive reaction.

"And what will he do?" he asks stamping out his cigarette.

"He'll… he'll… I don't know," she lowers her head and removes her arm from around Dave.

"Well, I'll tell you something shall I?"

"What?" she looks up at him.

He grabs Karen by the arm. "I'll do what I want, not what Daddy wants, is that clear?"

"You're hurting my arm," he lessens his grip. "Dave… he will help us, not tell us what to do. Dad will make sure me and the baby are all right."

Dave walks back to his bike. "I've told you, you're getting rid of it."

"Dave think about it," she runs after him, putting her arm through his. "You, me, the baby, we could be a family."

Dave stops and looks at her. "I'm not ready for all that family shit," he turns away and walks on. "Tomorrow you're going to the doctor's to get it sorted, right! Now lets get back home I've got some business to do."

"I hate you, I hate you," Karen screams as Dave carries on walking.

"I don't give a shit," he answers uncaringly. A couple passing by see and hear their argument. Dave stares at them, the couple look away and carry on with their Sunday walk.

Suddenly the lady screams out. "Alan! She's in the water. Help her! Help her!"

Dave looks back, Karen's nowhere in sight. "Karen! Karen," he runs to the spot where they were last standing.

Karen splashes around her head bobbing in and out of the water.

"Dave!" she splutters as she struggles to keep afloat.

Dave runs over to the rocks and sees Karen. "What the fuck!" he runs down to the river bank. "Kaz what's the fucking big idea? Get out! What are you playing at?"

The man runs to Dave. "Aren't you going to help her?"

"Why don't you?" Dave looks at him.

"You're younger than me," the man argues.

Karen vanishes under the water.

"Kaz!" Dave calls to her as he starts to panic.

"Save her, she's drowning," the lady, cries from the top bank.

Dave throws his jacket and boots off, diving into the water he swims to where he last saw her. He dives under a couple of times and emerges calling out her name.

"She's under the bridge," the man shouts.

"What?" Dave shouts not hearing the man for the noise of the falls, but tries to look where the man is pointing.

Karen emerges from the water under the bridge clasping at anything to hold onto but is swept down the fast flowing river.

"She's over there! She's over there," the lady runs with her husband over the bridge to the other side.

Dave is swept along with the current as he furiously looks around trying to see Karen. "Karen," he screams as he finally sees her, face down in the water lifeless drifting towards the riverbank.

The man scrambles down the bank and wades in as Dave swims to Karen. Dave pushes the man away and grabs Karen around the waist and lifts her out of the water placing her on the bank. "Oh God Karen, no, no don't do this to me," he looks at the man. "Help me then!"

The man pushes him out of the way and tends to Karen checking her breathing; he rolls her over on to her front and straddles over her pushing on her back trying to empty her lungs of water.

Dave jumps up. "What are you doing?"

"What's it look like, I'm trying to save her."

Dave paces back and forth. "Give her the kiss of life, hit her chest or something, don't just... are you getting off on her?" The man looks at Dave and carries on, Karen splutters water, coughing then starts to vomit. "Get off her," Dave pushes the man aside, his wife stumbles down the bank taking her coat off to wrap around Karen. "Leave her," Dave shouts at her.

"She needs an ambulance, there's a cafeteria across the bridge, Alan go and phone for an ambulance."

Karen climbs up on to her knees crying, spitting sick and water. "Why didn't you leave me?" she looks at Dave. "Why didn't you let me die?" she stumbles to her feet and staggers off, cold and wet, falling to her knees and getting back up.

Dave goes to help her. "Get off me! Just get off me," she cries as she stumbles up the bank.

"Will you be all right dear?" the lady asks approaching Karen. Karen hands her coat back coughing and crying.

"Get her to a hospital," the man tells Dave.

Dave follows Karen up the bank saying nothing. The lady stands with her husband looking shocked but the man just shrugs his shoulders.

Whitby O'Fair

The afternoon sun shines over the steps to Whitby Abbey. "Help!" Sam screams laughing.

"Don't run," Christian catches Samantha in his arms. "Once you start running down these steps you can't stop."

"Oh you saved me," Sam jokes. "You are my knight in shining armour."

Chris looks into her eyes. "And you shall be my maiden."

"54, 55, 56," Wendy counts the steps as she walks down.

"78, 91, 103, 51," Paul counts loudly to put her

off.

"Stop it… Orr you've made me lose count now, come here you," Wendy chases him back up the steps.

"Don't worry Wend take it from me there's one hundred and ninety-nine of them," Paul tells her laughing as he hops up the steps to avoid the vicious attack Wendy's handing out to him.

Chris and Sam laugh, watching their antics. "Why do people insist on counting the steps?" Sam comments. "Why don't they just walk down them?"

Christian looks at her puzzled. "Because it's fun," he puts his arm around her as they carry on down.

"Count Dracula's famous in Whitby, you don't see people running around with wooden stakes and garlic," Sam points out.

"Good point, remind me next time we come, to bring some with us, we might start a new craze."

"Don't be stupid!" Sam laughs.

Samantha, Christian, Wendy and Paul fill the afternoon with as much as possible, fish and chips at the famous Moby Dick fish shop, followed by the usual candyfloss and ice creams. They muck about in the amusements later, spending most of their time popping in and out of the many tourist shops.

Christian buys Sam a blue lucky duck from the glassmaker's shop to match the colour of her eyes. Then they all go to the Whitby fair, which has been coming to the town for many decades.

Chris and Sam ride on the hundred-year-old merry-go-round. Sam watches Chris every now and then. He looks at her and reaches out his hand. She ignores it for a second embarrassed to reach out and hold it while people stand around watching, but then nervously she takes his hand, a shiver of excitement runs through her body. 'I can't believe Chris really likes me,' she thinks to herself. 'And he's the first real boyfriend I've ever had.'

Behind them Paul hangs on for dear life as Wendy swings up her leg trying to kick him off. She laughs hanging on as Paul grabs her leg and lifts it up. An attendant steps between them grabbing her leg and helping her to straighten herself, while he lectures them both. As the attendant walks away Wendy takes one last kick at Paul. They reach over to each other laughing trying to kiss as the merry-go-round horses bob up and down.

The night sky turns red as dusk falls. Beads of white lights drape around Whitby harbour as the main town closes for the night, leaving the coloured lights flashing from the amusements and the sounds of loud sirens, music and excited holidaymakers echoing out over the bay, bringing excitement to this old historic harbour.

Wendy and Paul race each other along the jetty,

Sam hand in hand with Chris walk in silence. Every now and then the sea breeze would blow Sam's long hair over her face. She gently brushes it aside.

Christian walks Sam over to the rails, they stop to look out over the sea.

"It's been a lovely day," Sam thanks Christian.

"It has hasn't it… it's funny."

"What is?" Sam asks trying to keep her hair off her face.

"Over a hundred years ago Captain Cook sailed from here and discovered my homeland, Australia."

Sam looks over the sea watching the seagulls swooping down to catch fish. "Would you go back one day?" Sam asks.

Christian leans on to the rails looking at the waves breaking against the jetty wall. He breaks the news to Sam. "I'll be going soon."

Sam turns her head sharply and looks at him. "What do you mean? How soon?"

"The end of summer," he looks at Sam.

She stands for a moment looking at him, confused, the sparkle she has felt all day fades as she looks away, glancing over to Wendy and Paul who are kissing each other, in love.

"My mother and sister live there, I said I would follow them when my apprenticeship finishes."

"What about me?" Sam asks.

Chris steps behind her and puts his hands on her

shoulders. "I don't know."

She turns to him now angry at what she's just learnt. "Why tell me now, three weeks we've been seeing each other, why didn't you say something on our first date?" She turns back, tears filling her eyes.

"I should have said something but I couldn't, I wanted to see you again." There's a silence between them. "I'm sorry Sam," Chris turns her around, she holds her head down, hiding her tear-filled eyes. Chris kisses her on her forehead.

"Do you have to go?" she asks trying to be strong.

He wraps his arms around her and holds her close. She closes her eyes and a tear falls on to his jacket.

"No! But I've always wanted to go and see where I was born, see what it will be like to live there," she pulls away from him and walks slowly along the jetty. "I was five when I came to England and since my mam and dad's break up, we've all started going back and I feel if I don't go now I might regret it years later."

"So you decided to tell me now?" she looks at him. "After I've..." She stops in mid sentence and carries on walking, wiping her tears away. "Three weeks you've led me on, we have a lovely day together, you lead me to believe you want to be with me and now you tell me you're trekking off halfway round the world," she walks back towards the town.

"Sam!" Chris catches up with her and takes hold

of her arm. Stepping in front of her he forces her to stop. "Sam I'm sorry, I didn't want to lead you on, I wanted to tell you from the start, but when I'm with you I find myself… clamming up…. I've never felt this way about a girl before, I want to give you a choice."

"A what?" Sam snaps staring at him.

"A choice…to see each other, spend this summer together."

"What as friends… I don't think so." Sam tries to walk on but Chris stops her.

"Yes, if it will give us a chance to have a summer together to remember, who knows you might join me in Australia."

"Or what?" Sam asks brushing her hair aside becoming more annoyed.

"Sorry?" Chris asks.

"You said you wanted to give me a choice," she looks at him waiting for him to give her a reply.

"Well… after today, you go your way and I'll go mine," Sam pushes past Chris and calls out to Wendy and Paul to tell them they're going home.

Christian follows as Sam walks at a fast pace ahead of him, hurting inside and angry to have just fallen in love and lost it, all in one day.

Driving home the sun finally sets over the North Yorkshire Moors. On the back seat Wendy, with her head resting in Paul's lap, sleeps tired from a beautiful day out. Paul with his head back gently snores. Sam sits in the passenger seat looking out of the window across the moor, as it falls into darkness, all kinds of thoughts racing through her head, wishing she'd never heard of Australia. She glances slightly watching Christian drive them home, thinking, 'I could spend the rest of this summer with him or say goodbye tonight.' He turns and smiles at her knowing he's hurt her and reaches out to hold her hand. She lets him. "I suppose now I've met you, we could see what happens?" Sam says smiling back at him. She looks out of the passenger window again now knowing this could be the happiest summer of her life but at the same time, possibly the most painful.

An Apple A Day That's What They Say

Dave and Karen pull up outside the doctor's on Coatham Road. Slowly Karen climbs off the bike and removes her helmet. She looks at Dave but he avoids looking into her eyes and rides off. She walks towards the main entrance.

Entering the foyer she sees the surgery full. She queues waiting to see the receptionist, looking around she seems to only notice children with their mothers. A toddler plays with the magazines and newspapers on a small table while the mother chats to another mother, rocking her baby to sleep in its pushchair. Across the waiting room a four year old stands crying, his mother trying to shut him up. Karen looks at another young girl. 'Could she be fifteen, sixteen?' Karen thinks to herself. 'Looks like she'll drop a baby at any moment.'

"Can I help you?" a stern voice asks over the counter.

"Yes can I see a doctor please?"

"What is your name?"

"Er… what?"

"Your name please?" the receptionist asks impatiently.

"Oh! Karen, Karen Sinclair."

"Who is your doctor please?"

"I don't have an appointment," Karen points out.

"Which doctor do you normally see?"

"Doctor Stanley."

"Monday," the receptionist comments. "She's very busy on a Monday, but if you care to wait she will be able to see you in about an hour's time," the receptionist explains.

"How long?" Karen questions.

"If you would like I can make an appointment for next Wednesday?"

Dismayed at the thought of waiting until next Wednesday, she agrees to wait.

An hour and half passes so Karen approaches the reception desk. "Is she going to be much longer?" she calls over to the receptionist.

The doctor buzzes through. "Send in Miss Sinclair please."

"You can go through now, last door on the left."

Karen marches down the corridor, stopping outside the doctor's room she pauses, ready to turn back. Closing her eyes she knocks on the door.

"Come in!" the doctor calls. Karen enters and shuts the door behind her. "Come in, take a seat please," the doctor asks as she looks through a mountain of patient files, not even glancing up. "I'll be with you in a minute," she announces scribbling notes. Karen sits, her back straight, hands on knees, legs together. "Now," the doctor looks up removing her glasses, they fall and hang on a chord around her neck.

Karen for a minute stares, afraid to speak, then as if she only had ten seconds to live starts to real off her orders. "I want an abortion, I'm pregnant and don't want it, when can it be done?" she pauses.

The doctor leans forward, using her feet she manoeuvres the chair on casters closer to Karen. She takes her hand and holds it, tears swell up in Karen's eyes.

"Will it hurt?" Karen asks her voice breaking.

"Slow down," the doctor speaks softly. "What makes you think you're pregnant, how late are you for your period?"

Karen lowers her head and starts to cry, the doctor reaches for a box of tissues and hands her one. "I'm weeks late...I'm pregnant, I know I am."

"Have you been feeling sick on a morning," the doctor asks.

"A few times," Karen replies.

"How long have you been having intercourse," the doctor puts her glasses back on and pushes herself back behind her desk to make notes.

"About two, three months."

"And what kind of contraception have you been using?"

"Condoms... sometimes, Dave's careful he pulls out before he comes."

The doctor looks over her glasses as if to say 'well it didn't work did it.' "Wipe your tears now," the doctor tells her as she writes more notes.

"What are you writing? I don't want anyone to know," Karen becomes concerned.

"Don't worry, anything I write is between you and me only, now would you like to pop up on the bed so I can examine you and while we're at it we'll do a quick health check and see how you are, then

I'll need a urine sample and you can come back later this week for the results, OK?"

The Fisherman's Friendly Café

Later that afternoon Karen meets up with Dave in the Fisherman's Café on the esplanade.

Dave sits in the corner reading his newspaper, drinking a mug of coffee.

Karen enters the café and walks quickly to the table, she sits opposite Dave. "Hi Dave!" she says quietly.

"Well, what did the doc say?" he asks drinking the last of his coffee.

"I have to see someone on Thursday first, to talk about having an abortion, then they said it would be the week after if the test is positive."

"What do you mean if it's positive?" He stubs his cigarette out.

"They have to do all the tests first…can I have a coke please?" she asks.

Dave pulls out thirty pence from his pocket and puts it on the table. She looks at it, then at Dave. "You get it then," she tells him.

"You've got legs," he tells her and carries on reading his newspaper.

She slaps her hand on the money, picks it up and

walks to the counter. Dave lights up another cigarette.

Karen returns, slumping onto the chair, opening the can she takes a long drink from it.

"It's for the best Kaz, believe me you don't want to be tied down with a kid at sixteen," Dave tells her.

Karen looks out of the window to the sea. "Yes but what if…"

Dave interrupts her. "But nothing, I'll decide when I want to be a dad not you or any other girl, OK!"

Karen this time takes a small sip of coke. "There's another problem."

Dave looks over the newspaper at her, "What!"

"You've given me VD."

"I've given you VD!" he repeats loudly.

A couple of builders sitting in the corner overhear their conversation and spit out their tea laughing.

"Let the world know," Karen shouts at Dave.

"Jesus! It doesn't end with you does it," he gets up and storms out.

Karen shouts to him. "Well I didn't give it to you." She turns and looks at the builders laughing to themselves. "I bet you've had VD before."

"No love! We've never slept with you," they crack up laughing as she gets up and leaves.

The Tragedy Of Sex

Sally climbs out of Virgil's car, looking unhappy. Virgil jumps out moaning at her as they approach the house where Sally baby-sits. She rings the doorbell and the door opens immediately. The owners stand with their coats on, annoyed.

"Sorry I'm late, Virgil's car wouldn't start," Sally steps past them.

"You're here now, so help yourself to tea and coffee, Simon's tucked up for the night, we'll be back by eleven."

"OK Sal… I'll pick you up then." Virgil waves walking back to his car.

"Yeh OK! Ta," Sally shuts the door and hangs up her coat in the hall. She wanders into the lounge and turns on the telly, then picks up a magazine and sits in the armchair to read it. After five minutes she hears Virgil's car pull up outside. Jumping up she checks through the curtains and runs to open the front door.

Virgil bounds up the garden path. "There's nothing wrong with my car," Virgil complains entering the house offended at the excuse she made for being late.

"I had to tell them something, you were the one who was late," she follows him into the lounge, he slumps himself down on the settee. "Do you want a cup of tea?" she asks.

"No ta, turn the TV off."

"No, leave it on," Sally sits on the settee.

Virgil gets up and turns it off ignoring Sally's wish and plonks himself next to her. She turns her head away tutting to herself.

Virgil puts his arm around Sally. She sits with her arms folded.

Running his hand through her hair he tries to be nice to her. "How's yer sister?" he asks.

"She's all right," Sally uncrosses her arms and picks at her fingernails. Her face saddens. "She's out of hospital."

"Do you know why she tried to pop herself like?"

"She won't say."

"I know you said she was depressed but to try and kill yourself, that's a bit drastic." Sally says nothing. "I saw this programme once about twins and it said that you were supposed to be psychos."

"Don't you mean psychic."

"Yeh! That's what I said, didn't you get anything?"

"Well I was feeling tired that night, that might have meant something."

"Spooky, anyway come on Sal," he turns her head to face his and kisses her.

She doesn't respond. "I've been meaning to ask you, did you take some money off the mantelpiece?"

"When?"

"Last time you were here."

"No! Are you calling me a thief like?" he accuses her.

"Well they said they'd left three pounds and there was only two."

"Don't accuse people without proof," he snaps leaning back in the chair, giving up on any chance of getting anything tonight. "I may as well go if you're gonna be like this all night."

"No! Don't go," Sally looks at him, he turns to her and puts his arm around her waist, pulling her gently towards him. "This is our night let's not spoil it by being miserable."

"I'm not miserable."

"You look it… come on lay back, let's cuddle a while."

She lies back on to the sofa and Virgil slips between the back and Sally. "Wait!" Sally sits up.

"What now like?" he asks flopping his head into the cushion.

"I have to close the curtains, I don't want people seeing in," she neatly closes the curtains. "Are you sure you don't want a drink?"

"No I'm not in the mood for drinking, now come and sit down and stop faffing with the curtains." Sally sits next to him. Virgil gently pulls her back into the cushions and lifts her legs up on to the settee. "That's better," he kisses her.

Sally lays back and lets him. She rests her hand on his back the other arm is trapped between her and Virgil. It doesn't take long before Virgil undoes her blouse and slips his hand inside. Sally lies there, to her it's the normal routine she goes through every night that she spends with him.

It's not long before he has her skirt up around her waist, her knickers pulled down to her knees, his trouser belt unfastened and his button and zip undone. "You're dry tonight!" he says as his hand plays between her legs.

"I can't help it," Sally says embarrassed.

"Here take off your knickers." She sits up and does what she's told dropping them next to her on the floor. Laying back in the same position she takes as much time as she can to settle in comfortably, nervous at the prospect of what might, will be happening next. "Are you comfortable now?" she says nothing as Virgil pulls down his trousers to his ankles leaving his orange underpants on.

"You're not taking them off then?" Sally asks.

"No they'll be right down there." He kisses her tits while his hand squeezes them tight. He moves his leg over hers, worming his way between them, rubbing himself against her.

"Have you got one?"

"One what?"

"You know?"

Virgil lifts himself up off her. "I've told you, I want it to be right the first time, not artificial with a rubber on," he lowers himself back down putting his weight on her and bites at her neck.

"Don't mark me!" Sally reminds him as Virgil explores her body with his hands. "I don't want to get pregnant."

"You won't," he mumbles between the kisses. "Anyhow, I've heard you don't get pregnant on your first time."

"If I get pregnant..."

"You won't!" he moves over her lips to shut her up, in between kisses he tries to convince her. "Everything will be all right, anyhow you've just finished your period," reminding her what she said last week unaware of her lie.

She breaks from his kisses. "But what if I do?"

He looks up and stares into her eyes. "I'll stand by you, I've always wanted kids."

"You have?" Sally smiles trusting him, believing what he says. "How many?"

Virgil closes his eyes and becomes impatient with her talking. "Three!" he moves his head back down kissing her tits.

"I want to have lots of kids," she tells him as he pulls his underpants down over his arse. Virgil says nothing concentrating on what he wants. "Ow! What are you doing?"

"Sally! I'm trying to sha… make love to you," he says getting more impatient.

"Sorry… it was just unexpected, tell me next time when you're going to."

"I'm going to try now, are you ready?" Sally says nothing and just looks at him. Virgil uses his hand to find the way. "Open your legs up, I can't get it in unless you do." He pushes.

"Ow! It hurts!" she complains.

"Just relax," he snaps spitting on his hand and rubbing it into her. Sally turns her head, uncomfortable as it is, not daring to say anything more in fear of upsetting him. Virgil lowers his head between her and the settee as he tries again. Sally bites on her bottom lip, taking a deep breath in as he pushes, her hands grab and clench at the settee cushions, her eyes tightly shut trying not to show Virgil the pain she's going through. Suddenly she can't take anymore and breathes out. "Stop it! It hurts, Virgil please stop," she tries to push him away.

"Shut up Sal I'm nearly in, it'll stop hurting when I'm in."

"Ow!" she cries softly.

"Relax babe." He pulls back giving into her cries.

She breathes a big sigh of relief. "Wait a minute," she asks. Virgil spits on his hand again, snogging her he tries to get her in the mood then pushes again.

"Yeh, you feel good."

She cries out, his lips stopping her cries as he grunts back into her mouth. She tries to push him away but can't manage, after a few cries he lets her mouth go and lays his head into the cushions next to hers, pumping fast and furiously. Sally turns her head away from his, tears fall from her eyes from the pain as Virgil abuses her virginity for his own satisfaction. This is not what she expected, wanted, how it should have been. She expected what? Wanted it to be what? It should have been what? She was giving Virgil everything she had to offer, everything a girl could give to prove to him she loved him.

"Orr… Orr… Yeh… Yeh…" Virgil moans as he climaxes.

"Not inside me!" she yells to him pushing him away.

Virgil pulls out slumping down on to her stomach his erection rubs on the settee cushion as he finishes his orgasm. She breathes a sigh of relief as the pain eases away. Was it only two, three minutes, to Sally it felt like an hour of hurting, cutting, stabbing, so much pain. He lays on her breathing hard.

"Is that it? Can you get off now?" She shoves him away.

He sits up pulling his underpants back up. "I'll be back in a minute." He pulls his trousers up and heads for the bathroom. Sally pulls her skirt back down, lying on the settee not wanting to move too much in case it still hurts, she fastens her bra and shirt buttons. Carefully she swings her legs off the settee and sits up leaning over shaking, her face squints as she feels a little pain from her bruised skin. She finds her knickers and stands up to put them on. As she pulls them up she places her hand between her legs, it feels very wet and bruised. She looks at her hand and sees blood on her fingers. Looking quickly she sees blood on the cushion next to Virgil's spunk. She wipes her fingers under the material of her skirt and hearing Virgil coming down the stairs, she quickly turns over the cushion not wanting him to see the mess she's made and sits back down.

"Sorry Sal! I had to clean up." He turns the TV on and sits a cushion away from her. There's a silence between them. "Are you all right?" he asks her, still looking at the TV.

"Yeh… but you hurt me." she finishes wiping a tear from her eye.

"It'll get better as we do it more."

"I hope so."

He slides across to her. "Yeh, I heard it's not that great for girls the first time."

"I wish you'd took your time a bit more," she says looking at the TV.

"Yeh! I couldn't help myself, I wanted to feel you, you turn me on too quickly," he says as if putting the blame on her for his shortcomings. "What's today's date?" Virgil quickly asks.

"Why?" she looks at him.

"It's the sixteenth today isn't it?"

"I think so, why?"

"It's Eric's eighteenth birthday today."

"Who's Eric? I've never heard you mention his name before."

"Eric's a mate from college, he's having a get together at the Bay."

"Yeh, so." Sally guesses what's coming next.

"I said I'd drop in and buy him a drink, do you mind Sal if I nip down? I'll be back in an hour," he cuddles up to her. "Then we can have another go… eh." He tries to kiss her she turns away.

"No thanks not tonight, I'm hurting too much, anyway you're not going, not after what we've just done," she protests.

"It'll only be for an hour, I forgot to tell you last week," he explains.

She crosses her arms to show she's adamant. Virgil jumps up and kisses her on the cheek. "I'll see you in an hour then?"

"Virgil!" Sally shouts as he vanishes into the hall and out the front door, slamming it behind him.There's a silence in the room but for the voices on the TV. She hears him start his car and drive off.

Virgil pulls up in the Cleveland Bay car park. He straightens his hair in the rear view mirror before jumping out. As he walks towards the pub he sees some dirt on the bonnet of his car. He carefully rubs it off giving it a quick polish with the cuff of his shirtsleeve. Satisfied, and with a spring in his step, he enters the pub. His mates standing around the bar see him enter and give him their usual greeting. "Virgie Virgil's here." Virgil stands still and they all look at him wondering why he's not doing his usual strut to the bar.

Suddenly holding his hands out high, he loudly announces. "Virgie Virgil no more!"

A cheer erupts from his pals as he does his usual strut to the bar to receive pats of congratulations on his back.

Sally sits in a daydream alone staring at the fire, the title music from the TV show ending snaps her out of her daze back into reality, her bottom lip trembles as tears run over her delicate pale cheeks.

She buries her face in her hands leaning into her lap and sobs, now experiencing a new kind of pain.

The Comedy Of Sex

Paul walks nervously up the path to Wendy's front door, flowers in one hand, a small teddy in the other, he rings the doorbell.

Taking her time Wendy opens the door.

"Hi Wend, for you," he holds both hands out holding the gifts.

"Oh Paul! What's this for?" She takes them from him, first smelling the flowers then looking and cuddling the little bear. "Orr thank you," she gives him a big hug as he steps through the door. She closes the door and follows Paul into the kitchen. "I'll put them in water straight away." Grabbing a vase she fills it with water and unwraps the flowers plopping them in then separates them. "Oh they're lovely… do you want a cup of tea?" she asks.

"No thanks."

"Have you eaten anything? I can cook some beans on toast if you want."

"No thanks," he walks over to her pulling her away from the flowers, he looks into her eyes and kisses her.

"Oh Paul, I do love you," she holds on to him tightly her head resting against his chest.

"I love you too," he tells her looking over her head.

Wendy pulls away. "Come into the lounge I've

got a surprise for you." She takes his hand and leads him into the hall first. "Now close your eyes." He does as he's told. She walks him through into the lounge. "Stand there and wait," she commands as she picks up a small present wrapped in red crepe paper with gold love hearts on. Wendy switches the stereo on and closes the curtains.

"What you doing Wend?" he asks.

She stands in front of him holding out the present. "Now open them."

Paul opens his eyes, the room is lit with candles, the music starts to play Pelo Brisan and Roberta Flack's song 'Two hearts beat as One'. Paul looks at Wendy standing holding the gift for him. He takes her hands and raps them around his neck ignoring the small gift and he holds her tight as he dances with her to the music not wanting to say anything. Wendy closes her eyes and smiles. They dance together two hearts, two hearts that beat just as one. The music stops, Wendy steps back. "Open your prezzy now!" she whispers.

He tares open the wrapper revealing a white pair of socks. "Socks!" he questions.

"Yes I've heard you fellers always wear your socks in bed when you do it, so I got you a clean pair to put on," she laughs.

"No!" Paul says laughing and cuddles her.

"Only kidding, look inside them," she says and

helps him open one sock to find a gold chain with a cross on it.

"Oh Wendy it's beautiful, you shouldn't have."

"Yes I should, wear it for me tonight, here let me put it on you."

She unclips it and hangs it round his neck. "Now you mustn't ever take it off."

"I won't." They kiss. "Shall we?" Paul looks into her eyes as she takes his hand and leads him upstairs to her parent's bedroom. Again the room is prepared, the curtains closed, blanking out most of the evening light, candles placed on the dresser and bedside tables. Paul laughs and looks to Wendy. "Thank you."

"Thank me for what?"

"For being my Wend." They kiss again as Paul undoes Wendy's buttons on her blouse.

"Let me?" Wendy asks and takes her top off letting it slip to the floor then undoes Paul's shirt.

They stand holding each other kissing and caressing, stopping only for Paul to remove his shirt and Wendy to unclip her bra. "Can you get undressed in the bathroom?"

"Why?" he asks.

"I don't know, just do it for me," she orders him standing holding her bra on."OK! See you in a minute," Wendy says as she kisses him. Quickly undresseing she hops into bed. "Ready!" she calls to him. Still wearing his boxer shorts he returns putting his clothes next to the bed on the floor. She giggles at the sight, holding the quilt hiding her own body. He slips them off and climbs into bed. They look at each other. "Are you nervous?" Wendy asks.

"A bit." He leans over and kisses her, stroking her hair and face. "Are you sure your parents won't come back?"

"I've told you, it's Crystal's birthday treat, they've gone to London to see a show." They slip under the quilt both giggling as they play about under the cover. Then there's a silence. "No! I can't... I can't do it," she says pushing him off and sitting up clenching the quilt to her chest.

"What! What's wrong Wend," Paul sits up.

"I'm sorry Paul I can't do it."

Paul looks at her. "It's OK Wend, we don't have to."

"Close your eyes," Wendy tells him.

"What?"

"Just do it." she orders again, then jumps out of bed. She runs out of the room. "I'll be back in a minute." Dragging in another quilt from her bedroom she lays it on the floor at the end of the bed then pulls the quilt off Paul. He quickly grabs a pillow to hide his privates. Wendy lies on the floor arranging the quilt over her. "OK you can open your eyes now and bring the pillows."

"Where are you?"

"Down here."

Holding the pillow tight against himself he moves down the bed dragging the other pillow with him and looks over the end.

"I'm sorry, it didn't feel right doing it in mam's bed."

Paul snuggles between the quilts. "Now where were we?" he asks laying next to her kissing her, moving his hands over her body. Every now and then Wendy sighs softly. "You're shaking!" he tells her.

"I can't help it."

"I love you Wend," he smiles kissing her.

"Have you brought the condoms?" she asks.

"Oh... yes." He climbs out from under the quilt and crawls round to his trousers, fumbling in the pockets he pulls them out. "What flavour do you want?"

"Just bring them."

"Here they are." He finds them and crawls back lifting the bottom end of the quilt, sliding under he kisses her toes, feet, legs, tummy, breasts, neck and mouth. She closes her eyes as he kisses her eyelids and lays between her legs. "I'll remember this night for the rest of my life," he whispers in her ear. "I love you Wendy, I always will."

Wendy holds him tightly, kissing sometimes softly now and then with more passion as their bodies mould together, their hands exploring every part of each other. Paul stops and rolls on his back.

"Do you want me to put it on?" she asks giggling.

"No thanks, I'll wear it!" he jokes.

"You know what I mean."

"No I can manage, I've been practising."

"You haven't?" she giggles.

He takes the condom and opens the packet, looking up at the ceiling he fumbles under the quilt trying to put it on. "Are you sure you don't want to chew on a banana flavoured one while I get this on?" He pulls the condom back out from under the quilt to check he's putting it on the right way round.

Wendy lies on her side watching, giggling now and then. He reaches under the quilt looking up at the ceiling frustrated, glancing at Wendy giggling.

"It's not easy you know," he says embarrassed. "I may as well be blindfolded."

"Shall we do that?" Wendy suggests.

Paul looks at her. "Here hold the cover up but don't look." Wendy holds the cover. After a minute he pulls it down out of Wendy's hand. "Oh!" Paul gets frustrated. "It's no good,"

"What's wrong?" Wendy asks.

"I can't get a hard on."

Wendy giggles and kisses him. "Don't worry, let's play around a bit first," she pulls the covers over them.

Ten minutes pass, Paul lays on top of Wendy. He looks into her eyes while he guides himself with one hand.

"Oh! Wrong hole Paul."

"Sorry!" he tries again.

Wendy takes a deep breath and closes her eyes as she concentrates on the feeling she gets from the first sensations of Paul entering her.

Paul closes his eyes and releases his hand. Slowly he pushes then pulls out a bit and repeats to help it slide in gently, conscious of not wanting to hurt Wendy.

As Paul wraps his arms around Wendy's shoulders, Wendy folds hers around his back. His cross falls gently now and then over her chin as Paul for the first time makes love to her, each wanting to make this night right for each other.

"Paul hold me," Wendy asks, as a tear drops on to the pillow. Paul comforts her in a way as if wanting to protect her, she holds him tightly. "I love you," she whispers, her voice trembling, breathing deep sharp breaths. Wendy pulls away the cover trying to cool down revealing their naked bodies, beautiful as nature intended them to be, joined as one, giving and receiving pleasure.

"No! No!" Paul collapses over Wendy.

She opens her eyes looking over his shoulder. "Is that it… have we done it?" she questions.

Paul raises his head and kisses her on her cheek. "Sorry Wend."

"What, haven't we done it?"

Paul rolls over on to his back. "I can't… I can't seem to…" He thumps the quilt in frustration. Wendy giggles. "Don't laugh Wend."

"Sorry Paul, but it is funny," she cuddles up to him. "Maybe we are expecting too much to soon," she slides her hand over his chest. "We can try again later?" she says resting her head on the pillow next to his and kissing him on his cheek. Paul turns on his side folding his arm over the cover around her and gives her a reassuring cuddle.

They both lay together, their eyes closed, two lovers together sharing a moment in time with their feet poking out from beneath the quilt. Wendy's little toes pointing to Paul's new pair of socks.

Another Waiting Room

Wearing David's over-sized raincoat, Karen sits in a waiting room chair looking through the window at the rain pouring down on to the people outside. Some holding umbrellas walk on by while others dash about like drowning rats. "Serves them right," she mutters to herself.

"Sorry?" a nurse asks standing next to her.

"Oh!" startled, Karen explains. "No, I was looking out there at those idiots, fancy coming out in weather like this with no protection," she laughs at them.

"Yes, well… Karen is it?" the nurse looks at her clipboard.

"Yes."

"Right then, first we'd like to get you into your gown, if you'd follow me please," she leads Karen to a door down the corridor marked 'Private Care Patients'. The nurse opens it. "Here's your gown, if you'd like to get changed, I'll be back in ten minutes and we'll settle the paperwork and payment," the nurse hands her the gown.

Karen walks into the tiny room, the door closing behind her leaving her alone. The room is painted a soft pink with only a coffee table, one magazine, two metal and wood chairs and a grey metallic clothes rack with a mixture of metal and plastic coat hangers dangling at one end. She wanders over to the window and drops the gown on one of the chairs. "No protection, who am I to talk," she says to herself.

Sitting herself down she stares at the four walls then reaches for the magazine. There is a picture of a newborn baby on the front with the heading. 'Is there a choice for the child?' She throws it back on to the table and starts to get upset putting her head into her hands she cries. "I don't want... I want someone to love me, just to love me for who I am." She composes herself and stands to take her coat off and get undressed. Looking out through the blinds and down into the courtyard she sees a woman running, pushing her pram, stopping at the gates to check her child is covered from the rain. Karen turns and looks at the door, her coat half hanging off her shoulders she looks at the gown. Picking it up she throws it across the room and with her DM's she kicks the coffee table over. "No I won't, I won't," she cries out and makes for the door.

The nurse appears as she opens it. "What's going on?" the nurse asks her sternly.

"Fuck off!" Karen yells at her.

The nurse steps back shocked as Karen runs down the corridor putting her coat back on. She runs down the stairs into the courtyard. "Murderers, fucking murderers," she shouts running out through the gates.

All night Karen walks around the town of Middlesbrough, looking in shop windows Debenhams, Boots, Mothercare, cataloguing in her mind what she will need for her baby. She manages to scrape enough money together through scrounging to buy a burger from an all night food trailer, and settles herself into a shop doorway drifting in and out of sleep during the cold rainy summer night.

The next day Karen stands outside the hospital, as Dave pulls up on his bike. He hands Karen the crash helmet saying nothing, she climbs on and they ride home.

Feeling a bit guilty, Dave tries to help Karen into the flat but she brushes him off. "I expect you'll want to rest," he says.

She takes off her coat.

Karen says nothing and walks over to the mattress climbing under the sheets fully dressed. Safe and warm again she closes her eyes.

Dave approaches the mattress and sits beside her. "I've come to realise Kaz," he strokes her hair. "You've given up a lot for me, I'll make it up to you, I promise."

"Go away, leave me alone," she tells him.

He respects her wishes and gets up to leave. "I'll be back later, I'll bring you some chips if you like?" He walks back to the bed, leans over and kisses her cheek then leaves closing the door quietly behind him.

Karen hears his bike roar off into the distance. She rolls on to her back and looks down at the bedcovers, pulling them off she lifts up her jumper and t-shirt. Rubbing her hand gently on her belly, she smiles. "I'm not alone any more, I'll never be alone again."

Summer Ends So Quickly

With the coming of autumn, Redcar enjoys its last weeks of the busy season, soon the town will fall into a sleeping seaside resort.

For many teenagers, Redcar at night is one big party. From the amusements on the esplanade where thousands of coloured flashing lights create a tiny look of Las Vegas, to the many pubs, clubs and restaurants that offer food, drink, music and a place to meet and dance all year round.

One club, The Top Deck, beats them all and is the place to be seen in.

Christian, Paul and Wendy celebrate Samantha's seventeenth birthday at one of the top restaurants in town, Nino's by the Sea.

"We just laid there," Sam finishes the story. "Drifting around asleep in the sun, until the boat attendant rowed over to tell us off because he wanted to go home for his tea," Sam laughs.

"And he had the nerve to ask for another pound for the other two hours extra we had, after his language I told him to bugger off," Christian explains.

"Christian!" Sam slaps his hand for using such language.

"I take it he won't be letting you hire another boat in Locke Park again," Paul asks.

"I think if we go back, he'll have us walking the plank, ha harrr Jim lad, you'll not get me gold." Pirate Christian finishes his Irish coffee as they all laugh."Yeh, we've had a good laugh this summer." Sam looks at Christian and squeezes his hand. "I think I can say, it's been the best summer I've ever had."

He leans over and kisses her. "I'll never forget this summer."

A silence falls around the table. Wendy and Paul look at each other knowing Sam is not looking forward to Christian leaving.

"So how's the new job Sam, settled in all right?" Paul asks breaking the silence.

"It's OK."

"She'll be top editor before we know it," Wendy laughs.

"I'm only selling advertising for a newspaper," Sam states.

"Yes but we've all got to start somewhere, think big Sam and you'll go places," Christian tells her.

"We'll see," Sam smiles.

"Hey! Look who's just walked in," Wendy

nudges Sam.

"Who?"

"It's Mrs Summers with Mr Butcher."

"Oh they've been coming here for years," Chris informs them.

"You come here often Chris?" Sam asks.

"Only when I want to eat, come on we'd better get a move on."

"It's only eight thirty, it's early yet," Sam replies.

"I thought we'd have a walk along the prom and have an ice cream."

"Sounds good to me!" Wendy butts in.

"Why not," Paul grabs his jacket agreeing.

"OK then," Sam collects her handbag.

Yet Another Party For Karen

With music playing and bikers scattered all around, it's just another party at another house with the same old people.

"Just cheer up, you're always fucking miserable these days!" Dave snaps at Karen walking through the lounge into the kitchen to rummage for a beer. Like a lap dog Karen follows him.

"Kaz! All right, over here," Jenny spots her and calls her over. "Hey girls Kaz has arrived, come on have a dance."

"No Jen, I don't feel too good, I'll sit this one out," Karen turns and walks back into the hall. Jenny follows her.

"Hey Kaz haven't seen you for ages are you all right… Dave treating you all right is he? Let me know if he does anything to hurt you, I'll have him sorted."

"It's OK!" Karen snaps. "He wouldn't hurt me."

"He made you get rid of that kid." Karen looks at her annoyed. "Everyone knows Kaz, you can't keep a secret round here," Jenny informs her.

Karen says nothing and looks at her. Jenny shuffles closer to her, waiting for some partygoers to pass by. She looks Karen straight in the face. "You did get rid of it?" she asks. "Didn't you?" Karen puts her hand over her tummy and looks at it, then looks back at Jenny, tears swelling up in her eyes. Jenny pulls her towards the front door. "Are you telling me you're still pregnant?" A tear runs off Karen's cheek. "Oh shit!" Jenny looks around. "What are you playing at, how much longer do you think it's going to be before Dave notices, or do you think you'll just stand there, let it drop out and say, oh dear me it must have been twins… God Karen he's going to go ape."

"So!" Karen snaps.

"So… you have to go away, get away from him, he didn't want the kid from the start what do you think he's going to do when it's in front of his face, play happy families?"

"What's it to do with you?" Karen wipes her tears away and tries to walk away.

Jenny grabs Karen's arm. "It's got everything to do with me, I'm your friend… let me help you."

"How can you help, how can anyone help?" Karen sniffles.

"Look we can't talk here, come round my place tomorrow, we'll talk then, I'll think of something."

Karen looks at her. "I'll think about it."

"Don't think about it, make sure you do it."

"Don't say anything to anyone!" Karen tells her.

"Do you think I'm stupid?" Jenny replies. "Come on make like you're here to have fun, you'll be OK with me around."

Karen walks back to the lounge, she stops and turns to Jenny. "Thanks, I've no one else."

"Come on," she takes Karen's hand and they join in with the other dancers.

Lisa, one of the old biker girls and Ian's present lay, steps from around the side of the front door, smiling.

Jenny dances with Karen, their arms around each other's shoulders laughing together.

Dave walks up to them. "What are you doing?" He demands to know.

"Nothing," Karen tells him.

"Leave us alone," Jenny says turning her back to him, continuing to dance.

"She's not a dyke," he tells Jenny pulling Karen away from her.

"Dave! I'm only dancing with her, she's my friend."

"Go get a drink," he orders Karen.

"I don't want one."

"What's got into you, you don't drink, you don't smoke any more, you're turning into a right bore, now get in the kitchen where I can keep an eye on you."

Karen walks into the kitchen looking back at Jenny.

"And for Christ sake cheer up," Dave snaps

Upstairs Lisa drags Ian into a bedroom. "Come on I want to tell you something."

"What? It'd better be good I was enjoying a drink with the lads."

Lisa lies on the bed and slips her knickers off. "Give me one first."

"Away Lisa I can't just stand on command."

"Do you want to hear some good news?"

"What news is that? Ian asks.

"Not until I get some satisfaction and believe me, you'll get some satisfaction when I tell you what I've heard," she pulls him on top of her.

Ten minutes later Ian steps out of the bedroom smiling, doing up his jeans. Lisa steps up behind him and slides her hands around his chest. "I told you, you'd be satisfied."

"You bet that was the best shag I've had in ages."

It's Not Long Now

As the sun finishes setting, Sam, Chris, Wendy and Paul walk along the seafront enjoying the mild evening air. Paul and Wendy run around clambering over the seats tickling each other, every now and then Paul would attack Wendy's neck with a slobbering kiss.

"Slobber, slobber."

"Arghhh."

Chris and Sam quietly stroll along in front holding hands.

"It's not long now," Christian breaks their silence.

"Let's not talk about it," Sam looks out over the sea.

"I will write!"

"Stop it, not tonight," she kisses him on the cheek. "Thank you."

Christian looks at her. "For what?"

"For tonight."

Christian stops and turns to her, looking deeply into her eyes he leans forward and pulls her close to him. Sam's heart pounds hard as she fights to hold the tears back. 'I love you Chris,' she cries out in her mind as he kisses her.

"I wish I was never born in Australia." He whispers to her holding her tightly.

"I do too!" she replies quietly.

"I can't tell you how much you have meant to me over these past months."

"I don't want to lose you Chris," she holds on to him.

They stand holding each other tightly. Two young people with their futures ahead of them, destined to live their own lives separately as fate has never meant for them to be together.

"I've yet to give you your birthday present," he says reaching into his jacket pocket and pulling out a long thin box wrapped in gold foil with a card attached. "Happy birthday Sam."

She smiles and takes the card, opens it and reads it. Her face lights up. She opens the present revealing a red velvet box and on opening it she finds a pearl-like necklace. "I can't afford the real thing," he explains.

"Oh Chris, it's lovely," she holds it up admiring it.

"Here, I'll put it on you shall I, turn around,"

She turns her back to him, he drapes the string of

beads around her neck and fastens the clip then pulls her long hair through. Taking hold of her shoulders he tries to turn her back but she refuses to turn, so he wraps his arms around her and kisses her cheek. Sam raises her head still fighting back the tears, trying to be strong. 'How can someone so right for me hurt me like this?' she questions in her mind. 'How will I go on without him?' she spins round in his arms and cries for the first time. "Take me with you, don't leave me here alone."

A tear falls from Christian's cheek as he pulls Sam close to him. "I've thought about it night and day Sam, I want you to come with me but I can't see how, what would happen if you didn't like it there? You'll have no family, no friends," he tries to explain.

"I'll have you Chris, I love you," she cries in his arms.

"I love you too."

"Sam!" Wendy shouts running up to them.

Christian and Samantha compose themselves.

"Look what Paul won me, a lickle cuddlwy pig, he won it fwom the gwab machine inne lully?"

"How do you know it's a he?" Paul asks running up behind them.

"Let me have a look?" Christian takes the cuddly pig and turns it over. "It's a girl… it's got no bollocks… it's a bollockless pig." Paul and Wendy scream with laughter, Sam giggles too.

"Bollockless pig!" Paul repeats laughing aloud as they all walk on along the promenade.

"Come on, let's go to the Top Deck," Chris suggests.

Wendy and Paul look at each other smiling.

"No, if you don't mind Chris I'm tired," Sam says wiping a tear from her eye. "Let's go home now."

Wendy and Paul stop smiling. "Orr come on, just for an hour," Wendy asks.

"I want to go home, it's been a long day, anyway isn't it shut on Wednesdays?"

Chris panics turning to Wendy and Paul with help written in his eyes.

"As far as I know it's open," Paul blurts out.

"I'll let you into a secret." Christian runs in front of Sam and stops her.

Paul and Wendy stop and look on. "He's not going to tell her?" Wendy asks Paul.

"They've just started opening on Wednesdays for a trial period," Christian tells them all. "To see if it's popular and I have," he announces proudly, "four courtesy tickets from the manager's guest list."

Paul and Wendy look relieved. "Get away how did you get them?" Paul quickly jumps in.

Wendy looks at Paul. "Why are you asking questions?"

Paul grins back to her. "Sorry!"

"That's great Sam," Wendy runs up to her.

Sam still upset, runs past Chris leaving them all. "Sorry I don't feel too well."

Chris, Wendy and Paul look at each other. "Do something then," Wendy pushes Chris, "She's upset."

"What do you want me to do, drag her by her hair?" Chris whispers back.

"If that's what it takes." Wendy pushes him again to go after her.

Chris watches Sam walking away, he thinks to himself. 'What shall I do?' "I know," he looks back at Wendy and Paul. "Run."

"What!" Paul and Wendy ask.

Chris runs up to Sam yelling back to them, "I said run." Christian sweeps Sam off her feet and into his arms, and runs towards the Top Deck discotheque. "You're going to the Deck, like it or not," Chris tells her running across the road in between the traffic.

"No Chris, please… I don't feel like it, put me down!" she shouts at him.

"Sam… I love you, I'll always love you, but tonight is going to be the best night of your life."

"Put me down Chris," Sam cries into his shoulders. "Please stop, put me down… I hate you, I hate you," she cries.

Chris nearing the entrance to the discotheque yells to Paul. "Get the doors open!"

Paul runs on ahead and manages to open the doors in time for Christian to run through into the club.

"Hello Chris," the doormen greet him.

He runs into the foyer and up the stairwell. Paul and Wendy follow behind.

Chris stops and looks at Sam, with tears running down her face, she looks up at everyone standing in silence. "Happy birthday Sam," every one shouts. Recognising who's standing in front of her she looks around as they sing a loud chorus of Happy Birthday.

Sam, with tears and makeup running down her face looks to Chris, "I hate you even more now," she laughs and kisses him. He lowers her on to her feet as three cheers ring out.

"Happy birthday Sam," Paul and Wendy hug her.

"Quick! A hanky Chris," Sam grabs his handkerchief to wipe the makeup and tears away. She turns to everyone as the room goes quiet. "Well... where's my drink?"

"One drink coming up," Geoff shouts from the back.

"Oh! Who invited him?" Sam laughs blowing Geoff a kiss.

The DJ starts the music, streamers fly around the room and the lights dim for the party to start.

Wendy walks up to Sam. "You had us worried, for a second I thought you were off."

"Come on Chris, I'll get us a drink," Paul drags

him away.

"I'll catch up with you later Sam," Chris shouts.

Sam runs over to him grabbing his jacket collar and steals one last kiss before she's whisked away to meet all her friends.

At the bar Paul orders the drinks. "Anyway Chris, don't forget me and Wend when you're in Aussie, you've become a good friend to us both."

"I'm just sorry I'm not going to make it to your engagement party."

"Don't worry Wendy's making up the numbers with her friends," Paul jokes handing Chris a drink. "I'll tell you something Chris, I never thought her mam would ever let us get engaged, but when she found the empty condom packet at the end of her bed, she had us lined up, out the door and heading for the registry office."

"At least it's not a shot gun wedding," Chris jokes.

"Yeh, I thought Wendy was going to end up at my funeral the way her mother reacted, when she found out that we were as she put it 'fornicating and copulating' in her bedroom," Paul and Chris laugh together.

"A toast Paul, to friendship," Chris announces.

"Thanks Chris, I appreciate that… to friendship."

Sam wanders around the dance floor ecstatic at

seeing her schoolmates, friends and family all there to wish her a happy birthday. "Sally! Sue!" Sam calls out as they approach her. "How are you both?"

"Happy birthday… we're all right, got our ups and downs but were getting there," Sally replies.

"What are you two doing these days?"

"She got dumped," Sue tells Sam.

"Thanks Sue," Sally walks off, Sue follows.

"Oh… OK," Sam looks at Wendy and shrugs her shoulders. Amanda approaches them. "Amanda!" Sam calls out, they hug jumping up and down in each other's arms.

"Hi Sam, happy birthday! Here's a little something I got you."

"Orr thanks, I'll open it later when everyone's together…I thought you were going back to London?" Sam asks.

"I am next week, I'm going to live back with my step dad, mum's staying here, she's moving in with Norman."

"I thought I'd ask Amanda if she would like to see you again before she went," Wendy tells Sam.

"Yes, I jumped at the chance, I wanted to say thanks and goodbye," Amanda hugs Sam again.

"Listen I'll talk to you later, you've got to give me your address before you go so we can keep in touch," Sam asks.

"Let me have it too!" Wendy asks Amanda.

"Yes OK, thanks, have a great night I'll see you later."

The party carries on until twelve, most of the family members have left leaving everyone else to dance until they drop. Most of Sam's friends including the lads they'd brought were dropping due to too much drink, but other than that and the cake fight that Paul started with Geoff, the night was a great success.

Finally after the usual Frank Sinatra's 'New York, New York', the slow dances arrive starting with, 'This guy's in love,' followed by Christian's request for Sam, 'Three times a lady.'

Taking hold of Sam's hand, Christian leads her on to the dance floor to dance alone. The remaining guests stand around watching, then one by one they join them and soon, lovers old and young all share Sam and Chris's moment.

At the end Chris picks her up and twirls her round nearly falling over, then grabbing from behind the DJ box a large bouquet of flowers and a very large box of chocolates, he hands them to her whispering the words "I will always remember you."

Alone they walk along the beach home, the lights from the promenade reflect on to the wet sand as the town closes for the night.

"Chris?"

"Yes?"

"You know when we…" Sam pauses.

"When we what?"

"You know get close," Sam tries to explain, embarrassed.

"I don't know, what do you mean," Christian jokes with her.

"Stop it… why don't you… you know go further?"

"You don't beat about the bush do you?"

"Be serious Chris," Sam tells him.

Chris steps in front of Sam. "Why do you ask?"

"Well you never push me to go any further," Sam questions.

"Well I… I don't know," Chris replies.

"Is it you don't want to do it with me?"

"No it's not that Sam," Chris looks around awkwardly, then into her eyes. "It's not that I don't want to."

"What is it then?" Sam questions. "I bet you've done it with other girls."

"Yes… I've been a wicked boy… but you're different… I don't know, I've slept with other girls but that was me being a lad, you Sam, you're something more."

"That doesn't explain anything," Sam walks on.

Chris follows puzzled where she's going with

this. "Sam!" he catches up to her. "When I've gone, you'll most probably meet someone else, who'll be as special to you as I am now."

"I doubt that," Sam says walking on.

"Girls who want to have fun lose… what us lads want, in the girl we choose to marry."

"It's all right for you lads to sleep around, but not us girls, is that what you're saying?"

"That's life Sam," Chris stops her again. Running his fingers through her hair he kisses her. "You're different from other girls, the man that marries you, will be the one who will spend the rest of his life with you because you will be his girl. Making love should be between two people that intend to be together for the rest of their lives."

"You sound like my mam, we're in the eighties now," Sam reminds him.

They walk on arm in arm. "That's the problem, what's going to happen by the year two thousand. God knows what excuses will be made, and where will it end, girls as young as twelve and thirteen getting laid because they think it's the only way to get a boyfriend? If I was a girl I would want the first time to be for the right reasons."

"And they are?" Sam asks him.

"What's this twenty questions?" Chris jokes.

"No come on, if you were a girl?" Sam waits for him to finish what he started.

"Well... one, the right person who truly cares for me as much as I did them, two, the right time when both feel it's right, not one pressurising the other."

"And three," Sam asks.

"Who said there's a third?"

"There's always a third with you."

"OK three err... the right place, like not bent over backwards with your legs akimbo sticking out the back of a Mini Cooper or on a school field or your first time is a quickie at a party," Chris stops and turns to face her. "I'm not a girl, but I respect the fact that a girl has something that should be looked on as a precious and valuable possession."

"What's that then?"

"Her virginity... it's the last thing a girl loses and the first thing a woman gives away and when you choose to make love for the first time you will only have that one opportunity in your life to make it right for you, because from then on, you will remember that moment and the person you shared it with for the rest of your life," Sam kisses Chris.

"It's still our choice," Sam comments as they head for home.

The Twins Separate

Sally and Sue walk home after Sam's party.

"You said yourself, they only care about themselves," Sue argues with Sally.

"But we can't afford it," Sally tries to explain.

"You have your hairdressing job, I'll get a job soon," Sue says believing she will.

"It's been nearly three months since we left school and you haven't had a job yet."

"I can't help it if we're in a recession, anyhow, I've got an interview at the shirt factory in Dormanstown, they pay well there, the money will do us."

"I don't want to move, not yet," Sally states.

"Why not? Sal… I hate it at home, I'd rather live on the streets than live another day in that house."

"Can't you wait a little longer? When you get a job, we can find a flat then."

"You don't want to help me do you," Sue snaps at Sally.

"What do you mean?" Sally replies.

"Oh fuck off then, I'll sort it out my own way."

Sue walks ahead and opens the front door.

"Sue! What's wrong? You've been horrible to me ever since you left hospital."

Sue turns and grabs Sally by her coat and slams her against the front door. "I'll tell you what's fucking wrong shall I? I've helped you, I've looked out for you since I can remember and when I needed you, you just fucked off with your little boyfriend and didn't give a toss about me."

"Sue, you're hurting me," Sally holds her wrists trying to pull them away.

"Do you know, I've listened to you crying yourself to sleep for the past few weeks, and I've laid in my bed thinking to myself I wish you'd shut the fuck up, because I don't care, what have you got to cry about? You think life's shit just because your boyfriend dumped you."

"No it's not that!" Sally starts to explain but Sue interrupts.

"Well you try living my life and then you'll see what shit is," Sue lets go and runs upstairs.

"Sue… I want to help you, but you won't let me," Sally stands in the hallway trembling, shocked at the sudden unexpected attack from her sister.

Their mam opens the dining room door and looks into the hallway. "What's all this noise?" she yells. "Adrian's asleep in his bed, do you want to wake him?"

Back Now At Karen And Dave's Flat

Karen enters the flat taking off her jacket. Dave follows her turning on the lights, chucking the bike helmets on to the sofa and throwing his jacket on to the floor. The flat is a mess.

"Put the kettle on," Dave tells Karen.

"I'm going to go to bed."

Dave looks at her heading towards the mattress and smiles to himself. "Yeh, I think I'll call it a night too."

Karen immediately changes direction and heads for the bathroom.

"Where you going?"

"I have to go to the toilet, do I have to get your permission now?"

"Well don't take all night like last night." Dave walks over to the mattress takes off his clothes and climbs into bed. From underneath his pillow he pulls out a dirty magazine and starts to glance at the pictures. Lying on his back he folds the mag to hold it in one hand and slips his other hand under the quilt to rub himself off. "Come on Kaz, I want to go to sleep," he shouts, the toilet flushes and Karen wanders back in. Turning off the light she climbs over Dave into bed still wearing her long thick jumper.

In the dark Dave tuts and puts down the mag rolling over to Karen. "Take your jumper off then," Dave tells her.

"No I won't, I'll leave it on thank you." He tries to kiss her but she moves her head to one side rejecting his advances. He slides his leg over hers. "No Dave! I don't fancy it tonight," she tries to roll over, turning away from him, but Dave pulls her back.

"Well I do," he snaps climbing on top of her.

"Dave please!" she calls out.

"It's been a week since I've had a shag," he persists and pulls up her jumper fumbling with his hands to pull her knickers aside.

"Well I don't want to," Karen tries to push him off.

Dave grabs her wrists and pins her to the bed. "Shut it," he snaps again staring her in the face.

She turns her head to one side signalling to him to get on with it.

"There was a time when you couldn't get enough of it," Dave reminds her getting into position. He lays his head next to hers, half his face buried in the pillow as he fumbles under the sheets. "God you're getting fat, when are you going on that diet you keep telling everyone about?" Karen says nothing, closing her eyes she feels him selfishly satisfy his urges. "That's it come on you beauty," he shoves into her.

"Ow! Do you have to hurt me?" Karen cries out shuffling to make herself comfortable.

"It's not my fault you're dry," Dave pulls out his hand, spits on it and slides it back down. "Here this always helps," he tells her rubbing it in.

Karen turns her head and closes her eyes again, disgusted at the thought and feeling as his hand rubs against her.

"Oh yeh… Yeh that's better," Dave starts to pump Karen, puffing and grunting as he lies on top of her banging away. She lies looking at the ceiling, now and then her face flinches as a sharp pain shoots through her body from his uncaring demands. "Open your legs!" he tells her. Karen moves her legs slowly, not to assist Dave but to try and find a more comfortable position herself. After a few minutes Dave collapses on top of her. "Oh this is hopeless," he moans. "Don't just lay there like a sack of spuds." He carries on puffing and panting.

Even though in Karen's mind, she knows if she responds it'll make Dave come quicker, no way was she going to do this, thinking to herself 'I'm not letting you have all the fun'.

Dave puffs and pants then stops again. "Fuck!" he shouts into the pillow muffling his voice. A small grin appears on Karen's face knowing he's on a loser.

Dave struggles groping with his hand next to the

mattress on the floor. "Where's that fucking lighter?"

"What do you want that for?" Karen snaps watching his hand grabbing for it. "You're not having a fag while you shag me."

He flicks the lighter above Karen's head and starts to pump her hard. "That's it… Yeh," Karen hears the rustle of paper above her head. "Come on! Come on! That's it," Dave bangs away.

She tries turning her head to look above her where Dave's lighter flickers in the dark. "What are you doing?" she asks turning her head from left to right. She sees the dirty mag leaning against the wall as Dave looks at it while he screws her.

"Get off, get the fuck off me," she shouts kicking trying to fight him off.

"Come on Kaz a little longer," he keeps banging away wrestling with her.

"Fuck off, get off me." Karen twists and turns trying to shove him off. "No one screws me reading housewives monthly."

"Yeh! Come on Yeh," Dave collapses on her, Karen stops struggling as the flickering light goes out. Panting he rolls off her. "At least it got you going," he laughs.

"Fuck off bastard!" She rolls over turning her back to him and tries to go to sleep.

The Show's Nearly Over

Christian enters the lounge from the hall as Sam's dad sits on the sofa to eat his dinner. Bobby, on the floor next to the fire, munches away at a packet of crisps, and Ann, her legs tucked underneath herself, reading a comic, cuddles up on the chair. Samantha follows Christian into the room.

Mam enters from the kitchen. "You're all packed then?" her mam asks Chris.

"Nearly, I'm still deciding what to take and what to leave," he replies.

"You've got your passport?" dad asks drinking from his mug of tea. "You can't go without it," he laughs.

"Three days and you'll be in temperatures up into the nineties, while we all look forward to the winter," mam says with her usual loving giggle.

The taxi bibs its horn. "We'd better go, the taxi's here," Sam says picking up her coat. "We don't want to miss the show."

Bobby jumps up. "I want to give it to him now."

"Oh go on then, be quick about it," Sam tells Bobby.

He dashes into the kitchen then back out with a present for Christian. "This is from Ann and me," he hands it to him. "Go on open it."

Christian rips off the paper to find a cuddly toy

doll with crossed eyes and on its front printed the words, with the letters not in the right order.

'TO MU
CHSE XM
AKE SYOU
REY ESGO
SCRE
WEY'

Not knowing or understanding the meaning or connection with him flying to Australia on Saturday, he accepts it's their way of saying they'll miss him. Christian laughs and hugs tiny Bobby then goes over to Ann's chair to kiss her on the cheek. As usual she reels back in horror at being kissed by a man, but this time she quickly steals a kiss from his cheek. "Thanks." He smiles at her.

Chris walks over to Sam, looking back at the family that he has grown to love as his own over the past few months and the house that has become his second home. "Thanks," he says his voice breaking.

The taxi bibs its horn again. "Come on he'll go without us," Christian heads for the front door.

"See yer Saturday," Bobby calls.

As Christian walks to the taxi, Samantha kisses her mam goodbye.

"Samantha?"

"What mam?"

"Give your mam a hug," she asks.

"Oh mam," Sam hugs her. Her mam has a tear in her eye. "Are you all right mam?"

"Yes dear, it's just that you've grown up so quickly over the last few months, you're not my baby girl any more, you're quickly turning into a young woman," she hugs her again. "Now run along, one day you'll understand."

Sam runs to the taxi and climbs in, Christian waiting, holding the door open, climbs in after her.

Her mam walks down the garden path to wave them goodbye.

Coffees To Finish

After watching the Cannon and Ball show at the Middlesbrough Town Hall, Samantha and Christian finish off with dinner for two at the Dragonara hotel. Their last evening together.

"I hope Cannon and Ball get the message we sent them, isn't it exciting, we're having dinner at the same hotel they're staying at," Sam says excitedly.

They both relax, finish their coffee and mints after enjoying another fun evening together.

"I'm sorry you're missing Paul and Wendy's engagement party," Chris reaches out and takes Sam's hand.

"Do you think I'd be enjoying it, with you flying off to Australia the same night," Chris squeezes her hand and says nothing. "Here…" Sam reaches into her handbag. "I was going to give you this on Saturday, but you may as well have it now," she hands him a small black velvet box.

"What is it?" Chris asks.

"Open it and see," he opens the box to find a silver pendant on a chain.

"It's a St Christopher," she tells him. "He's the patron saint of travel, wear it and he'll protect you on your travels," Sam stands and takes it from him. "Let me put it on you," her hand shakes as she places it around his neck.

"Oh Sam you're shaking."

"Oh am I? I didn't notice."

Christian stands and turns to her. "I'll miss you so much, I think I'm making a big mistake," he kisses her.

"No you're not, now sit down," Sam orders him back into his chair. Sitting down herself she looks at Christian admiring his chain and pendant. 'What did I just say?' Sam thinks to herself. 'You're leaving me here in Redcar without you,' "What am I going to do?" she speaks out loud.

"What?" Christian looks up hearing her words.

"Nothing I was just thinking out loud… Christian… I know you have to go, you've explained many times but I want you to know I'll remember this summer as one of the happiest I've ever had."

Christian smiles. "I'll tell you something Sam…"

"Don't say anything," Sam interrupts. "I want to ask you something."

"What is it?" Christian asks.

She takes hold of his hands and without hesitation asks. "How much is it for a room?" Christian looks into her eyes. Samantha smiles, "I want to remember you for the rest of my life."

The door of the hotel room swings open, Christian and Samantha stand holding hands, staring into each other's eyes. Christian leans forward to kiss her, she folds her arms over his shoulders not wanting to end this moment, knowing as soon as she did her next few steps would be her last as a young girl. Christian cuddles her before sweeping her up off her feet and into his arms to carry her into the room. Sam giggles nervously as he nudges the door closed and walks towards the bed, the foot lights from the bedside cabinets dimly light the room, just enough to help him see his way in the dark. Kissing her he gently lets her down, back to her feet, her hands still clasped around his neck she slowly lets go and lowers them to her side. Sam not taking her eyes away from his kicks off her shoes and slips off her jacket feeling a sense of calm fall over her.

In bed Samantha holds the covers tightly to her naked body, as Christian climbs in under the sheets. Leaning forward he kisses her carefully releasing them from her hands, reminding her how beautiful she is and she should have nothing to be shy about. Soon with every kiss, with every touch a different sensation runs through her body bringing her to discard her inhibitions, letting Christian playfully kiss and tease her.

Soon the moment arrives. She lays beneath him feeling his hot breath on her neck as his soft lips caress her. Folding her arms over his shoulders she holds him tightly. Samantha smiles, for this is the night she has chosen to lose her virginity and say goodbye to the girl, to become a woman. The moment in her life, she will remember, for the rest of her life.

Sally

Sally sits at the dining table and puts her arms around her mother's shoulders, both cry into each other's arms. Her mother's face covered in bruises.

Sue sits opposite in her dad's armchair staring, not giving a care.

Their father enters the kitchen from the backdoor

a bit worse for drink and locks up for the night. Stepping into the dining room two police officers standing by the television set, approach him.

I am Detective Jeffries and this is WPC Swan, Mr George Peter Robinson, I am arresting you for the assault on your wife..." Their father stands for a second swaying on his feet from the drink. "You bloody cow! Come here!" he shouts. Before the detective can take hold of him he dashes round the table and tries to hit his wife. Sally stands to move away, but gets his fist in her chest. She crunches up and slumps to the floor winded.

"Sally!" Sue jumps up screaming. The detective grabs him from behind and throws him face down on to the table. He yells out swearing and threatening as cutlery spills off the table on to the floor. The police fight to cuff his hands behind his back.

Their mam cradles Sally who lies, gasping for breath. "My baby, my baby," her mam cries looking up to her husband yelling. "Why! Why!"

Sue kneeling by her side turns and sees a knife on the floor. Without hesitating she grabs hold of it and lunges towards him, stabbing him in the back. "You pervert!" she cries out. "You fucking pervert."

He reels back giving out a horrifying cry. Spinning round he falls to the floor collapsing over the detective. The WPC stumbles, grabbing the knife in Sue's hand she falls to the floor dragging her down with her. Sue cries out again. "Mammy why didn't you stop him, why didn't you stop him?"

Sally coughs and splutters, a trickle of blood runs from her mouth as she falls unconscious in her mother's arms.

Karen

Dave pushes Ian about in the kitchen as party-goers gather in the doorway. Ian shouts something at him and Dave flips, his fist flies into Ian's face. Grabbing his hair with his other hand, he lays his boot not once, not twice but three times into his face. Blood splatters over David and the kitchen cupboards as Ian slumps to the floor. With one leap Dave jumps on Ian's head with his boots.

Other bikers dive to Ian's rescue. Dave thumps his way out of the kitchen grabbing Karen, who is by now screaming and shaking uncontrollably. He dashes out of the house dragging her behind him into the darkened street. Turning he slaps her across the face throwing her against the wall. He then drags her crying to his bike shouting at her to get on. Sobbing she does as she's told and holds him tight as he speeds off, both not wearing their crash helmets. Jenny dashes out of the house and can only watch as she sees them turning the corner, riding out from the

Saltburn housing estate.

Karen screams pleading with him to stop. Ignoring her cries Dave races down Marske Road with confused and angry tears running down his face. He wipes them away, looks on and then closes his eyes as he accelerates full throttle. Hitting the curb with his front wheel the bike spins out of control, off the road crashing through a hedge and a fence into a ditch. He and Karen are thrown into the air.

Slumping to the ground, Karen's arm bends behind her back. Her leg twists as she tumbles ten, twenty yards, finally coming to rest on her back. A splinter from the fence protrudes from her stomach. Dave knowing how to tumble in a crash suffers a broken leg as he lands a few yards from her. He crawls to her crying, calling her name as she lays unconscious, unaware of the terrible injuries she and possibly the baby have suffered.

Amanda

Amanda sits looking out from the window of the coach. In the distance, lit by the full moon, the silhouette of Roseberry Topping and the Cleveland Hills pass by. She settles down to the six-hour journey back to Pinner in London, remembering the summer with mixed emotions, but happy she's going back home to be where she belongs.

Wendy

In the dining room, Wendy laughs with her friends around the food table, showing off her engagement ring Paul had still kept for her.

"Come on Wendy!" her mam calls her over holding the cake. "Are you going to cut the cake?"

Dad grabs it out of her hand. "You know what happened the last time," he laughs. She hits her husband on his arm for his remark nearly knocking the cake out of his hand.

"I'll go and get Paul." Wendy tries to leave the room, her relatives stopping and grabbing her on the way to wish her well, finally she escapes from them into the hall. "Uncle Bob, have you seen Paul anywhere?" she asks him.

"I think I saw him chasing your sister upstairs," Uncle Bob points with his pint of beer.

"He's always fighting with her," she laughs and runs upstairs. Walking along the landing she looks into the bedrooms for Paul, she finds cousin Andrew in one of the rooms. "I hope that's not Crystal under that Quilt, I said I'd tell on you two if I caught you again?" she tells them walking towards her bedroom.

"Now stop it and get downstairs." She shouts back.

Opening her bedroom door she calls out Paul's name. She finds him laying on the bed kissing a girl with his hand down her jeans. Wendy stands shocked, her heart thumps into her mouth and her voice cracks as she calls his name once more. His head slowly looks round to see Wendy burst into tears and run away, quickly he jumps off the bed and runs after her calling her name. Crystal sits up, fastens her jeans and shuts the bedroom door, smiling to herself.

Samantha

Standing alone on the roof top terrace of Teesside airport, her long blonde hair blowing in the wind, Sam places her hands in the pockets of her thick knee-length cream coat, trying to keep warm on this cold night, watching the plane as it revs up its engines to gain pressure. Slowly the wheels start to turn and very soon it roars along the runway.

With tears running down her face she waves. "Is that him?" she calls out, thinking she saw him for the last time through one of the planes windows waving back to her. Then up into the air banking to the left Christian's plane takes him off to his new life. Samantha places her hand back into her pocket and stands listening to the last sounds of the engines as it flies into the midnight clouds.

In a dreamlike state, Samantha remembers back to the one and only morning when she lay with Christian, her head resting on his chest as he sleeps, lost in his own world of dreams. She recalls how happy, peaceful and secure she'd felt with him in that hotel room. 'Did she make the right choice?'

Her mother's words echo in her mind bringing her back to reality. 'It… is for the love between two people,' she smiles and looks to the sky.

"It! Is that, it! Is that love?"

Virginity "Is that it?"

Place a request for Karens second book

L O V E

"Is it that?"

Read the girls story
following on from that terrible night.
Find out where they have all ended one year on.

Which of the girls
Rebuilds her life,
Shares her life,
Changers their direction in life,
Returns to her old life,
and enjoys a new life.

Wherever fate chooses to send them
Can they find love?
Will it be love?
What is love?

L O V E

"Is it that?"

Coming soon

Log onto karenlouisetaylor.com and leave your details.
The information held will only be used to market the book and will not be passed on to any other parties.
Karen promises that you will be the first to know when the book will be available.

Virginity "Is that it?"

T h e b i g
40
That is it?

Copyright ©

There comes a time in life when we stop and look
where we have been and where we are going.
Karen, Amanda, Sally, Wendy and Samantha
have reached that time.

and then there will be

L i f e
It is that!

To be published in 2024
when the girls face retirement.

Virginity "Is that it?"

Now you have read Karens book
why not visit her web site.

Details of film stars auditions are found on

karenlouisetaylor.com

And join the many thousands of readers to her chat room.
Also you may wish to visit her sponsors web site.

www.condomclive.com

It is not a porn site.
Send an e-clive-a-gram to a friend.

International Ambassador to Condoms for (I.S)
Licence to thrill &
World Population awareness campaigner.

Have fun be safe.

Intelligent Sex.